Ravens
Reafan K

For hearts of oak and all who fight.

Julie, Gabriel, Ava, Barbara and Ray.

Three Crows Books
Copyright © 2016 Reafan Kenning
ISBN 978-0-9956677-0-9

TABLE OF CONTENTS

HEIM

Her back snagging on the tree as she stood up, pushing against it, red hair falling over white skin. Skirt almost crimson and feet bare on the leaf and stone. Not knowing why, just reaching for the night visions, somehow wrapped in the wild honeysuckle and bramble. Thorns in her fingers and bark scratches on her back and the stars calm in an empty sky. Swinging the tech up to greet them, up from the ground, courtesy of the unknowing military, small mechanical repository of hope.

Bright sparks in the green vaulted circle and all just as her eyes had told her, still but for the small creep of a distant satellite, looking back down at her in its retrograde, navel-gazing strategy. But there, moving fast, suddenly brightening, directly overhead. Coming to a standstill. Holding the night visions still, pulling back a few inches and looking quickly at the featureless sky above her before allowing herself to see again the intense pulse of light centred in the green image of the analog scope.

All the nights she had been scrambling about the wild woods were strung out behind her like a rosary, every bead fingered and worn, every dark homecoming a small tight fist in her stomach. But today she reckons with the future, securing it to the unrelenting past. Suddenly looking away, a small creaking in the litter of the forest floor, something in the shadows.

Who is it?

Her voice staggering through the trees, orphaned from her elation, waiting for an echo.

I know you're there.

But she was surprised when the shadows slid apart and something moved forward, a man holding up his hand, fingers spread wide, devoid of device or intent. Long hair.

I'm sorry, I didn't mean to frighten you.

That was all she needed, immediately looking back up

through the scope. But it had gone. Looking again. No. Not like this. Sitting down heavily on the buttress of an oak tree and leaning back on the bark. Moonlight sliding off waxy holly leaves. Bright red berries. Moths landing on her red dress. Strange churring call of a nightjar.

He had sat down on a rock, forearms crossed over crossed legs. Looking at her and waiting.

Did you lose something?

Outdoor jacket, black jeans, hiking boots.

Yes. I waited forever.

Standing, walking over to him, leaves crumpling under her soft soles. Damp earth. Kneeling and looking at his face. Not much older than her. Intense, maybe, but kind.

A light. I saw a light.

Your night visions.

Yes.

I didn't see anything.

No. Only with them.

I wish I had seen it.

She smiled.

Then you lost something, too. I'm sorry I couldn't show it to you.

He smiled back. She studied the loss in his face, tightness of the jaw, pretty eyes. His hands dangling from wrists like pale squid. Washed up mariner. What could she give him? Take his cephalopod fingers in hers.

I waited for that light for years. Then I saw you and it was gone.

I'm sorry. Really. I'm... sorry to do something like that to you.

Yes. You even look like you know what I mean.

He sighed.

Yeah, I think so.

She watched his other hand tense on the granite, nails into the quartz flecks.

No. It's not your fault.

He looked away. Curses written on his skin like tattoos. She pulled his arm.

No. It's... strange. Something else.

He opened his free hand and the one in hers turned in time, fell back.

Like what?

Yeah, like what? What are you doing wandering around here anyway?

My auntie told me to come.

Grinning at her.

I'm listening.

She told me to go walkabout. Head West.

To find what?

I don't know. Just keep going. You maybe. Lights in the sky.

So you just went? Where do you sleep?

He shrugged.

Got a back pack. It's warm. Ish. So what about you?

You've seen what I'm doing. Shall we build a fire?

Yeah, why not. Anyone going to hassle us here?

She smiled.

I don't think so.

She made a ring of stones in the small opening and he wandered in with armloads of wood. Seasoned, not rotting, not pine. Done it before. She pulled some paper out from her own pack and layered up the twigs, crosshatching bigger pieces at the top. He threw her a Zippo. Smoke through the trees, the two of them settling upwind on the dry earth, dog fox somewhere coughing out his call. Glowing ash ascending and hovering, sparks on their clothes. The beech and oak rich with sprigs of rosemary.

Looking at his black hair, blue eyes. Him just letting her. The woods darkening away from the fire, helicopter drone in the distance. Scar on his cheek. Maybe a fighter.

I'm Ava.

I'm Gabriel.

Squatting on her bare feet, arms around her legs, knees up to her chin, skirt smoothed down. Him cross legged, taking his boots off.

You're tired, Gabriel.

Yeah, been wandering around a bit.
I haven't told you anything about myself.
I noticed.
Rocking herself and clutching her legs a little more tightly.
My Dad told me to come out here.
Laughing now.
Maybe not just like that, like your auntie, if that's true, but over time he showed me things...
She paused, watched the fire spit on the grass.
If you're looking for encouragement, take it as read.
Kind and clever.
Why not come and see him?
You're inviting me to meet the old man?
Offering him dimples.
He don't have a gun.
Wondering why. Tell Dad the aliens brought him. They tell you the world is just a machine. Random mechanical sequences. But I like him.

The path home familiar, banded series of quartz granite rocks, myopic bustle on badger trails, acorn fattened ducks asleep by the pond. Small breezes of daredevil bats on impossible trajectories. The woods giving way suddenly to orchards, greengage, apricot, Ashmead's kernel, scattered rows of beans, broccoli, rhubarb, a Mandelbrot's set of plenty. The endless labour. Open invitation to the old house. Georgian windows, painted render, militant beauty of honeysuckle and rose. Simple, elegant. Dada lives, my Dada.

Frog on the doorstep, in and out of cat's teeth. Delivered at our feet as we crack the door. Thank you puss, come on inside. Shushing Gabriel into the pantry, see if there are any lights. Droning fridge.
Been on the hunt, then?
Dimly making out Dada, lights off, feet on the big table.
Have kill to show.
Easing Gabriel forward into a handshake.
Welcome, have a seat, Ava may put the kettle on if we're lucky.

Pushing out the shaker chair. Not so old but craggy, white hair, hands like claws as he puts a match to the candle by the apple bowl. Gabriel sitting silent but only for a thank you. Men in my life like a river, carrying me to the sea. Dance across the water to you, sailor boys. These two grinning at each other.

Name's Sebastian. Around here they call me Bastian.

Gabriel.

Cups of tea all round. Pot on the table with a cosy. Fridge wheezing like an old pig.

So what happened, Ava?

Don't know, Da. A light came just as I looked up with the night visions. Then Gabriel arrived and it disappeared.

Leaning her forehead into his, his hands stroking her hair.

I was sad to lose it but I'm not now.

Him smiling as she leans back.

And now you've bought this boy to us. Not something she does every day, Gabriel.

No, I wouldn't think so.

Da, he said he was here because his aunt told him go walkabout.

Da raising his eyebrows theatrically. Relying on whatever residual deference could still be mustered for the seniority of age. Gabriel charmed.

Auntie Vera. She'd just got arrested and I visited her in jail. She sent me on a mission, probably to give me something to think about while she was away.

May I ask what she was in for?

Gabriel sighing.

She advised clients as a psychic. In some cases regarding finance. One guy lost a lot of money, pulled a few strings.

And was this psychic advice genuine?

No. She scammed him.

Da laughing.

And are you implying that she is scamming you with this walkabout business?

I thought so but now I'm not so sure.

Didn't stop you going though.
Gabriel laughing, rubbing his face.
No.
So you think that although she's a scam artist she's also a genuine psychic?
Maybe.
Has Ava told you what I do for a living?
No. Manage a permacultural paradise?
That's very kind. I'm a dowser.
Gabriel grinning hugely.
I'd love to learn. Who do you work for?
Corporations, sometimes governments, agencies, private individuals. I'm trying to tell you we're not cynics. Sceptics perhaps. Your aunt sounds like a riot.
Yeah, she is.
The love in him obvious, seems more like a Mother than an aunt.
Could you do with somewhere to sleep, Gabriel?
Thanks. A shower might make me a better guest.
Done. Would you show him to a spare room, Ava?
Thank you, Da.
I'll see you in the morning, Gabriel.
Resting his hand on Gabriel's shoulder, giving Ava a hug and a look, walking into the dark house.

Show Gabriel his room, the bathroom, come back and watch moths flip flop around the candle. Crickets and scents through the open window to the garden. Miss you, Mama, wish I had an auntie Vera. Need to get her out of jail. Forgot to ask how long she's supposed to be in there. At Her Majesty's pleasure.

Do some yoga on the soft pine floor, feet gripping the boards, flame radiating out from the knots, parallel lines in between. Cat, dog, headstand, plough. Pranayama breathing in lotus, settling in for a mindful moment. Sometimes nothing, sometimes calm. Today plasma configurations like strange petroglyphs, electromagnetic, neon bright, an auroric script across the inner sky. To echo a light among the stars fled so recently at the boy's advance. A thousand days of darkness and then a flipped switch. Better get to bed before anything else happens.

Padding past Gabriel's room, crack of light under the door. Could go in. Inner Dada says no. Back to my own south-facing little sanctum with the empty double bed. Smiling softly at the darkness as eyes adjust. Crack the window open behind the curtains. To let the night in my veins. Spread eagle on the bed. Sleep come free me, that's enough for today.

SILVER

Out in the far corn fields bringing the bacon home. Squeezing
two men into a metal egg with goggle eyes and muscular
extrusions. Deep compression of our little lives. Bas relief
iconography of St Nicholas on the inner hull. Intercede with
Him tonight for these two, both merchant and sailor,
deserving of your good grace. Up real close with the company
man, expensive cologne even here. Under the Arctic ice and
down to a foreign landscape, in demand after aeons of
existing hardly at all.

How are you feeling, Bastian?
All the better for your saintly image on the hull, Nikolai.
Nikolai grinning.
My beatific conscience reaches from East to West without regard.
Gesturing expansively in the interstitial volume of the sub.
Regardless even to the possession of faith or otherwise?
Most acutely when otherwise.
Bastian grinning in return.
I better have a word with the company's personnel department.
*Big company, Bastian, top of it way up in the clouds. Who knows
what goes on there?*
Bastian twisting to look him in the eye, already intimate
with proximity. Nikolai looking back.
What's going on here, Nikolai?
We're paying you to find the black gold, no?
Bastian turning away, switching on the camera. Endless
blackness. Sediment drifting in the current, following them
deeper. Never had chance to say goodbye to Ava.
*You could fish out here for a long time without catching anything,
no, Nikolai?*
It's a long journey. The sub is slow.
You're not an oil executive.
No.
Just wait then, don't get claustrophobic. Breathe. Fish
appearing now. See. Just wait. Don't get intense. Minutes

scraping away the time. He'll talk when he's ready, it's only been...

I'm sorry to be this way, Bastian, it's not easy. Not easy to arrange this meeting. And I wanted to have a little time to get a look at you.

So who are you?

I am an oil executive, at least on paper. It's a position that allows access.

To me, for example.

Yes.

Intelligence, then.

I hope I do the word justice. But nothing monolithic. Agendas vary.

What's yours?

As regards you, to introduce you to some friends. Scientists mainly.

You will know my science is limited.

Yes.

You want me to do woo woo.

Yes.

Blimey.

But I still want you to find oil and gas. Russia needs to keep the Europeans warm.

However you don't really care about that.

Personally? No. Or rather, that's not a problem I need to worry about.

What kind of scientists?

Ones who want to save the world.

Ha ha.

Fish getting weirder as the sub descends. The men's breath synchronising.

What would happen if I told you where to get off?

Nikolai glancing out of the window. The mind-bending pressure.

I would ask you not mention that we have spoken. It wouldn't be in anyone's interest.

I'm sure. And that's all?

That's all.

Dowse him like a vein of ore. Fish on a line.

What do you expect me to believe, that Russian intelligence work for Jesus?

Who do you work for?

No-one.

There you are, then.

And if someone found out I was involved in your little plan?

Depends who you mean.

The Russians.

You don't think I represent my authorities?

No.

So you might trust me, then.

Might.

With the Russian authorities I would hope to have enough backing to photoshop you out.

The British? The Americans?

Depends on your grasp of geopolitics, Bastian. You would be out of my hands. With your prior agreement I would get your family out as soon as we had serious concerns. Beyond that... it's possible I could help you...

But not very likely.

Speculative. Experimental.

The sub creaking. Water scalloped light refracting repetitively across the endlessly concave inner surface.

What about your President?

What about him?

Come on.

It's not easy, Bastian, I can't talk about him.

He's Orthodox.

Yes.

Mother told him to carry a cross.

Nikolai looking away, answering to the darkness outside the window.

He was in a car crash. Being near death changes you. Doesn't it?

Wants me to talk. Wants all manner of things.

But you already know my story, right, Nikolai?

I'm sorry. Everything digital is a forever server farm. I know something happened to you.

It's not data you're asking for.

Nikolai reaching for his shoulder, squeezing the deltoid muscle.

Push the boat out, Bastian.

Nodding. Dog in the back of a car.

Alright. I'm on the operating table and I'm looking down on these guys. They've got scalpels and saws and drills and the side of my head's all mapped out in a grid. I'm screaming at them to stop but they can't hear me. They're saying there's a tumour in my head or a number of them. In the temporal lobe and maybe more spread around the right hemisphere. Never seen anything like it.

They found me passed out in a field behind the house, couldn't wake me up, decided I'd had some kind of seizure. Now they've got me lined up for the cure. But I've not got cancer. If I had cancer I'd have been feeling ill. But I feel fine, or did until just now. Next minute this lunatic is lowering a circular saw onto my skull and it's starting to look red and I can feel the vibration in the bone. If you ever want to know what fear is.

As all this is going on the ceiling starts peeling apart and there's a dark vortex appearing, pulling me away from the operating room. And then it's light and more love than you could ask for, the whole show. I wouldn't have been surprised to meet Jesus. Maybe it was only a few seconds, maybe it's forever. It printed me like branding a cow.

Losing that place was worse than the cutter's bloodbath. No warning. Suddenly I'm on a dry hot plain with strange stone structures scattered around. There's people screaming and there's fire coming from the sky, like lightning arcing across the horizon and machining the ground with vast dendritic grooves. Like they were doing to my head.

We're running. I'm trying to herd my kids towards one of the stone structures. There's some kind of sanctuary there. I can see the lapis lazuli around my wife's neck, the look in her eyes. You have to fix this. You have to save them. I'm trying to carry them and hurry them and not leave anybody.

It's Ava. She's on the surgeon, pulling his hand away, scratching his face. They're trying to pull her off. He's dropped the saw and it's cut his forearm, blood spattering on my face. Somehow I get to grab his wrist and now he's really looking freaked. There's a man behind Ava and he's taking them all down just like that, four of them lying on the floor. Ava's pulling me up and crying and the other man's saying have you cut through the bone? *And no they haven't, they only just started and all this has happened in no time at all. Ava's laughing and crying and after a while she kicks the surgeon in the head as he's lying on the floor.*

That's when I knew I had an angel looking after me.

Nikolai smiling.

It's an honour. May I?

Fingering the scar where it crosses the hairline.

Ava said they weren't following procedure.

No.

There was no follow up. Not from them, not from us. Why were you passed out?

I don't know. I don't know about any of it.

What's the last thing you can remember?

I'm not sure.

Not good.

No. They say a walker found me but I never saw him. Or I can't remember.

Worse.

Why do I want to trust this man? Is he just that skilled?

They really messed with me, Nikolai. It's not like I just got over it. Ava's still disturbed. How do you ever feel safe after a thing like that?

I don't think you do, brother.

Am I your brother?

Aren't you?

You're going to screw up my life. Our lives.

You just finished telling me you're already screwed.

Like it can't get worse?

It can always get worse but at the moment you're a rabbit in the headlights, waiting for road kill.

Somehow the rods are in my hands. They're going to move. They're moving.

Well, here's something for your pipelines. It's gas. You can pay me. Don't start a war over it.

Nikolai smiling.

Gives me some breathing space. Given that I employed you over some resistance.

Oil as well.

Good, they'll wrap me in the flag. You know what happened with the fall of the Soviet Union?

I doubt it.

What they did with Gorbachev was interesting but we can talk about that another time. Afterwards various governments, banks, corporations, NGO's came in to help with the transition to democracy. Instead they asset stripped the place, made fortunes, put Russia back to the Middle Ages. The triumph of the West. There were people not eating, physicists selling nuclear secrets to feed their families. It was gas that put Russia back on its feet.

And a strong man.

Nikolai spreading his hands.

You think someone who could face all this out could be a pussycat?

Two men grinning. Conspiring. Breathing together.

I'm not their apologist, Nikolai. Sounds like what they were doing to me in the hospital isn't that different from what they were doing to Mother Russia.

Not that different from everyone else.

No. Go on then.

Alright. You're contracted for three weeks but this is only the first day. You've already done what the company mandated.

I could probably find more.

Let's not.

Ring those bells, Nikolai. On your feet or your knees. Black flowers on the vine, black starburst in my eyes. Put your muscle to the rope, cast iron to the spine, sing our song for us. Ring those bells.

Your orthodox priests use no instruments. Only the voice,

Nikolai?

Only the voice is free to all. But they allow the bell.

The bell.

The bell is a singing icon and its iron is alloyed with divine grace to disperse and destroy the forces of cruelty and of demonic suggestion, and to becalm dumb beasts and all of Nature, and to turn them to the good of humanity.

And did your peasants use instruments in the songs they sang against the Tsar that the Church supported?

Da, probably.

Hmm.

Our songs came from Mount Athos in Greece, after Rus was founded a thousand years ago. Now the monks there have been declared schismatic by Ecumenical Patriarch Bartholomew 1ˢᵗ, Archbishop of Constantinople, because they object to his attempted rapprochement with the Catholics. He is first among equals in the Eastern Orthodox Communion but they are the embodiment of our spiritual tradition. The monastery is to make way for developments that may assist in receipt of European Union funding. The monks throw petrol bombs at the bulldozers.

And where is your strong man in all this?

I've told you I cannot talk about him. It's not for spurious reasons. But I'll tell you how the Church survived in the Soviet Union? The state did a deal with the Church. Many bright people were to be found receiving education in the Orthodox monasteries and seminaries. The Church allowed the KGB to recruit for the intelligence services and in return they were left alone, allowed, despite communism's internationalist credentials, to continue with a nationalist bearing.

A little sulphurous.

Certainly. Our strong man, as you call him, is of course ex-KGB. The relationship between Church and state is now more traditional. There is a perception in Russia, as in many parts of the world, that there is moral degradation in the West, related to the near-death of religion. That in the West you have thrown out the baby with the bath water and are now like rudderless children, lives full of entertainment, sexuality, marketing. The man who interests you so

*much has said that secularism devoid of spiritual values is the road
to hell, and that he will fight it. In this context the Church is not an
artefact of history but a potential vehicle of renewal.*

But supporting the Church is not what you want from me?

No.

*Orthodox Church services are about the whole congregation
singing.*

Yes.

Not a spectacle.

No.

Could ring the sub like a bell. Diving bell. Any piece of metal.
Summon to worship and drive away evil things. Cleanse and
illumine the sea.

Will you sing for me, Nikolai?

And he did. Held my arm at wrist and bicep and closed his
eyes and looked at me as his voice echoed in the metal
chamber. Brother of the deep. Alive among the glistening
unconscious fish.

Afterwards the silence stretched on and my hand stretched
open, band of gold against the straining tendons. So long
gone, so long alone. A love gone dark. A touch on my cheek.
Finger of a strong bony hand lifting away a tear. Gentle
gesture so anomalous to the culture of my home. To bridge
the division of men.

You have crossed over, Nikolai, from another century. How
have they let you live?

WIRE

See who's at the door, Gabriel.

Sitting on the back porch rocking chair, watching the swallows skim past her in small groups. Sometimes time seemed to slow and she looked in their eyes as they looked into hers. They seemed to be getting on.

There's someone to see you, Ava.

Gabriel's hand ushering through the bars of light across the doorway.

Hello, Ava.

Mum!

Gabriel retreating.

I'll put the kettle on.

Sit down. Here, take the rocker.

How about you show me around the place?

Walking through the beans and peas, bolting leeks, Mother choosing the rudimentary gazebo they had made last autumn.

Rustic.

Yes, mum.

He always had green fingers.

Yes.

You don't miss London, then?

I'm sorry.

Nervous, fingers twisting around each other. No wedding ring.

You didn't give us any notice. I may not have been here.

No, I came on the spur of the moment.

Dad's not here.

I guessed.

Do you miss him?

What? Of course not. You know his views.

Do you know mine?

What?

Do you mind if I call Gabriel?

Gabriel appearing. No tea.

Please sit with me Gabriel. Mum, Gabriel, Dad said he could stay with us for a few days.

Hello, Gabriel, how do you know Ava?

It's alright, Gabriel, you can justify yourself later, we were just about to have an exchange of views and I'd like you to be with me.

Because I don't trust you. Because I still love you. Because we're about to have an argument.

If you were younger I would feel I had to protect you. He has you completely brainwashed with that Neanderthal stuff, hasn't he?

Yes, I believe you would and yes, I'm completely brainwashed.

I've come a long way, Ava, I was hoping for something different.

Feeling petulant, upset, like a child. Dad says don't feel bad, everyone feels that way. I want her to love me. I want her to not be who she is.

You want to know how brainwashed I am? I'll show you. I have an old poster of yours rolled up in a tube. It's Gloria Steinem, making the sign for vagina with her hands. She's wearing a t-shirt and she's smiling. Her t-shirt says I had an abortion. Part of one of her campaigns as editor of Ms magazine. I take it out when I think of you and I cry.

You've been told your body is not your own, but it is.

Did you ever tell me that all the women who started the feminist movement were insistent that the only way to free women was to destroy the family? Like ours, for example.

Well, it turns out to be true, doesn't it? Your Father wanted to control me.

I see your Family Planning Group, with its fingers in every Government pie, is lobbying for post-term abortion. Up to the age of three. You've got abortion on demand, you've got women to smile about it, you've got no-fault divorce and now you want to murder not only foetuses but live babies, live children. You think objecting to all this is controlling you?

Yes I do. If you stopped being so dramatic and emotional you would see that there are hard choices to be made and for women to be imprisoned by primitive biological conditions is no good for anybody.

I was listening to a professor of Bio-ethics recently, telling us how child-bearing was oppressive to women, men get away with it, and children should be gestated in tanks. I guess you wouldn't have to have sex with men. You could abolish the family and have them all raised by the state.

Come on, choice is always better.

Like you chose to be a lesbian? To explore your vagina?

Gabriel shifting uncomfortably. Tight gazebo. Motes of dust in the sunlight.

Now just a minute, I don't need to be lectured by you. These ideas come from him, they're not yours.

And are your ideas your own? Did you know Gloria Steinem was paid for by the CIA? Now why would that be?

Don't start with your wild conspiracy theories.

Ah, that's the phrase when you can't cope with the truth.

Stupid girl.

Yes, maybe, a bit damaged. I was thinking recently about why you and Dad got together in the first place.

And what did you come up with?

It was sexual.

And did you discuss this with him?

Yes.

And?

He said it wasn't my business but that it was true. Is it?

Well, it's not like we had much else in common.

Smoking weed, being angry.

How clever you have become.

And now?

Now what?

Breath catching in her throat, tight lungs. Her pupils widening. Like the experiments where the subject reacts even before the event. The words.

Is the sex better, now?

Ava! I knew I shouldn't have come.

Why did you?

You're my daughter.

Not one of those abortions you're so happy about.

That's it, I'm going.

Gabriel standing up.

You stay away from me, I'll find my own way out.

Just like you did before, Mother.

Gabriel hovering, uncertain. Like a prisoner by the cell door.

Yes, I do want you to hold me. I'm sorry you have to wait for permission.

I love her, I miss her, I don't want her here. It took me so long to get away from her. The things she said about Da, the way she kept him away from me.

Hold me fish-man, mariner, sail the sea with me, my hands are shaking. Pulling him onto the floor and into the sunshine, feel the grass, scent of fennel and turkey fig like coconut. After a while his erection against my hip like the engine of a boat.

I'm sorry, Gabriel, I'm not ready for that. I'm not trying to tease you.

No, I'm sorry, the thing's got a mind of its own. And you can't help being beautiful.

Happy, now, like the stroke of a bell. How easy for him to please me.

So you've learnt how to charm the ladies.

Well, the evidence is there for all to see.

Laughing.

Just keep your arms around me. I'm going to cry.

Long cry. Long, long, long. Patient sailor.

Well, that's broken the ice, you know about my parents. Tell me about yours.

Ah, well I never knew my Dad and my Mum died after a long illness.

Oh, God, I'm sorry.

Yeah. I was really brought up by auntie Vera.

The one in jail.

Yeah.

Is she a good woman?

Heart of gold. Bit wild. Had to make a living for us all. Well, didn't have to but did.

You love her.

Yeah, she's like my Mum. We didn't have nice stuff like all this.

But she sent you to me.
How about that.
You like my Dad.
Sure.
He trusted you. With me.
I was surprised.
You do hocus-pocus like her?
I learned to turn some tricks. Not like her.
I mean the real stuff.
Oh. I've not known what to do with all that.
But you have it.
I don't know. I don't know anything much. I'm wandering around like a dog with its ear chewed off. Looks like you're going to befriend me.
Oh, is it really like that?
Your mum don't compromise.
No.
It's just, girls like you, all this privilege, they just want a pet that behaves.
I'm not like that.
No, I don't think you are. Only here, nothing is mine, it's all you and your Dad and all this beautifully tended land and oh, I'm just catching a plane for Moscow, expenses paid.
What can I do?
Nothing. Maybe I'll just rob a bank.
You have things.
A two-man tent and an auntie in jail.
You have more than most men I've met.

Looking away. Up at the sky. Shipwrecked boy. You always think you're the one got it bad. He understands what I'm saying, he just doesn't believe it.

I can hack.
What?
That's how we have money, Vera and me, her scams aren't so hot.
What do you hack?
Rich people's accounts. I try make sure they're nasty bastards before I do it. A little here and a little there, they don't even notice.

So far.

Like Robin Hood.

Funny. I'm not proud of it. But it's something I can offer.

To feel like a man.

I suppose. Maybe I can protect you.

What?

He talked to me before he left.

He didn't mention it.

He said you had dreams. He had them, too.

Yes.

I hope he's ok. He thinks something is going to happen.

What?

He doesn't know.

Strange, Da talking to Gabriel and not me. Maybe he wants to make him feel better, more included.

I dreamed of strange people, not quite human, lots of different ways. I mean they were human to look at but you know dream logic, somehow they weren't. I didn't like them, they didn't understand what they were doing. They kept coming back, so many nights, it was like being haunted.

You think they were connected to the light you saw in your night visions?

No, they were just regular but weirded out.

So it's not about aliens.

No.

That narrows it down a bit.

Thank you.

But you think there's somebody up there?

Don't you?

Seems likely but I've never seen anything. You can't buy those night visions over the counter.

No. Third generation tech and then some.

But you can see stuff not visible to the naked eye.

Yes. All kinds of stuff according to Dad. He was using them for a while before he gave them to me. The military pick up on it regularly. They have dual visual and night vision on their jets. Chase stuff around. Seems they're not keen on the rest of us knowing

*what's going on. But I'm driven to it. The other night was my big
moment.*

Then I snuck up on you.

*Yeah. But the big deal is that I knew when to look up, if it wasn't
just a coincidence. And then there's you, another coincidence.*

You think they beamed me down?

Maybe they could beam auntie Vera out of jail.

Maybe we've known each other forever.

Biting her lip.

I know.

It's like someone's stirring the pot.

Yeah, bit of spice going in.

Hey, let's dance!

Pulling me up, humming an old time tune, hand in the small
of my back, whirling me around.

My, you know how to show a lady a good time.

That's what they all say.

You know ballroom dancing?

Yeah.

Don't tell me, auntie Vera.

Yeah.

Nimbus and cirrus spinning around the blue sky. Left arm
out in a blur. Centrifugal, centripetal. Like a gyroscope, more
than the sum of the parts. Open my mind. Open my heart.
Spin me around sailor boy and I'll fall on you and laugh and
the world will be once more the way it was.

Taiga

Taiga arcing away forever on each side of the river as we push upstream in canoes, following the morning sun. Nikolai pushing away the ice with a long wooden pole. Husky in the boat, white fur, dark guard hairs, blue eyes. Rows of boats ahead with dogs and men, outboard motors. Blue sky empty of clouds. Trailing fingers in the water, clear as a bell, air full of spring, geese flying slipstream in formation. Compete with the dog to spot pike, green and carnivorous, when the boats are tied.

Branching up tributaries with motors raised, pulling the boats up the rapids with ropes tied to trees, fighting the current. Freezing water sapping strength, muscles burning, dogs barking from the bank. Sedentary weakness. Slipping on rocks, laughing in the white water, inhaling and coughing. Pushing on to rows of logs on a shallow bank, roping up to a crankshaft, shouldering around like oxen at a grinding wheel and winching the boats to safety.

Boats hidden in the boreal forest, larches at all angles. Trail leading ever deeper, could walk forever, walk away from a life or a shadow of a life. In the fading light there are log cabins covered in moss, small lights, a fire. Greetings and men kissing beach other three times on the cheek.

Privyet!

Dobryj vyechyer!

Introductions with fluent English. Furnished with a small cabin, stove set with kindling, baskets of wood, kettle. Small oil lamp, table, chair, bed. See you in the morning. Grain patterns on the planed log walls and pine smell from the firewood, still a little green. Stove crackling easily and through the window glass everything made from larch or beech, sylvan outpost at the edge of the world. Could fall off forever.

Morning sharp and fragrant, easing in through the cracked door.

Dobroye utro, Bastian.
Da, dobroye utro.

Stepping out and sitting on the bench at the other side of the
door to Nikolai. Neither man quick to speak. Occasional
glances and smiles in the green forest light, making tea and
watching the sun move higher through the trees.

What would you like to do?
I thought you might have some kind of plan.
Plans change. The place has affected you.
Yes.
You could be alone for a while if you wish.
Yes.
Be ready in an hour. In the cabin over there you will find soap and
towels. You can wash at the spring.

Doing as told. The cabins all roofed over with soil and moss,
spread randomly through the trees but not quite natural.
Trees bent to grow as cover for the cabins. One or two
younger trees roped at angles. So not easily seen from the air,
like the cover for the boats. Same again where the spring
formed a pool big enough to lie in. Cold as a heart attack,
sweet as a nut, drinking on all fours and finally lying face up,
trying not to scream. Current force fed into the old body,
tripping the rusty switches.

More tea at the cabin and then Nikolai leading the way, just
a backpack each and the blue eyed husky trotting silently
behind, tail curved up, beautiful as snow. Long into the
evening coming suddenly on a large yurt, circular and domed
with a corrugated steel tube and hat emerging from the top.
The door opening and a bearded man coming out to smile at
Nikolai and give him hugs and kisses. Being introduced and
welcomed and leaving the two of them chatting on in Russian.

Walls hung with beautiful cloth, floor covered with rugs
over something like rattan, all laid over wood raised from the
earth a few inches, except in the centre where a stove sat on a
wide stone plinth. Low bed, a small chest, three stools, kettle,
rifle, baskets of logs and kindling, axes and tools, a lamp.

Book by the bed. Russian.

You can stay here.

Nikolai leaning in.

Thank you. You two heading back in the morning?

No, we're heading back now.

What?

Neither of us has covered this sort of distance in the dark. We're giddy at the thought.

You serious?

We have a torch and compass, it's not cold. What's the worst that can happen?

The two of them giving him bear hugs and gone as if ever having been there at all was unlikely.

Pack of wolves turn you into a dog's dinner?

Nature red in tooth and claw, not having taken the wild out of wilderness, not like at home where anything above knee height has been slaughtered to extinction. Anything with teeth, anything unwilling to bow the knee. Finger and thumb on incisors where the points have been rubbed away. And what about when the Russian bear comes calling at night?

Looking for a snack.

Lay the fire in the stove, cutting edge tech with glass doors front and rear to open the fire. God bless these merry monks. Mess about with the rifle a bit, get it to fire at least. Kicks like a mule and leaves you deaf. Supposed to line up bottles or cans. I'm better when I move.

Warm in the yurt, no need for the fur hat. Ava with Gabriel, it'll be alright. Who'd be a Dad? Ava, my girl, you're the best thing. You'd like it here. Kneeling on the rugs in that regard, to protect you, see that you unfold. Forgive me these risks, there's no progress else.

Sounds of bird and beast, unfamiliar yet the same, insects, leaves rustling, wood crackling, wind in the flue. Far from despair, only Mother Nature, like eyelashes on my cheek.

The morning bright and clear and every morning so.

Wandering the trails. Back home these would be made by badgers. Unfamiliar flora and fauna. If in doubt don't put it in your mouth. Mainly larch as even in the hot summer months the permafrost allows only trees with shallow roots. Further south the forests blossom but Nikolai brings me to nowhere, the way it was once everywhere, where a squirrel could go from tree to tree.

The days all the beautiful same and after a few there's not been a breakfast yet. Lapping at the streams and sucking the moss. Fires at night, smoke drifting or spiraling up towards the numberless stars, whispering that once in the distant past they had been torn down and the sky had been broken. In the days when there had been another sun. The best sun.

Pools of water in the empty hearts of old trees, chipmunk dens and odd feathers and bones among the leaves. Reaching in to dark openings in the larch, see about getting bit. Fingers touching something made by hand, wrapped in tarred cloth. Here in the middle of nowhere. Sit down and scrape away the tar, unwrap the cloth.

Round head like a frame drum, skin over the wood, leather sewn on for eyes and mouth. Bright blue beads around the frame and simple clothes over a stick body. A fetish gift from an older time, an assimilated culture once fired by its own animus. Thank you Grandmother. Turning the doll, sewn with the will to keep us from harm, to stand guard in the long night.

But you have been here already, just outside the firelight, ahead on the trail. Yesterday you stood in a glade among the phosphorescent moss and broken branches and looked at me. Now you are here in my hand, pulling me free from my moorings. Let me sit on this buttressed tree and wait for you. But after a while running, trying to hold the memory of the yurt, the way home. Stumbling on roots, stopping to vomit dry with nothing to heave. What can I give you, Mother, please not myself.

Waking on the rugs, no memory, it was only seconds ago. Too much light. Torn canvas of the yurt, splintered frame and sagging poles. Crawling to the flickering sunlight where half of the yurt was no longer. Claw marks like a spray of knives. I never saw him, I never heard him, he didn't touch me. I saw her. Dark and humid, she held my arms and looked at me. The great drum face, old skin pulled tight, patchwork green cloth under the iridescent blue beads.

She will not hurt me, she needs no reason. She stuck her finger in my wrist, slipping into the ulnar artery. Releasing herself into my blood, like soil and electricity, vegetal and fleshly, her unwashed breath on my face. Long, long, long, until the lodestone sang from fingertip to brain and my heart burst red.

BROTHERS

They had been to see the yurt and fix it and talk among themselves.

All hail the bear wrestler!

Opening the cabin door to assess the shouting. Line of men bowing and grinning.

Three days is long enough. Come out and tell the tale. The fire is lit and your audience waits.

More grinning. And so the ballad of the crazy Englishman passed into the litany and the men marveled at the solitary stigma on his wrist.

He was chewing your arm off but you bravely slept!
The bear knew you were crazy and ran!

And they slapped his back and held his arms and smiled to bring him back lest he wander too far into his mind and lose the way. For your brothers and sisters are all the world and there is no world other.

Eat some soup, you fool!

Ava and Gabriel loose in the world, children there are monsters.

Around the fire the story unfolds and spoons are pressed to my mouth and spilled over my shirt, they seem to laugh at everything. The fetish on the splitting block resting on the axe, inside me.

Every night, brothers.

Yes, you are. Yes, you are, my brothers. Nikolai carrying armloads of wood, shirt off, muscles like an ox. Put down the wood, Nikolai. Standing in front of him, palm on his chest, push him, push him, wet eyes. All of life. All of life, Nikolai.

At night she leans over me. She is inside me. Her face begins to disappear, I disappear with her. It starts in the middle, starts eating her face, sucking her in like a black hole, starts slow and ends with nothing. She is gone, I'm gone. Nothing. Every night.

Nikolai setting me down like a child, holding my wrists over each other to stop my hands from shaking.

It happened to me, it's happening now, all around us, it's not from the past.

What is it, Bastian, what is happening?

Death.

Eyes looking at me, at each other, looking for meaning, who would know?

Who is she, Nature?

Yes, Nature. All Life.

Who would kill her?

Yes, who would kill her? A thing without blood, a thing with no history, out of nowhere.

Dark, silent faces around the fire, waiting for the fetish, I am the fetish. Waiting for me to speak, for her to speak. For me to find the words.

We won't be ourselves. Something else. We will be something else.

Spine

The bell sounding through the window, man stood by embers
from yesterday's fire, holding up the iron. The beginning to
days unlike to any other. Paths and trails to outlying
structures, martens in the trees with pine cones in their
dextrous paws. Resin on the trees like vegetal blood. Monks
and men, fish smoking over charcoal. The forest whispering at
night. Come closer.

Nikolai lifting a door from a small earthen mound. Dwarf
shrubs and mosses obscuring its radial symmetry. Like a
burial mound. Sudden electric light, smooth surfaces, monitor
screens. Nikolai grinning.

Cables from the river. Micro-hydro. Miles of it.

You want to wire me up to this stuff?

Yes.

What have you found out so far?

You know about the Schumann resonance?

*Natural resonance of the Earth, generated between the surface and
the ionosphere, as in between one sphere inside another.*

*Just so. And the frequency of relaxed attention of the human
brain?*

Exactly the same. They're identical.

Yes, they are. Hell of a coincidence.

Obviously not.

*No, and that's why people who are deprived of access to the
Schumann resonance, such as living underground, start getting
anxious, depressed and ill. Even being in a building rather than the
open air will have some effect in that direction.*

So, you live in the taiga.

*I wish I was here more. Perhaps it would speak to me like it did to
you.*

If that was the taiga it did more than speak to me.

*Yes, that's why I've moved things on so quickly. The problem with
the Schumann resonance is that it's not just rock and earth that
shields it. So does electromagnetism.*

Of which there's no end.

Mobile phones, WiFi, TV, relay towers. Electromagnetic smog blocks our access to the natural signal of the Earth. Our brains can't cope with it. Like the Romans who lined their aqueducts with lead and made themselves crazy with the poisoning, we are losing our sanity.

I know from my own work about the Earth. It's magnetic fields and the magnetic fields of our brains, the way they work together. You're talking about being cut off from that, too.

I am. Sun, Earth, human, magnetic fields like nested boxes, like Russian dolls. Information flows between them like water. In my life I am gifted with privilege, I am in a position to know things hidden from the world. Let me tell you about science. Do you know what electromagnetic theories are based on?

Yes, Maxwell's equations.

Maxwell's equations. The jewel of mathematics, expressed in quaternions. Later translated in the late nineteenth century to more conventional maths by Heaviside and used in that form ever since. Simplified but eviscerated.

Science has bifurcated. In the early part of the last century a curious thing happened. Field theory was discarded, unable to cope theoretically with the newly discovered weak and strong subatomic forces. So then we had relativity and gravitational theories, later at odds with quantum theory. The problem, though, is that field theory was, and is, engineerable. Electrogravitics, anti-gravity and a host of other exotic phenomena.

Let me guess. Not everybody discarded it.

No. The Nazis, for example, with their non-Jewish science. A million miles ahead of the West or the Soviet Union. The post war race for Berlin was more about places like Pilzen, a race for technology that would never be made public. Now we hear wonderful things from cosmologists. The universe we can see is only a tiny part of what's out there. Gravitational theory demands more. Black holes, Dark matter, Dark energy. All invisible. But electromagnetic phenomena alone account for everything from the shape of galaxies to the endless anomalies of our sun, which, by the way, they keep trying to tell us is thermonuclear despite the evidence clearly indicating it isn't.

The sun is a purely electrical phenomenon, strung out with other stars like Christmas lights on electrical threads, themselves twisted in pairs like DNA helixes. Information flows along the electrical highway throughout the entire galaxy which is, in turn, strung out with other galaxies along even greater electrical pathways. When you pick up magnetic lines with your dowsing rods you are accessing information flowing from horizon to horizon in the known universe and beyond.

I'm beginning to see why you want to get away from the electromagnetic smog.

Yes, in the last century field theory and other electromagnetic work began disappearing from university courses and libraries.

So who has it now?

That's a big question. Call it black ops, call it cabals within government and the corporations that make their tech. It's not a power structure of a recognised sort. The point is that the technology they are developing is off the scale. It facilitates strategies that are increasingly divergent from conventional frameworks.

But as you know, I'm no science whizz so...

So this tech around you can measure brain activity in all kinds of ways but particularly in relation to the magnetic fields it generates. One of the things we have discovered is that when people are engaged in psychic activity their right brain generates a strong magnetic spike at guess what resonance?

Seriously?

Seriously. The very same Schumann resonance.

You're saying the Earth's magnetic field is the medium for telepathy?

A medium, at least.

A medium that spans the known universe.

Certainly, there are no barriers. Space is not empty, it is full of plasma shaped by magnetic fields, mediated by electrical currents.

That is, a sufficiently sensitive brain could access what?

Everything? All the information out there?

You tell me.

Because I have a sensitive brain.

Yes.

You want me to be an oracle.

That might be helpful but no. There's more.

Hmm.

What do you think of full spectrum dominance?

Think of over reach.

Well, attempts were made to shield from psychic activity by means of magnetic fields. Interfering with the magnetism of the brain. You have a well known professor in the West who works in this area and describes how one day they were having technical problems and so used a computer with a well known operating system as a patch to generate magnetic fields. On that day all psychic activity was blocked. Turns out that the operating system, at use in most homes in the West and across much of the world, put out its signal, or smog, at all frequencies simultaneously, blanketing all frequencies. Total spectrum dominance.

Did the people who designed it know this?

I'm sorry to keep saying this. You tell me. Either way our consciousness is being blocked by artificial magnetism in general and these effects in particular. Apart from driving us crazy these things are blocking our sensitivity at all levels, not just psychic tricks but empathy. The higher functions of cognition and emotion, these things that are central to our evolution beyond the animals, and ultimately our connections to each other, the Earth, the universe. Perhaps even to God if he is other than these things.

You're saying our evolution is being curtailed.

I am.

And you want me to...

Tell me what to do about it. Do something about it.

But I'm crazy. Talk to dolls.

No-one thinks you're crazy.

No. I can see that.

No-one has tried to define your experience for you. But the timing is interesting. It seems we have allies.

Even if it's just my unconscious.

Even so.

You ever think that reality is less objective than we're told? That it's malleable and subjectively created?

It's a mystery beyond imagination, Bastian. These guys who think they have it taped, that we're almost at the point of understanding everything, these guys have lost the plot. It's a mystery what happened to you.

You've been waiting patiently and now you feel it's safe to nudge a little. Let's go outside.

Sitting down on top of the dome, Bastian cross-legged, Nikolai following suit. Cold morning air and damp vegetation. Low light flickering up through the larch and birch.

Maybe it's just the taiga, Nikolai, it affects you. But since that night I've been aware of things differently. I can feel the life in things, plants animals, humans. Just talking about it accelerates it.

Advanced case of biophilia.

Advanced heart attack. My thymus gland must be in overtime. I know the heart has neural material. It's like I can feel it talking to my brain, it's like my skin is dissolving. I'm looking at this tree and I can almost see light moving through the bark, sap through the capillaries, oxygen coming off the leaves. It's inside me. Jesus, Nikolai, I don't think there's any way back.

Sounds beautiful, Bastian.

Beautiful here. Being in a city would kill me.

Perhaps, but you can speak for life.

What?

The one that spoke to you, the fetish.

She is life.

She is life.

She didn't ask me if I wanted her to push into my veins.

Are you sure?

No.

Well, then.

Well, then, what?

What are you going to do?

How should I know? You're the head honcho around here.

No, I'm not.

Ah, yes, Jesus. You think he would approve of fetish dolls and craziness?

How should I know?

I suppose you never met him.

I met somebody. So did you.

Yes.

Who's to say which is which and who is who?

Who is?

Well, there's only us here, Bastian.

What about the bear that came with the fetish?

He's a bear.

But also something else.

We're all something else.

What if I go out tonight. Can I call him back?

The Westerner plays with the Russian bear. What if he's in a bad mood?

I know. You're asking what I should do.

You're going to talk to the animals.

Maybe. If I can. You don't like it?

What about people?

Talk to people?

Yes.

Which people?

People who can hear you, people who can talk back.

You have such people?

Maybe. So do you.

Don't mess with my daughter, Nikolai.

If you thought I would do that you would not have invited her.

No.

Let me tell you what our governments are up to.

Alright.

But she is with me, Nikolai. She is watching from the trees. The cracked leather of her face and the smell of the earth. You don't know, Nikolai, to have pushed the boat out so far.

Do you know how you found Saddam Hussein when you lost the weapons of mass destruction?

No.

Down a hole with some cash and a bunch of Mars bars. You have a guy who does the right brain thing with the magnetic field increase.

He concentrates on a person and after a while the other person's brain waves start to mirror his. Next thing, he's reeling off their memories. He tells the military that he remembers Saddam getting himself in the rat hole and bingo, all the angels sing.

Shit.

Yes.

And that's why you have all this tech under out feet?

Yes.

Do you have anyone who can do that?

Not until now.

You want to weaponise me?

Yes and no. Not to be part of anything military, not to hurt people, nothing geopolitical.

Not trying to fry people's brains at a distance? Not to tell them in their sleep to kill themselves?

All this goes on, yes, but it's not something I would want for you, not for anyone.

How do you know I could do that stuff anyway?

I don't but I do know some things. Being in intelligence and it being my business to know.

What things?

How do you think I came to watch over you, invite you here?

I've been thinking about it.

There's a woman.

Oh, Lord.

Yes. She saw you. In her dreams. She said there was a light around you.

A light.

She told me to find you.

When was this?

Ten years ago.

Where is this woman?

She's here.

Here? Doesn't that put the brothers off their prayers?

Probably.

Are there other women here?

Not at the moment.

Hmm. Where are you hiding her?

She's in a place like where you met the fetish.

Alone with the bears.

Yes.

So much for chivalry.

It's her choice.

Hmm.

I brought you here to see if you had these abilities or perhaps others. Just now you told me how your experience has changed you. I am tempted to see this as a syllogism.

You believe in me because fate tells you to.

Like we said, it's a mystery.

I don't fancy being hooked up to your machines.

Alright.

No persuasion?

I like crucibles. Throw in some ingredients and turn up the heat. I don't need to be in charge of what gets cooked up.

So long as it's spicy.

The fetish and the bear, they're beyond my plans.

I hear you. So what's next?

Well if you're going to turn your nose up at all my shiny machines how about meeting the woman who asked that you be brought here?

Alright. What's her name?

Olga.

Does she know I'm here?

I don't know. I haven't told her.

Why not?

She's busy.

Doing what?

God knows.

FUR

Pulling away from the warmth of his body to look at his face.
Not the same.

What happened to you, Dada?

I don't know. Nikolai thinks it's ok.

Nikolai does.

*Me, too. I'm sorry, it's just my humour, not quite up to the
moment. You look great. See you have Gabriel with you.*

Just tell me.

I will. Let's walk.

Leaving her things by his cabin and strolling into the woods
arm in arm.

What about Gabriel?

Nikolai will look after him.

Alright.

Peeling resin off the trees and sniffing at it. To find the soul
of the place. Dada has gone away. Where is he? He is a fetish
man. He is in the resin from the trees, I can smell him. Cross-
legged and talking, back against the tree, he is in my spine.
Changes. His changes changing me. A data-mining algorithm
in my head. What is he looking for? He is looking at me.

I'm not myself Ava.

I know. What are you?

*This man, Nikolai, he wants the light to grow. He wants me to look
for where life exceeds itself. Where the threads meet. Or people.*

Or the fetish wants it.

So it seems.

She is life?

That's what we said.

We.

Another we. You and me are still we. You and Gabriel, too.

It's that obvious?

Smiling, now. Looks more human. Telling the story. Says the
fetish follows him around, would I like to meet her?

What? Is that safe? How would you do it?

I think it's safe depending on how you define it. You'll have to be sharp, I've not caught up with myself, yet. I think you may have to want it.

Want a bear in the night?

See, that's how blind I am. There's a danger to this experience that I haven't understood. Maybe we should see Olga.

Why Olga?

I was winding up to it when I heard you had arrived.

Alright, but let's go see what your Nikolai has done with Gabriel.

Walking into a circle of men by the fire, clapping and laughing. Nikolai and Gabriel stripped to the waist, wrestling. Gabriel has no chance but it hasn't stopped him. More like Nikolai teaching him moves.

Were you expecting this, Da?

No, but I'm not surprised.

Why?

It's a welcome embrace.

One of the men listening and nodding at her.

Yes, Gabriel said he didn't believe in Jesus so Nikolai challenged him to a fight. Fighting is a good way for men to get to know each other.

The sweat making them slick. Not the sort of thing you see back home. Dada watching me and grinning. Eventually grabbing them both by the shoulder.

Stop messing about, Nikolai, we were supposed to be off to see Olga. Let's bring the kids.

We stink like her goats, maybe she won't notice.

Freezing white water in the stream carrying away the smell. The water tastes different, different minerals or maybe just clean. Inhale it into the nostrils, splash the face. Not like home. Where the countryside is a market garden. Here the wild back of beyond.

Walking behind Gabriel, pushing him in the back. Him stumbling into Nikolai and apologising. Edge of hysteria, perhaps. Should be worried about Dada but that's not the mood. Olga-bound with sail set high. Somewhere there's a hard landing but not yet.

True to the tale there's a yurt surrounded by goats you would best be upwind of. No tethers.

Visitors, at last. I was beginning to think you had forgotten me.

Disembodied voice, eventually centring on a tree some way behind them. Olga stepping out and forward, an unlikely babushka.

As I could hear you a mile away I thought I'd check on what comes this way. Please come in and have tea.

Olga and Nikolai hugging and grinning. Like two old boots, these two. Brief chat in Russian before introductions. Ordering the men to milk the goats for the tea.

Sit, Ava.

Watching Gabriel chase goats past the doorway of the yurt, men laughing.

What are you doing with Gabriel?

I'm not doing anything with... I love him.

Smiling. Why do I want her approval?

I'm glad.

How come everyone speaks such good English?

Why are you here?

My Dad...

I want you to be my Mother.

Your Father is not the same.

I know.

Will you marry Gabriel?

I've only just met him.

Or divorce him?

I don't think so.

You have the right. You don't need a reason.

My Mother had a reason. It didn't make sense to me.

Do you know what the main cause of death in black people in the West is?

No. Violence?

Abortion.

The fire crackling, silence outside.

You have the right, Ava. Gabriel will not be able to stop you.

My sister is dead. I never met her. My brother, too.

After such an act a woman will never be the same. Your Planned Parenthood people started with the Ku Klux Klan, to murder black people. They soon went on to whites. Now they are campaigning for post-term abortion.

I...

We remember communism. They said we would be equal. Some more equal than others. Now they do the same in Western social policy. Political correctness comes from the Communist manifesto. Your feminists are communists, funded by your intelligence agencies. Culture change agents. They aim to destroy the family in order to free women. Your women are so brainwashed they don't know this even though it is explicitly stated. They aim to have childhood run by the state, population reduction, mass infertility. You know these things?

Yes.

You know that they want to destroy your men so they cannot fight against the state, to stop them protecting their families? You must protect Gabriel so he can fight for you and your children.

You are my Mother.

I will protect him. As my Father has protected me.

Good. Every year your women are more liberated and yet every year your statistics show they are less happy. Why?

We have to have careers, children, beautiful sex lives. Without all these things we are failures.

You have been told that having children makes you just a cow.

Yes.

So your men are just donkeys.

Yes.

Now you can be a donkey instead of a cow?

Yes.

What do you think about raising children?

It is the deepest thing in the world.

Yes, it is. The greatest intelligence is what it needs.

My body cries to me, Olga. For children.

I believe you. Your body and brain are completely different from those of a man. You cannot be like him, nor he like you, however much you pretend, however much your schools brainwash you. This is what you call hate speech.

Biology.

Yes, biology. Something to rise above, to leave behind. In order to become alienated from yourself and your world. Children are what will make you happy, Ava. There is nothing superficial about your biology, it is divine.

Tears running onto my hands. Strands of eye-liner threading the water, salt stinging where scratches part the skin. I can't stop, I don't want to stop. The madness in our lives. The damage we carry. It was her that told me to do it, I can't take it back, I was so young.

I'm sorry, Olga.

I am sorry, too, Ava. Let me hold you.

The comfort of her breast. Madonna mine, intercede with Him. I need you, I always needed you. Where have you been?

Where are the men?

They have left.

Why?

Because I asked them to.

You never spoke.

Olga, are you real?

Yes, Ava, Olga Volga, here I am.

What is happening?

Do you know about the Holy Trinity?

Father, Son and Holy Ghost?

It is not the right way of saying the truth.

Do the monks know you think like this?

Yes.

What is the right way?

Have you seen Osiris, Isis with her child Horus?

Yes.

To be a whore is to be with Horus, with child.

No.

Yes. In the Judaic tradition the man who brings the wine at the wedding can only be the bridegroom. The man who brought the wine was Jesus. With his wife.

They had children?

Such is the story. Either way the empire lied. The old Fathers lied and now the feminists lie. For the same reason, to divide us and rule us. The King is dead, they tell you, long live the Queens. They would have us crawl in the dust.

So what is the Holy Trinity?

Father, Mother, child. From the beginning and always. This is our survival, our evolution and our humanity. Family is far more than meets the eye. It is the crucible in which our souls are made.

Our home.

Our home.

BEGIN

The women talking. Olga wants us to push off. Nikolai
leading on through the forest, life straining through the earth
up to the sky. Lipids in the leaves, sterols and aromatic oils,
soft wet electric discharge oozing from the trees. She is
everywhere in these things and in the soil under my feet.
There is earth in my brain.

   This is what she told me today.

   DNA. Three billion base pairs in the human genome.
Adenine, Thymine, Cytosine, Guanine. Each base pair is two
bits of data having four possible combinations. Four base pairs
make eight bits of data; a byte. The human genome has
around seven hundred and fifty megabytes of data. Less than
a movie.

   Or maybe it was a memory.

   Is this true, Nikolai?

   The math is basic.

   *She says that amount of information couldn't come close to
encoding the complexity of the human body.*

   No.

   The geneticists lie.

   *Science is magical thinking. We came out of nowhere for no reason
in a big bang.*

   Why does she tell me this?

   Because science does not tell us who we are?

   She is saying death.

   That science will kill us?

   Maybe. Or we should kill it.

   Science is neutral.

   She tells me to wait.

   What for?

   I don't know.

   She stands behind the birch. I can smell her breath. I will lie
down.

   Nikolai and Gabriel come to sit with me, Nikolai puts his

hand on my chest. After a while they back off and I can see only the sky through the leaves and branches, faint cirrus above like feathers. I can hear them talking faintly, like whispers, Gabriel's rough tenor.

Your brothers are not like other men I have met, Nikolai.
No.
They serve Jesus Christ.
Yes.
It bothers me.
Why would it bother you what they believe?
Because we're not on holiday.
No. What bothers you?
What you're all up to.
You don't believe in Christ.
No. I think it's all some bullshit empire building propaganda.
From Rome?
Yes, but not just that.
Russian Orthodoxy is not the same as Catholicism.
Not much accommodation with Zionism either.
Not at any level.
But it's still Sky God and what you can't see.
Some people have experiences.
Like Bastian. Does that mean his fetish doll is real, is a God, a Goddess?
It means there is something mysterious and powerful going on, no?
Perhaps, but... I don't want to insult you, Nikolai, but you it seems to me your Church has been built on dogma by illiterate men with limited minds.
Is that not so of all religions?
I think so.
What do you think is happening to Bastian?
How would I know?
Come on.
Alright. He's in touch with something.
What about you?
Am I in touch with something?

Yes.

Not like him.

In so far as you are.

I don't have the words.

But you don't like Christian words.

I'm not a propagandist.

Nor are the brothers here.

But you're still...

You know what we are?

Well, that's why I'm asking.

The brothers here are in transition.

As in?

Olga has plans for them.

Olga.

Yes.

Who is she?

To them she is Sophia. Intelligence.

And to you?

We help each other.

To do what?

No reply that I can hear. Survive, Gabriel. We are helping each other to survive. Is that purpose enough? The voices have gone, leaving birdsong from strange birds.

Dada?

Sweet Ava.

Are you alright?

We're not machines, Ava.

No.

They can't copy us. Replicate us. The fetish told me that DNA is not enough to build us, not by a country mile.

Ava reaching for my hand, twining her fingers in mine.

Evolution, Ava. Mathematics. There's a law that's the opposite of entropy. States of disequilibrium tend to jump spontaneously to more organised forms. More complicated forms. It's exponential, you can't see the end. There is no end.

Evolution.

She talks about causality. Maybe I'm just remembering something

I forgot. There are experiments where effect precedes cause. Not just quantum physics. The intelligence we are evolving is the same as the one that created us. She whispers about past, present, future. She is a crow that would bend the laws.

Why?

So that we survive. We, her.

Why would we not survive?

Can you not think of reasons? She will take me there, I think. Like a bad dream.

Olga thinks you're ok.

That's good.

It's weird, she's like my Mother. What have you brought us to, Da?

I'm running on instinct. I hope it's ok.

Ava looking away, biting her nails.

Olga told me about Rome. How the slaves were run by women. They would take the women from a new group of slaves and kill a few of their children in front of them. They would tell the women they had to control the men and make them good slaves or more children would be killed. They got people to police themselves. She said this was what they did with black people in America, black women controlling their men and poor whites. The eugenicists even attempted to breed powerful black women for the part.

America is like Rome.

Yes. What happened with Mother, what I did... I know the eugenicists, they are still with us. The women are still being used to control the men and make them subservient to the state.

Olga.

Olga. Olga Volga. She said I had to help. How our families were being destroyed. How we couldn't even replace our own numbers without immigration. About the promotion of homosexuality to erode the family, control population. About trying to destroy fertility. She said we needed to love the children. Pre-school club, post-school club, holiday club, free child care. Just tells them they come second, third, fourth. Never first.

What does she want you to do?

She said that if the women don't look after the children and support their men there will be no-one to oppose the global technocratic dictatorship. She wants me to be good to Gabriel, to make him strong. She wants me to forgive myself. She wants me to fight for our families, our future.

    She wants you to think about marriage, children.

    Yes.

    She told Nikolai to bring me here.

    Do you know why?

    No, I don't. And I haven't spoken to her yet.

    Ava smiling the smile she knows I love.

    She sent me to ask you to go see her now.

Hovering outside the yurt. Can't remember what happened to the others. Goats, penned in and leaning on the wooden fence, catching the fading sun. Never trust a goat.

    Hello, Bastian, thank you for coming.

    Beautiful woman. Not so young.

    Sorry, I was miles away.

    Yes. Come in.

The wood stove crackling and her putting the kettle on one side. Aromatic smells. Glancing at each other, proffering little smiles and settling down with tea. Intense milk of the goats.

    I'm sorry, Bastian, I don't seem to be very chatty.

    You asked Nikolai to bring me here.

    Yes.

    How did you do that?

    Ah, now that's a bit of a story.

    Opening his hands and waiting. Nowhere else to be.

    Your daughter is a beautiful girl. Very talented.

    Smiling at her. I like you.

    Yes.

    We have many talented people here.

    And you have plans for them all?

    I'm not the only one with plans.

    She's not like everyone else. Ava trusts her already. But then I trusted Nikolai.

Alright.
Then stay, Bastian.

FIELD

Domes full of silver tech and the backwash of blue lights. Uncomfortable rows of small, caged animals. Dome encircled with aquaria, small colourful fish and bubbling pumps. Nikolai's dream dome.

Know anything about fish, Ava?

Know how to cook them, Nikolai.

Here the pike need wrestling before cooking.

Like Gabriel?

He's a lucky boy.

Olga's worried he might not be.

Ah, that you might blame the culture instead of the state.

Something like that, I think. Use the state to protect us from the culture.

We had such fun here with communism. The political one. You have the culture change agents.

She said women choose compliance, that's why they do well at school. She said we had to fight against the thought police, the ones who control the language.

Are you interested in astrology?

Not really.

They say we are entering the Age of Aquarius. Procession of the equinoxes. With Aquarius on top, Leo is on the bottom. I think Olga is saying that the suppression of masculinity and the suppression of individuality are one and the same. That a female dominated society is conducive to collectivist, state-mediated totalitarian solutions. Insect nation.

We bought it, though.

So did we. How can anyone disagree with equality? You want children?

Yes.

Then you will be dependent either on Gabriel or some other boy, or the state. If you are dependent on the state you will be dependent on men's taxation collectively rather than on your husband. You can easily pretend you are not and that you are economically equal.

Or not have children and be equal.

Who could disagree with equality?

Children growing in tanks in the warehouses of the state like fish in aquaria.

Do you really believe in astrology, Nikolai?

Well, what do you know about the sun?

Ah, I see. The sun's electrical and magnetic fields affect the Earth and all living things. Presumably there are resonances with the planets.

Tesla was obsessed with resonance. But you haven't told me what you know about the sun.

Why do I get the idea you already know?

I'm sorry. I haven't interfered because of your age.

But you felt free to interfere with my Dad.

Yes. But then he was having some problems.

Yes, thank you, Nikolai. I mean it.

So tell me what it's like to see magnetism.

Alright. It's blue, like lines of force superimposed on visual space. It's beautiful.

Do you see it all the time?

I think so but it's faint so you get used to not seeing it a lot of the time.

Around people?

If I focus.

People are different? To each other?

Very. My Dad's different. More different than anyone else I've looked at.

Can you see yourself?

No.

Me?

Hmm. You're different in another way, but not like Dad.

What do these differences mean?

No idea. Well, not no idea but I don't know.

What can you tell me about it?

I can tell you I see magnetic fields, that they're everywhere, that they change all the time. But I can ask you something.

Alright.

Olga.

You looked at her.

Yes.

And she's different.

More than different. I wasn't going to talk about this but now I want to. All my life my Dad showed the most radical divergence I could see but now...

Now?

Not like the rest of us.

Ava, please tell me what you see.

No. You tell me. She has affected me like no-one I have ever met. I left my Father with her, a woman that asked he be brought here. I want to know.

What do you want to know?

What she is?

What rather than who?

Yes.

I can't answer such a question.

Why not?

I don't know the answer.

That's not very reassuring, Nikolai.

No.

Then what can you tell me?

Like you say, that she is not like anyone else. That I have worked with her for a long time. That I trust her.

With her or for her?

Hmm. Well, honestly I'm not sure but if it was for her I wouldn't mind. It's not about me or her but what we're working towards.

Which is?

Well, the idea of you both coming here is that you should know.

I'm listening.

Have you seen any changes recently?

As in?

The Earth's magnetic field?

There have been changes all my life. What do I have to compare them to?

Well, you know that the field is weakening, shifting?

Leading at some point to a magnetic polar reversal.

Yes, there are gaps appearing and local reversals.

I can see the orientation beginning to shift, the lines are moving to the east. The North Pole is wandering.

It always does. But recently it has accelerated to such an extent that its location is being kept secret.

Secret.

Years ago flights across the pole were difficult because compasses go crazy. The Americans thought we might use this phenomenon to launch a sneaky attack on the land of the free. So, back in the 40's, Major Maynard E White takes the 46th Reconnaissance Squadron, the first operational unit in the Strategic Air Command, to investigate. He comes up with a grid system which is still in use today. He gets a bunch of physicists to look into what happens when magnetic North coincides with geographic North. In every experiment the sphere turns over or destabilises. Guess where magnetic North is headed?

No.

Oh, yes.

You think the Earth is going to turn over.

Maybe. But the magnetic reversal is for sure and it's not thousands of years away the way it's sold in the media.

That's why they're hiding magnetic North.

Yes.

So what happens with magnetic reversal?

What do you know so far?

Birds get confused.

Yes. Not only birds.

What else?

All manner of things. Let me show you some fish.

This is why you brought me here.

Yes.

Alright, then.

See this tank here with the small silver fish.

Yes.

Different markings, two species?

I suppose.

They've been together for months, they don't interbreed.

Alright.

The ones with fewer markings were the originals. When they were gravid, that is pregnant, we subjected them to particular changes in magnetic fields. The spawn are the other ones you see.

A new species?

New genome.

Jesus.

Well.

Playing God out in the taiga.

I hope not. It's not even hard to do.

That's even worse.

Yes.

Looking at the fish, seeing the little lines of force around them. Evolution happens in sudden jumps. All that gradual change through competition stuff is just ideology for the eugenicists.

When the Earth changes its magnetic polarity evolution happens in one generation?

Yes.

Jesus.

It's more complicated than that but yes, it's the magnetism. The whole universe is an electric phenomenon.

You've got these laboratories out here to jump start evolution?

No.

Thank God for that.

Thank God.

What, then?

First step is to let you know that opportunity sits on your shoulder.

To evolve. Change our DNA.

Yes.

And what's the second step?

That there are problems with evolution.

Problems.

Yes.

There are more steps?

That's where you come in.

Sitting down next to a tank with the strangest looking fish. Maybe they Frankensteined them.

What do you want me to do?

Look at the sun.

Go blind.

We have filters, clever software, you will be able to see the heliosphere almost down to the surface.

I'd like that, the sun is like a friend.

Also the Earth.

I can do that already.

Not from space.

Every three sentences you open another world. You and your orthodoxy.

I...

You can get a rocket? Slip me a Soyuz? Or an Angara?

Maybe, but there are other choices.

Exotic ones?

Maybe. Or just less public ones.

Dad said you likely pumped the Nazis.

Hard to think of a pie they didn't have their fingers in. We've come a long way since then.

What else you want me to look at?

Planets, people, the way things join together. Maybe you'll lead us.

Off the beaten track? Like my Dad?

Yes.

Hard to know who's pulling the strings.

Yes.

Watching him trying to cut the brush from the jungle. The opener of ways. Open our mouths with iron instruments. Poor Nikolai. No good deed goes unpunished. Take us with you to a sticky end. Where's my sailor boy? Will you take him too? You don't know where we're going, Nikolai.

STIGMA

Here she is. She is here. She is on me like a succubus and her loamy breath is in my nostrils. She is whispering to me and she is full of fear. She tells me she is so frightened she might void her bowels. She wants to show me, she wants protection, she wants to be loved.

Under her skin there are things moving that she cannot remove. They are taking away her will. Her dress has pulled back at the top and the leathery skin is exposed, cracking and flaking across her shoulder, pulling strands of the epidermis down to the tissue underneath. The reek of poison and rotting flesh. A taste, black and alien, it is the taste of metal.

Flashes of boreal forest, black streaks on the lime green leaves. A pine marten slipping from a branch onto the litter below, unable to co-ordinate its limbs. No birdsong. An image of change, blue and gold streaming between plants and animals and humans, degrading to black, disorganised and disrupted, isolated and aimless, deteriorating, displaced by something that was not life. Something invading the forest, circumscribing the globe, regimented and empty. Leaping from orbit to assail planets and suns.

See the vortex growing in her solar plexus, sucking at the earth and sap of her body like a black hole eating all things in its reach. Life draining from her body, tearing her apart, slowly at first and then accelerating, twist into the void in her guts. Reaching out, give me your hand. Her finger penetrating the artery, injected herself into me, pouring her life into my veins as she corkscrews into nothing, into a place where there is nothing but death.

She lives now only in me and she shows me my daughter. The metal table and the stirrups. The glistening instruments. A Mother's encouraging words. You're doing the right thing. Pulling him away. My boy, my girl, my future. Colour me in blood. My hands will be claws. Screaming no but it is too late and a life floats in a slop bucket. My mouth is full of ash and all things have come to an end.

Ava, my beautiful girl. Could I but help you. The fetish lives in me. You still live, Ava, there can still be children, there can still be life. My tears with yours, we will make an alchemy, a future, and you will have life still. Your body is young and though the scars will be forever you will bring joy into this world. If I knew how to pray I would pray for you. I pray for you. It's only humility after all. Hold on, my girl.

Spine shifting on the bed. My spine. Hand on my hand. Olga Volga. Is it her? Is she the fetish? Through my eyelids I can see her, hear her breath. Nikolai's friend. Like I can see the light in trees and animals and people and she is an explosion at my bedside. Who brought me here. These gifts I can hardly bear, Olga, this remaking of me. I have brought my daughter to you.

We hunted badgers, watched foxes by moonlight. Gathered fruit from the trees we planted, scraped up horse manure and carried it to the vegetable beds. We played football. We held hands when the drugs brought her down. We held each other to make the world safe.

Be gentle with my daughter, Olga.

Yes.

Don't do to her what you have done to me.

Do you regret what has happened to you?

No.

Well, then. Tell me what happened.

You don't know?

No.

Massaging tendons and muscles in his hand as he spoke. Surprised by tears on her face. Leathery skin like the fetish.

I grew up in a place like this, Bastian, an endless forest with the cold and the boundless stars. The communists left us alone at that time, thinking us too marginal to be of interest, if they knew of us at all. There were villages strung across the taiga, not just Asians but Russians as well. My Father was Orthodox but we had no priests. He came to escape the authorities and brought us to live where the kindness of people still opened its hand to you, teaching you skills and the strength of mind to survive.

Soon I was learning from what was left of the shamans and playing with boys who tried to teach me their overtone singing. The doll you describe was not forgotten when I was young. She would guard the house at night and when owners were away, not so much from people but from dark spirits. You suspect that I am connected with her, the one who is inside you, but I am not, or not consciously. She is as much of a surprise to me as she is to you.

I have lived in forests all my life and I have seen bears many times. They have come looking for food and we have lost dogs to them, dogs who tried to guard us, but I have never seen a bear behave anything like the one in your yurt.

Scars on his wrist itching, the bear may have had something in its saliva, some infection.

Olga.

The statement of her name a way of coming to terms.

How did you become friends with Nikolai?

Nikolai is a complex man. Do you know how he became involved with intelligence?

No.

Through the Orthodox seminaries. That's how they recruited intelligent men.

Not the only one apparently.

No. He grew up in a religious family and learnt his reverence from an early age.

He has had some kind of experience. To do with Christ.

Yes. More than one. He has had an unusual career path.

What do you know of his experiences?

You can't figure him out?

No.

I know everything about them. He is my brother.

Watching her build up the fire and shut the stove door. This family affair.

You don't look like him.

My Mother went to the city to sort out some affairs. My Father didn't want her to go but was unwilling to try to stop her. She was a *very strong willed woman. She never came back. I was five.*

I'm sorry, Olga.

Yes, so were we, we cried for such a long time. Later my Father married another woman, one who had lost her husband to the communists. He discussed it with me and said my Mother would have wanted it that way. Eventually I agreed and before long I had a baby brother.

What happened to your Mother?

We never found out. There were stories.

Did you love your new Mother?

She died, too.

I'm sorry.

Yes.

You grew up with just your Father?

Yes.

Ava's Mother left.

I know.

We seem to be short of them.

Yes.

Do you have children?

I have not been able to have children.

I'm sorry.

Me, too.

No husband.

He left me.

Because of the children?

Yes, and because of me.

What did you do?

I wasn't like him. Later I understood that I was asking too much of him. He was an honourable man but I was beyond his capacity.

I'm sorry.

Yes. Things happen around me. Things he didn't like.

I know how he feels.

But you like it.

I don't know about liking it but I'm not running.

Good. I'm not so strong, Bastian, or Nikolai either, we need help. Your help.

Reaching for the knife next to the wood axe. Looking down at the wrist. Scars on the artery, fresh blood.

Like stigmata, Olga?

Yes.

Do you remember Odin?

I don't know.

Me neither.

Gleaming point of metal opening the lateral wound. Blood dripping red on Olga's matted floor, crimson against the white skin. Olga taking the knife from his hand, wiping it on her dress, holding it to the fire. Dipping it in the water bucket. Sliding it fresh and sharp on her own wrist and holding up her hand to him as the blood runs slowly down across the tendons and bones. Reaching wrist to wrist, hands and fingers stretching, arcing like slow-motion birds, blood on blood. Since ever we began we give one to the other.

Leaning on each other's shoulders to find home in each other's bones. The guile in my skull, your spine will hold me straight. Smiling and laughing quietly, away from the humdrum and toil, old friends, warriors well met in a quiet harbour.

I have been calling you for so long, Bastian, but you didn't come. In the end I asked Nikolai to bring you.

He said you dreamed me. A light.

Yes, a light. Around your skull, like a halo. Made me laugh. Are you a holy man?

Not so as I've noticed. Some people tried to put a hole in my head. Nikolai helped me. Because you told him about me, it seems. I owe you my life, my daughter's life.

I didn't know, Bastian, why you were in my mind, why I wanted to bring you here. It makes me nervous. What to do with you if you got here. You've made it easy for me. Thank you.

You have had a privileged education, your English.

Yes, my Father.

He is still with us?

He is dead. He made me promise. On his death bed. To fight.

And that's what you want of me. To fight?

I think so.

My Father told me about a dream. The 60's. A dream that lied. He said that he brought me out of that time like you ride out the flood. That it was only the dimming of the light. In my youth he told me to hold on because it was going to get worse. It took me a while to understand. He told me I would have to fight.

Yes.

It seems like a child's game when I think of what you have had to go through in Russia.

Tsars and politburos. Russia teaches us to think in longer cycles. I have waited twenty years to see you.

I have dreams, too, Olga, the ones where you see what will be. One morning I told my wife that I dreamed I was walking in Norfolk, a part of England I had never visited. I could see the streets around me and when I awoke I could find them easily on the map. That was when we went to libraries. I told her we had to go, she told me I was an idiot.

I went with my daughter on my back, like a rucksack. Footfalls in the steps of the previous night. When I got there, there was a house, a house in a financial bracket far beyond me. It had land and was in need of repair, at best. A man asked what I was looking at and ended up inviting me in. He was in a worse state than the house. He asked me to help him with some things. He had been in intelligence, reporting back from Berlin in the 30's and then during the War.

When I saw his rods I brought out mine and we started to laugh. He took me to some places, the two of us larking about like children. A year later my wife divorced me, took Ava and what little I had, I was homeless. This man took me in, said I could work for my rent while I found my feet. Showed me how to work with sodium and gold. I remember shining a torch through the glass and seeing the distillate levitating up to where the beam had been. One day it turned red. The next day he died.

I had come to love him. I just kept working, disengaged, maybe it was delayed shock or perhaps the gold. The ambulance had taken the body. Two days later I found a note with an address and telephone number, just sitting on the kitchen table under a vase with cut flowers from the woods. Name, address, telephone number. A relative or friend perhaps, someone to take care of matters.

The man thanked me for calling and said he would like to visit. I said alright. He asked me for identification. Only a debit card. He said he would do the rest. Two days later he came back. I was wondering how long he would give me before I had to leave. He showed me some papers, said the house and land were mine. That's where Gabriel found us.

It was a dream that had me running hither and yon and it infected me. Now I am infected by a fetish. The night before Nikolai brought me here I dreamed the same kind of dream again, all these years later. Your secret little base. I followed the river with the pike and the blue-eyed dogs, followed the trails. Just as I was pulling back a branch to see where I was I saw you.

You know where we are? That's hilarious. Nikolai's security...

Yes, but that's not my point.

Your point is your life is dominated by this kind of synchronicity and now it has led you here and you want me to offer you answers.

Something like that.

I don't know, Bastian, the fetish is yours, you brought her to me.

And she is life.

Yes, perhaps.

Only now she is dead. She is all around. She left a part of herself in me.

And now me.

She's showing us the future?

I think so. Where the present goes.

When she died there was nothing. Just artificial things.

Cyber things.

Yes, or just not alive. Mechanical.

But she lives on in you?

The first thing she gave me is biophilia. All living things, I can feel them. I can feel you.

You could ask her for more.

Be even crazier?

Yes.

Ask for what, how she died?

Yes. Look for solutions.
I think...
You think you are the solution.
In a way. And you.
The thing she did to you?
Yes.
When I look at you I could cry.
I'd probably cry with you.

Wind in the leaves strengthening, pulling at the fire in the stove, flames leaping eagerly.

I will carry this with you, Bastian, if you will allow.

Watching the fresh wound open as she flexes her wrist, hand face up, reaching forward. Blood arcing across her snow white skin.

SEED

Maps laid out on the round stone table, lines tracing the continent. All around the world, latitude and longitude like two doves with strings tied to their feet flying around the navel of the Earth. The work done and the work to come. Talk growing heated as time grows shorter. Cycles within cycles, the sun, the moon, the wobble of the Earth. Procession of the equinoxes. Pulses coming to the sun along the electrical filaments of other stars, the wiring of the galaxy. Rocks in space like angry bees, the remains of older times.

We have tried to focus the flows but urgency has seen us slip off the course that we prepared. Now that road is closing, its time over. Now there is a new plan. Survival. The preservation of our work in the bodies of the survivors and the will to begin again. And if we fail there is a fallback, a desperate failsafe prepared for whomever of us remains to stand in for memories lost.

The knowledge of the cycles in the stonework, maths, geometry, keys to the Earth's place in the cosmos. Because this will come again. The next wave. Let them know resonance and how to lift themselves and the Earth.

But with the others the plans fragment and discord threatens all our labour. Intervention brings incalculable risks and yet passivity may be the death of all we have worked for. We wanted time to tell of the changing orbits, of discharges between the worlds, of how we shaped ourselves. We wanted to continue.

But the chances grow slimmer and there is an obligation. The others need help, also. Yes, we will use them but they need us. It is for the benefit of all. So we have slipped from the stream and cast our own plans. The resistance is fierce but we press on, our minds are set. We will carry the costs and outcomes ourselves.

Stepping out to meet the woman. Lovely she is in her simple shift. Dark hair and eyes, light brown skin so different from my own. The crude jewellery, so dear to her kind. She is like a child, arcing her neck to look up at me. Fear and excitement. We have met only once before and never in private. She looks at me in wonder and she weighs what manner of man I am. Not like you. Still our blood will flow together and your children may yet be our future. If we succeed, if they are allowed to live.

She is like the earth and smells of the earth. We are distant though we share much. It is not the first time her people have been changed, yet she is unaware. She trusts in her choice because she sees prospect, an increase to life, and because her heart calls to me. Betrayal of my people and perhaps of hers.

Her eyes wander over my long limbs, she turns over the long fingers on my bony hand and fingers the metal, a work unknown to her. The gold reflects on the white skin she strokes to see if the colour comes off. She looks at my face and I kneel so she can touch my cheekbones, so long next to hers. She strokes my red hair and looks into my slanted green eyes, along the length of my skull. She puts a hand to the back of her own small round head and looks at me as much as at a snake as at a man.

I am unsure how we will blend, if our bodies will have the clay to make a new shape, but we will soon know. I am the first but others will try and we will not be mechanical but will be together as man and woman, sharing our lives and ending the separation of our peoples.

Already we have altered the seeds of plants and grasses to make them productive and brought animals into husbandry to ensure their survival. We will bring them through the waters and teach them the crafts to give them a hold. We will show them the states of the noble metals to electrify their consciousness and allow our seed to grow in them as the generations advance. Perhaps we will one day remember ourselves in the vehicles we have created.

There are men in our village who are not happy with these arrangements. There will be much bitterness.

It could be done in a different way but then there would be deception. Which is worse?

If they did not know…

The truth would come out soon enough.

Yes, that's true.

I don't want to start this work with lies, there is already enough darkness in it.

What do you mean?

You understand there is a difficult period ahead with the weathers of the Earth. The destruction you have seen so far is only the beginning. We have told you the truth but not all of the truth. We cannot be sure what is coming but the world we know will come to an end. We are few in number and may not be here when all is done. You will more likely survive if much reduced. Nevertheless some of what we offer you will endure.

Then it is not us you wish to help.

I believe in my heart this is for you also. Not all our people would wish such an outcome.

You are divided?

Yes. We do not yet know the price.

To you?

To both of us, but yes I mean to us.

You will be at war.

Perhaps.

You lead your people. You will be responsible.

Yes.

Then come, touch me, because my heart craves your beauty and your guile and I wish my sons and daughters to be more than we are.

Lovely she is and there is guilt for the passion of our work but the stars turn and reflect in the polished black obsidian prepared as a gift. That she can see herself. As I come in her I see the future unfolding and I know there is hope. Light ripples in my spine and I know what we have to do. I see the paths trace forward just as I see their genesis in the distant past. I see the where the streams converge and I reach out before me and behind me to fuse them into one and I know it can be done.

Her head on my shoulder, moving with my breath. Her dark hair and the smell of the earth. Calm before the storm.

When you came you went away.

Yes.

Where did you go?

To make the way for our children.

Hand on her stomach, tear suddenly on her cheek.

Yes, be a husband to them. You wish more than one?

Many.

Will you stay with me?

As much as I can.

ANCESTRAL

So my greatest asset is that I'm nobody?

I'm sorry, Gabriel, we have a problem with facial recognition software. The panopticon likes to watch.

And it would know everybody's face but mine.

Something like that. We have assets but it's not long before their faces get known.

How do I know that this isn't some game? That I won't just be a cut-out?

Nikolai shrugging.

That's up to you.

A bit uncompromising. Trying to make my lost sailor into a man. Big bear leaving us with a smile and stalking off into the woods. To think his giddy thoughts.

Well, Nikolai will be rubbing his back on a few trees. What are we doing?

Well, I'm getting a bit pissy.

I noticed.

Don't like being bossed around.

Is that's what's happening?

I don't know. I don't know what I'm doing, Ava, that's the truth. I can see you think this is all about not having had a Dad and you may be right. But I don't want to be led around like a child if my life is at stake. I can't just trust.

My Dad trusts him and he's not so gullible.

And then some. Dada showed me where the primrose path goes. Anyone who tells you you're a victim and you need their help, they're the ones who want to abuse you.

So what, man up or ship out?

Find myself shrugging. Like Nikolai. Not knowing what to say. Say nothing. Watch the scars twitching across his skin. Smile. I love you, sailor boy.

Your Father injected me.

What?

The fetish. He passed her on to me like a drug. I think he's been cutting his wrist.

Tell me, Gabriel.

He injected me. It was like an injection. I'm not even sure what happened. He was with Olga and something was happening between them.

What was happening?

You'll have to ask them. I'd like to know myself.

Gabriel!

Alright! He held my wrist and the blood drew me...

There's blood on you.

A little. I think it's theirs. I met them in the woods, just walking around. Olga looked even weirder than usual, the two of them gawping about all saucer-eyed like some kind of chemical. I sat with them and they were beautiful, so beautiful, like the forest come alive and speaking to me. I said I want what you have, help me. Like hearing my voice speak on its own. They looked at each other for a while and Bastian took my wrist and Olga held my forearm and I could see her, Ava, so help me, the fetish.

She put her nail in my artery and she was inside me and everything your Dad said was just the way it was...

Holding him now, I didn't see before, he's coming apart at the seams. I'm with you. After a while he pulls back and looks at me. Strange smile.

The thing is this whole conversation with Nikolai, he didn't know. And with you, it's like listening to a part of me, like a shell, it was me but no longer something I cared about. It works on its own.

Your personality.

Yes, damaged responses. I'm not angry with Nikolai inside, just my mind thinks I should be. I'm not angry about the fetish, it's...

Hands on his face, palms on his temples, shakes of the head. Trying to get something out of his skull.

It's the best thing. It's, she's... trying to kill me, I'm tearing apart. I'll be glad when I'm dead.

No.

No, not death. Life, to live, to remember. Myself, ourselves. You. Remember?

Yes, like a false self created by trauma or ignorance but not just that. Her image isn't even that old, I don't know why she holds it.

She showed me the past. Is it real? It seems real.
What, Gabriel?
You know about other races?
You mean like other humans?
Yes.
Neanderthals, now Denisovans, hints of others, getting more
complicated. Then hominids and all.
That's it?
I think so.
Don't think so. I'll tell you.

And he did. The tall skulls, the long limbs, the DNA. Nikolai came back and sat and listened and the box was opened and it was full of lies, laid at our feet like gifts pulled from the rotting innards of a vagrant reptile, stinking and vile.

Gabriel, I'm sorry, I didn't realise what had happened to you.
It's alright, I think it's good, I didn't mean to be angry with you, I just couldn't stop myself.

Letting him curl up on the ground. Like a child's skeleton exhumed in foetal posture.

Why did they do this to him, Nikolai?
I don't know, Ava, he said he wanted it.
Why did no-one tell me?
I don't know, they didn't tell me either.
Do you know what he was talking about?
I think so.

How skeletons have been found, often very large, with elongated skulls. How these skulls have a larger cranial cavity than normal skulls. The systematic disappearance of these artefacts despite residual written and photographic evidence from modern times. The global nature of the phenomenon and the oral traditions, often giants with red hair, blonde hair, blue eyes, green eyes.

How when Montezuma came to South America the Inca thought it was the return of Quetzalcoatl, who had brought civilisation across the ocean, because they remember him as having white skin and a red beard. The natives having brown skin, dark hair and no beards at all. The Native Americans said over and over that they did not build the mounds, which were the work of red-headed giants they once fought with and who had been exterminated.

How these people have been found all over the world. How so too has the binding of babies' skulls to make the shape, the one you see on images of Akhenaten and Nefertiti. These deformed skulls, which have normal cranial capacity, are confused with skulls exhibiting larger capacity, no deformation and differential structure to normal skulls. How the deformation is associated with royalty and is said to be a characteristic of the ancestors.

How there are many examples and traditions of these people in the Middle East, including stories regarding the origins of mankind.

So you are saying this has all been covered up.

Yes.

Why?

Nikolai sighing, a guardian weary of his charge.

You have been told that civilisation began around 3,000BC in the fertile crescent. Now we have Göbekli Tepe, sophisticated and vast stonework from around 10,000BC. It all goes out of the window. In truth there are many other sites that go back further. Glib archaeologists tell us they are very recent works without having a shred of evidence to support them. They ignore the evidence of stonework we can only just replicate with modern technology. You know the way it works, the ones with qualifications and a nice job are so desperate to believe the dogma that they are the easiest to brainwash. Same with politics.

There was a global civilisation before the end of the last ice age and it went down with the flood. All the lies are for the middle classes. The elites know the truth full well and work to make it invisible. They have stolen our history.

You think Gabriel is remembering an older civilisation?

An older race. How we come to be as we are.

How could he know this?

Your Father did something to him.

Yes, he said he passed out, that it was like a dream but not like a dream. Look at him, he's gone.

He said that underneath it all he was happy?

Yes.

So let's not worry yet, your Father is alright.

Sort of.

Yes, sort of.

Why have they stolen our history?

To steal the present, steal the future.

What is it about the past that is such a threat?

That there are possibilities in us that they would rather we not remember. You and your Father are testament to the truth. That is why you are a threat.

And Olga.

Olga, yes.

You're talking about evolution.

Yes.

But there is more.

What do you mean?

I can tell by looking at you.

There are all kinds of knowledge...

I saw lights in my night visions, they came when I asked.

Ah, I see.

Well?

Well, we're not alone. You know that already.

So our evolution isn't just terrestrial.

No.

And our future?

Is what we make it. That's why I asked you to come.

My Father.

Yes.

Because Olga told you to.

Yes.

And she is what?

My sister.

Your sister and what else?

You will have to speak to her.

And what about you?

You mean do I have abilities like hers? No. I have had to resort to other means.

To create this wonderland in the taiga?

Yes.

You could have told me about the past. Why is Gabriel having this experience?

Perhaps so you can know who you are.

Gabriel's hands twitching like the paws of a dreaming animal. Maybe it's harder on him, he's younger, more damaged, less thought through. A mass of scar tissue.

You want him to spy for you?

Be a messenger.

Like when you sent someone to find my Dad.

Yes.

Olga has given you a list.

Nice to see him smile, different lines on his face. Hard to imagine his life. The corridors of power and the pulling of strings and the endless danger. Dad said he was like a saint, ringing the Church bells with an iron hand, calling the faithless to prayer. Man and boy, these two, keep them safe for me, keep them away from harm, Nikolai, saint of the sea, both their minds are lost to me now.

DEATH

Two of us sitting on rocks above the damp soil, together in the green light of trees. Good to have company. Don't feel like an animal. Animistic quality of blood rituals. Odin drinks the blood of a God to gain wisdom, using his wits to steal it. Iron, magnetite, oxygen. Archaic rituals, blood, pain, stress. Cultural dissonance of an ancient fetish embracing injection, mixed metaphor of old and new. No literality then, imagery spinning out of the synchronous discovery of a hidden artefact.

Does she have a personality?
The fetish?
Yes.
How to know such a thing?
Nikolai wants Ava to talk to the sun.
He's a busy bee, Nikolai.
We're being lucid, Olga.
So we are.
Are we married?
Hmm. Well, we're not married to Gabriel.
I hope Ava will forgive us, me.
He said he wanted it. I believe him.
Me, too.
You saw her death, then.
No, but I think I understand it.
She is life. It's about the end of life.
Yes.
There's more?
I think so. Some things Nikolai explained to me.

Olga and Nikolai, the glimmer twins. Sending him out across the stars on his solar boat. Don't come home until you bring me fresh meat.

Alright.
I think it's about the singularity.
As in when machines become so clever we don't know what they're up to?

Yes.

Go on.

Nikolai says there are three elements. The first is, as you say, when programs can redesign themselves in ways that lead them beyond our understanding. Not far off now. We won't know what they are doing and we won't be able to check on them.

What could possibly go wrong?

There's a lot of people pushing hard on this one and, of course it's part of the security state apparatus.

So billions in black projects. What you see is only an echo of what they have in back.

Yes. Next is manipulation of DNA. Every kind of crossbreed and enhancement. Also XNA. Artificial DNA that doesn't biodegrade. The erosion of the line between biological and artificial. It starts with GMO's, getting DNA in your system that doesn't belong there, but that's more about ending fertility. I've been talking with Ava about this. Women freed from the oppression of childbirth, fertility replaced with rows of birth tanks run by the state.

The technocratic future is presented as immortality, freedom from disease, intelligence enhancement, games involving imports from other creatures. Want your children to be stupid when all the others are smart? But the enhancements will be for the elites, the rest of us have devolution via toxicity to the embryo, to the brain. We already have aerosol application of gene change via virus, knock out targeted parts of the brain, on and on. The elites will be transhumanist, engineered biology, cybernetic implants. Where today we have web and cloud they will have access to the hive mind. Everything you know comes from the hive, you can be monitored, hacked, excluded from credit, terminated.

Lastly there is nanotech, the least known outside of small circles. Tiny robots that can be programmed to do just about anything. Target people by genetic signature, as specific or broad as you like, have the nanobots dismantle us at the molecular level, use our bodies to replicate themselves. Or use anything to hand.

You mean indefinitely?

Forever and ever, amen. Forget the weather weapons and the nukes, you don't need them. No mess, no fuss. Already nanotech is in the food, in the air and water, you can't see it without the sort of tech not many people have. It's in your body and mine. It can take over all life.

I see.

Yes. Nikolai could explain this all better. The air is being sprayed with all manner of metals, often at nano scale. There are effects on fertility, intelligence and so on. They spray aluminium and then engineer aluminium resistant plants! Then there are those nice people wanting to bring free WiFi to the poor in Africa by means of orbital drones and there are others messing around with frequencies that can affect the brain directly. The metallicisation or whatever you call it, of the biosphere, allows for direct control of nanotech, computers, machines, implants.

The more we buy into the machine mind the more easily we can be controlled. My guess is the biological component will decline as time goes on. Either way this thing will not only be able to control all your implants and upgrades but also the nanothech which will be in every living thing on Earth, even down to rocks. It can convert all life to more of itself as it reinvents itself, winding its way ever further away from its creators.

This is what the fetish showed me.

The future, yes. And not just here. Imagine this on probes going out through the solar system, a system we are already leaving. There is life everywhere, Bastian, of every kind. Worlds without end, amen. This thing could kill them all.

Olga, I know when you say it, I can feel her inside, her fear.

Me, too.

This is the taste of metal she gave me.

Yes.

You know there is life elsewhere?

Yes. You do, too.

I've seen... things. Why would they do this?

Olga sighing, shifting.

You know about the suicide banker Ava told me about?

Stayed in the burning tower because of the put options available on the biggest deal of a lifetime. Burnt alive.

Yes. I have studied psychopaths or sociopaths. A mind-bending pursuit. They are like machines, no empathy. They don't care who suffers, who dies. They have OCD rituals in place of a heart, in place of a life. They are paedophiles. They run our world.

No rhyme or reason, then.

No. Just the hunger for power, status, recognition, an individuality with no connection to others of its kind or to Nature.

To life.

Yes, no connection to life. Biological but functioning like a machine. They are the ones who are dismantling the family, bringing in cultural Marxism to dehumanise people, make them obedient, to prepare for transhumanism and the hive mind. Singularity.

They fear her because she evolves.

Yes, evolution, the one thing that cannot be controlled, only eliminated. Superceded by the biological version of the command economy and eventually replaced by algorithms and quantum computing.

When she takes me I know that evolution can inhabit places a machine can never know.

She knows things a machine can never know. Past, present, future. There are jumps in evolution that are not linear, nothing to do with gradual responses to environmental change, competition. They reflect blueprints from a level of awareness we cannot understand and yet can be intimately involved in. The ones that are not psychopaths. In our hearts we know. Empathy, the gift of the fetish. To not be separate from life, to not see the future as empty.

She is in us to survive death? Like an ark?

Yes, it would seem. But not like moving to another world. In any case the machine will follow.

Another way, then.

Yes. I was listening to one of the geniuses working towards singularity. He was asked if God existed. He said not yet. Like pride in a child that surpasses you. A new God to whom we can offer obeisance.

Worse than the old God.

Nikolai is no fool. He knows the real God. He works for the real God. It is a consciousness expressing itself through evolution, ours and others. It always moves to greater intelligence and self *awareness. Such qualities lead to the development of personality. Psychopaths have little personality, only repetitive drives. Machines have no personality. It is God that becomes a person.*

That is why everything they do, even unwittingly, is for the hive mind. They are isolated from the whole and yet without authentic individuality.

Yes. The death of the fetish is like the death of God. Nikolai is a devout man. He will not allow it.

He serves evolution because that is how the will of God expresses itself.

I think so. In you, in me, in the fetish, all life. It is the mystery. Of how I could see you and call to you and all that has happened. Of all this.

Waving her hands expansively at the forest, the sky, the vertiginous light running through it. Olga Volga, you make me feel like I am home.

Blue sky stretched over the skinless day. Nerves reaching out fibrously to touch the luminous trees. This thing like an infection. Interrogating us the way an ocean speaks to sea walls and dams and dykes. The two of us joined by a mossy umbilical. Is this what you prayed for Nikolai? It's coming to you like it came into us. It's going to find you.

Gabriel says he's ok. I'll find him with roots growing out of his legs but I don't know who he'll be. Are you set, Nikolai? Off through the trees he'll be out here somewhere. Why not back to the little village or the domes? But that's not the way, find him alone in the trees and open his veins before he knows. A man who walks in the darkest places on Earth and comes out smelling of roses, see how immune he is to this. What will your brothers say when they drag you in and prop you up by the fire?

The whisper of him coming to me through the rough bark like a scent. Walking and running, losing all compass and understanding. Why? All this anger and the simple object of its ambition. Currents in a tightening gyre. To blame another, to protect yourself. What, then? To turn back? The simplicity of who we were, wondering only how to make ends meet and where our place might be.

And the helpless observation. Watching night step in and the stars go out. Our families, our land. Even our selves they would twist until we are a mockery of the life that bore us. No, there is no succour there to hold me and tell me it's alright. It's not alright. Why, then, this vengeful chase? An anger that stems from fear, as always. Not myself. Something else. No longer about me. Easier for the elders than for Gabriel and me.

She is inside me now and she is not interested in the shame or the fear or the anger. There is no judgment. Only to move on, stand up, fight. This is what she says. Yes, I have said I will. She says she has used me, that my anger has taken me into the forest and that she wanted me here. That I do not know myself. That nothing is as it seems.

Choose to see. The flow of force arcing and splitting like a wave on the rocks. Something ahead distorting the pattern. Been following these lines all along. Feels like it could pull you in. Shimmy up this leaning tree for a better look before drawing any nearer, scramble against the flow of descending ants and knotted branches. There it is and it looks familiar, like something in one of Nikolai's domes. Like a Rodin coil. It's a vortex, a whirlpool, but it's not clear if its force is directed in or out.

Spray and foam, dendritic arcs, double-knotted filaments, spheres of energy floating lightly away from the ferocious currents. The thing could be alive. Trying to look past the energy to the physical Earth, there doesn't seem to be anything unusual going on. Hints of spiral growth in the vegetation perhaps. You would never notice it if you weren't already looking. Nothing to draw you here without a fetish to make you come. How would I know this spitting beast?

Climbing down and inching forward. Doesn't seem to want to eat me. No physical effects to notice unless perhaps nervous system responses. Safe, then, at first blush. Alright to sit down. Could do with a flask of tea, really. No fetish to push me in. Seems getting me here is enough, at least for now. Crossing legs and straightening the back. Strange how old programs kick in. Might do some asanas. Close the eyes and the visuals disappear although the feelings stay. Still, much calmer. Let the breathing deepen and settle, try to relax the shoulders. Birdsong and rustling in the leaves. Force lapping at the feet. It's alright, just let the current take you, mind anchored in the body, body stable on the earth, not going anywhere.

It's like those magic eye pictures. As you let your attention slip away from the surface there are other images behind. There is a still, empty space like the eye of a storm, and through this opening there is a grassy, limestone plateau with groups of megalithic stones, arranged in circles. There are any number of circles but the image flickers, showing only five or six and what appears to be an archaeological dig. Different points in time perhaps.

Suddenly it's like being there. Can't see the taiga, rather the wind ripples the grass and raises goose bumps on my skin. Sunlight reflecting off the white limestone boulders and the blinding blue of the sky. Megaliths with animal carvings, constellations perhaps, strange images of people. Here the power is overwhelming, spiraling around a centre. Another vortex, larger, more powerful. No, no further, pull back.

The taiga. Thank God. Nothing has changed. Insects on my arm, wet moss under my feet. That's right, focus on the physical, get up, walk around, sit on this small rock and face away from the whirlpool, keep it behind me. Empty taiga. No, not empty, there on another rock, only a few yards away.

Hello, Ava.

Nikolai, you surprised me.

I thought I should wait.

Yes, thank you, I'm glad to see you.

Gabriel told me you were looking for me.

Yes.

To infect me.

Ah, yes, that was the plan.

No longer?

No. At least not in anger. Anyway I'm not sure I know how.

Are you ok?

I think so, will you give me a hug.

Nikolai shuffling over and putting his arm around me, leaning my face on his chest, musky male smell. Feeling safe. Warm body, warm heart.

You seemed very far away.

Yes. Nikolai, I'm sorry, it's just that all this is going so fast. When I saw Dada he had changed so much, and now Gabriel. They're the ones I don't want broken. Now me. The way I feel is shifting so quickly.

Olga said it was the breaking of a false self. I don't know.

Yes, but when that is something you identify with so strongly, it's such a threat. You saw how Gabriel was struggling.

Yes. He's just lying with his eyes closed. I think he's alright.

I think he will be. You have a big experience, it puts everything else into a different context. Something just happened to me. Can you see anything in this place?

Not really. I feel a bit... as if things are superimposed on each other, but nothing looks any different.

Well, there's something here, Nikolai.

Sitting up and sharing the story, just how far out it sounds, how far out it is. He doesn't doubt me. Thank you.

Sounds like Göbekli Tepe to me, or something like it.

Göbekli Tepe?

Southern Turkey. We've been told that civilisation began in Sumer and Egypt about five thousand years ago. Then Göbekli Tepe was discovered. Only a small portion of it has been investigated but the oldest parts so far are said to be twelve thousand years old. Supposedly there were only hunter-gatherers running around in loin cloths at that time. The architecture is stunning.

Yes, it was.

And the older is stuff is of higher quality. It declines over two thousand years.

So whoever built it has a history going back even longer.

Yes. This time was roughly the end of the last ice age, so before that. This is also the time and place that, as far as archaeologists tell us, the first agriculture was discovered. Modern seeds for wheat and barley and so on. Animal husbandry. All happened very quickly.

Then who built it?

Now, that's a question. The archaeologist in charge, very conservative, very reputable, said some things interpreted by some as this being the mountain within Eden in which the Watchers lived. Source of the Tigris and Euphrates and so on.

Watchers.

The ones who gave humans knowledge, bred with them, made them in our image. Associated with hybrid children known as Nephilim.

As in the Bible?

Yes. Elohim *in Genesis is translated as God but it is a plural word.*

So you're saying this is the literal setting for the Bible creation story?

Seemingly. Something happened there.

Alright, here's something Gabriel talks about. Jehovah told Adam and Eve that they would die if they ate of the fruit of the tree of knowledge but they didn't.

No.

Doesn't that mean Jehovah lied?

Yes, on a literal reading.

Gabriel gets annoyed.

I know.

So?

So much of the early Bible appears to be a reworking of old Sumerian creation epics, even down to Noah and the Ark. Enki and Enlil represented two factions of the Gods, one wanting humans to be wiped out by the flood, one wanting to save them. Enki, who wanted to save them, was the one who made them and educated them.

Made them.

Yes.

Why did Enlil want them killed?

Apparently the noise of their love-making was keeping him awake at night.

So Enlil is Jehovah and Enki the snake who tempted Eve?

Maybe.

You don't seem too worried about this.

I have other things to worry about.

What about the brothers?

They have things to worry about, too.

If this is the place where the creation myth happened, what was I doing there?

Good question.

Nikolai sighing.

You ever feel fishy? Feel like a swim, visiting the seaside?

Express my inner fish.

Maybe. Humans are strange aren't they? Not like other apes. Hairless, physically weak. A champion fighter could never take on a chimpanzee. What's the survival advantage of being weak and hairless?

Channel it into a big brain. Like brainy people having poor vision? Big brains are no good if something's eating you. We're told we evolved to be bipedal on the savannah. The same one full of big cats and packs of dogs. How would we outrun them as we're perfecting our locomotion over a few million years. Even now we have bad backs, ask your Father.

Go on.

Apart from species like the naked mole rat which lives underground the only mammals to lose their hair are the ones that go back to the water. They have body fat to float and stay warm and their throats are adapted to keep out water. Humans have all of these. Ape babies all sink, human babies float. Ever wondered why women have a layer of fat that men don't have? Why you traditionally have long hair? Think of yourself floating about with babies who are hanging onto your hair.

That's why we like having our hair pulled, then.

Could be. Do you know what vernix is?

Like a waxy covering babies have. Like cradle cap on the skull.

Yes. Only aquatic mammals have vernix. Seals for examples. But seals that come to shore to give birth don't have it, only seals that birth directly into the water. Vernix is an extreme aquatic adaptation and yet we have it. Have you seen apes and monkeys wade into water on your David Attenborough shows?

Ah, yes. He's a great British institution.

Talks rubbish about carbon dioxide but never mind, he's very charming. Apes will stand on their back legs for long periods of time as they wade deeper looking for food. Much safer than tottering about the savannah like a predator's wet dream. You mentioned brains. Not enough protein in the hominid diet to grow them but start eating fish and you have brain food. Even today the human body is adapted to a fish diet. Animal fats are bad for you, fish fats make you healthy, develop your brain.

Omega 3 and all that.

Yes, and the rest. So all that may have evolved in lakes in the Rift Valley. But the global myths about fishy ancestors offer another possibility.

I'll never look at a haddock the same again.

These days we can splice DNA from anything to anything else. Jellyfish to mammal is popular to make animals that glow in the dark.

Nice.

Trivial is standard, it seems. But your images may have been symbolic rather than literal.

If I saw Göbekli Tepe, then that was literal. Even the archaeological dig.

Yes, but based on a lifetime listening to Olga's tales and even one or two of my own, it can swing both ways.

Makes sense, Nikolai, you are a regular treasure trove.

You are the one with the abilities. I'm envious.

Well, maybe we'll infect you.

Yes, maybe. I'd like to get the others out here and see what they make of this place. Strange how it's been here all along and we never found it.

Strange how you tell me all this stuff they never tell you at school.

Humanity is far more mysterious than they would have us suppose, Ava. Geneticists know the official story is full of holes but if you speak up your career is gone. Microbiologists in particular have a very high death rate.

I've often wondered about genetics in regard to being rhesus negative.

You are rhesus negative.

Yes, and my Dad.

Did your Mother's body reject you?

Yes.

I'm glad you're ok.

What does it mean, Nikolai?

It means that all primates have a protein sheath in relation to red blood cells. Most humans do too, but some don't. There's no obvious explanation. It's most common in Western Europe, hardly any in Africa. The only other time we see foetuses being rejected in that way is when two different but similar species breed, usually in captivity. So horses and donkeys, for example.

So there are two species of humans?

Well, the number of humans existing in recent times has been growing. Neanderthals, Denisovans, we know there must be more. Whether they would be different enough to create rejection of the foetus is debatable. In any case we still have the problem of why there are no other examples of rhesus negative anywhere else among primates.

So if it was another type of human it might be different from homo sapiens?

Pandora's box of difference.

INFECT

The bright white lights and the knives. Again. Benign this time. To show me what is inside me. No real pain. Looking down the microscope via the monitor. What are these things come out of my flesh. They are fusion of technology and biology. They reproduce. They have attributes from all domains of Nature, no longer separate and inviolate but fused into a resilient organism with partly artificial chromosomes. They respond to magnetic fields. They are inside me, inside us all. They come from the planes with the heavy metals. They are the interface to the machine.

What are they doing, Nikolai?

You know what, making the machine God.

Sending it back in time to kill the real one.

Seems that way.

So now you have a strategy.

Your infection.

For a while they seemed to let Russia go, now you're in the crosshairs again.

Since Syria and Ukraine.

Yes.

It is only because we were weak. The doctrine is to prevent our return, or any power rising to control Eurasia. That's what frightens them. In the short run they want to prevent Europe and Russia integrating economically. Your puppet kings shoot their own feet to please their masters across the water. Behind closed doors the psychopaths sacrifice our children, sell us colour revolutions and R2P.

I had a Polish friend. When I was about ten this man appeared in my bed, disheveled, asleep. He had a phone call from his government. We have your wife and children. Come home and we'll make it you rather than them.

Yes, we have seen communism, our people are not as lulled by ideology as yours.

Ideology.

Cultural Marxism for you, the soft version, the less obvious one. Originally it was about distributing wealth. Now the rich get stratospherically richer as the poor slide into being welfare dependent scapegoats. Your banks are criminal enterprises. Ours, too, but we're working on it.

How did this happen?

Race, gender, sexual identity. You know who first used the word racist?

No.

Trotsky. The good communist. The same one who went to New York every week or two to get his million dollars from your banks to pay for our revolution. There were people holding onto their national identity, resisting communism, in Ukraine for example. This was a false consciousness, a petite bourgeois national fetish, unwilling to embrace the universal political creed. They were elevating their national identity above the collective egalitarian ethos and so were guilty of racism. Anyone who resisted was a racist. This was R2P, to save people from the racists, from their nation states.

In England they say only white people can be racists. If you do not actively embrace multiculturalism you are a racist. Town halls won't fly the English flag.

In London white British is a minority. It didn't happen by accident.

The British Empire justified its colonisation with a rhetoric of inclusivity, one big family. The cousins wanted to move into the big house.

And who can blame them? For trying to improve their lives, help their families?

But...

The white race has a powerful history, a powerful identity. To create a global Superstate it has to be destroyed. In the days of the Soviet Union resistance to your country being taken over by the red flag was racism. In Europe opposition to multiculturalism is racism. Sacrifice your country to immigrants because you are guilty or you believe it's about caring and sharing. You don't need to know anything about the cultures taking you over, you just need to feel warm and fluffy about them.

I've wondered about that. Empire is nothing new, nor slavery, nor oppression of any kind, excepting perhaps the surveillance tech, all the other stuff the machine God plays with.

No. Russian Orthodoxy was always pitted against Zionism. They are open about their desire to destroy Western civilisation, to control everyone else. Their exceptionalist creed controls the exceptionalist nation and it's obvious to us, opaque to you.

For us it's racism.

Yes. The Newspeak of your bought and paid for media. There are many levels of power working to destroy your civilisation, our civilisation. Look at Sweden. A paradise where the Prime Minister pottered around on his bicycle, rape was almost unheard of, people were at ease. Then they took out Olaf Palme and dismantled the place. Now rape is everywhere and it's the immigrants doing it. How strange that the feminist socialist controlled media try to prevent women from knowing the truth. Feminists are willing to sacrifice women to rape to protect their vision, the no longer white European paradise.

The white man is the enemy.

Yes. In the US, in Europe, everywhere.

I watched Ava so closely when her Mother left. I watched her acting out the ideology that tears families apart. How women will never be free until the family is dismantled. I think she is free of that now.

I'm sorry, Bastian.

I'm glad she's here. Glad she's with you and Olga.

Olga will help her.

Yes. It makes me feel safe.

Bastian, here in Russia we will try to protect the family, you can stay, she can stay, I will look after you.

If I survive.

Yes.

At home it's not even your culture and your family any more, it's your sexual identity. Primary school children being given drugs to delay puberty in order to allow decisions about gender reassignment. Parents excluded. Vaccinations, contraception, psychiatric treatment, all without your knowledge. Propaganda in the schools.

Being gay is a positive lifestyle choice, primary school children being encouraged to cross dress.

Ah, Bastian, I know. Post-modernism. There is no truth, everything is relative so everything is equal. There are no facts, only opinions. Here are some facts. Homosexual men are about half of the time willing to admit that they were raped by a man in childhood. A homosexual man is about ten times more likely to rape a child than a heterosexual one. The gay rights campaigners you see on the BBC are promoting paedophilia. These facts are in scientific journals and still to mention these things is hate speech. We are happy for everyone to live their life but we will not allow these things to be forced into the minds of children.

I remember reading Plato at school. The Republic. Timeas and Critias. Soon became clear he was into little boys. Contempt for women and relationships with them. Thought people should be allowed to breed by lottery but that he and his elite gay cronies should secretly rig the elections. This kind of bullshit has been with us a long time.

Childlike sexual identity, Bastian. Thinking sex is who you are. Like teenagers.

Running around shouting revolution.

Yes, revolution. The state will protect you from racism, the state will protect you from sexism, the state will protect you from homophobia. You don't need your family, you don't need the land, you only need the state. The lovely ladies in Washington standing up for women's rights while murdering half a million women in Iraq, R2P all over the world.

Videos where the most powerful women in America, the ones you just mentioned, bombing brown women everywhere, are trying to ban the word bossy because it's sexist.

Bossy women trying to ban the word bossy. Over here we can't believe what we're seeing. Maybe it's a game to see if we're paying attention.

Looking down at the lesions and the foreign fibres on the back of my hand, the scars from the fetish, her dirty nails and her loamy breath. Gold ring on my finger. Is a dream a lie if it doesn't come true or is it something worse.

Bastian, all this, it's all been done before, as the noose tightens sexual licence offers the illusion of freedom. I have seen them, brother, the dark rituals, the child sacrifice, the rape, the mind control, the false personalities. Demons from another time, they run our world. The families who own the banks, who own the corporations. They drink the blood of the young. They turn men against women, white against black, they make you less than a man, less than a woman. They have only death or slavery to offer us. In the small hours they know they are empty vessels.

So here we are, the war against the family, the stealing of the land, the war against European culture, the end of the white man. All the things that stand against them. Without a Mother's love the children grow weak. You know what they fear when you see what they want to kill. I was never a patriot but they want to end the nation state so you know you have to preserve it. They want an end to religion because for all its lies it offers values they cannot control, so we fight to keep the values they would bury. What should we do else?

In the West we deride your culture as the cult of masculinity, your strong man as a Neanderthal.

He fights against the machine, Bastian, no GMO's and their genocidal infertility but rather organic food to grow life in the bones of the children. Men to fight for their families, women to offer love when the men need to be brutal. Biology gives us the family. Family is all. You have women at work while the children grow with strangers, you have weak men. In Scandinavia half the boys grow breasts with the endocrine disruptors, substances that could so easily be replaced. They have doctors to say it's normal. We have been made scared of differences, we create uniformity to console the neurosis. Individuality is the force of evolution. They cannot tolerate it.

That's the thing, Nikolai, no more facts, only beliefs, beliefs that make the state your Mother and Father. I remember the lies at school even way back. How the Germans started the wars. Then the propaganda against the Germans, the Treaty of Versailles. The myth of the good war. Never mind that the Nazis and the Zionists worked together. Now we say your man is like Hitler.

They know what he wants. He wants democracy from sea to

shining sea. We could rescue the Europeans but your leaders fear their masters in Washington. They ask for their gold back and get laughed at. I have read your Tolkien and his Lord of the Rings, which sold more than any book excepting the Bible. What was he doing, Bastian?

A story for the empty places in history?

Just so. Reclaiming Western culture from the Middle East and the void of values brought by Rome. In their soul the people know what they have lost. That is why the sociopaths have been so fierce with Sweden. They remembered still the people's way, sharing, Nature, the old ways. How powerful and beautiful they were. All around the world people can still reclaim their lost heritage, each different, each beautiful, not lost in a mish-mash where our core values are that we have no values, where the differences that define us are lost. Social diversity is a reflection of genetic diversity and it is for the enrichment of all.

If he gives up on the West and its duplicity you will work with the Chinese and new lines will be drawn.

Yes, and they will lead to war. The West cannot cope with other powers. Their diplomacy has withered down to only naked violence. They have withdrawn unilaterally from our no first strike agreement. They believe a nuclear war can be won.

If I can't make it back to the city I will be stuck here, here in your cold paradise.

Let us hope not. But if you are you will be protected as best as we are able.

Yes, thank you. There was a famous psychic who spoke of Russia.

There have been many.

Edgar Cayce. The one who talked about the Hall of Records under the paw of the Sphinx.

Ah, yes.

He said that Russia would be the light of the world. That you would revive Christianity and be the hope of us all. Now your strong man is the leader of the free world.

Yes, he is. We pray for him that he might find the way, for our hopes lie on his shoulders. He is in our hearts.

What senses do we have? To know what is what and who is

who. All the broken bodies on the way to the top, even so there's always someone higher. A blind reptile eating its own young. Cut his strings and there's no-one there. Who are we dealing with here?

You don't think they'll just give him the bullet, like JFK?

Harder for them, obviously, but possible.

The videos of women celebrating their abortions. In the clinic with Ava, the tiny, perfectly-formed body, the proud Grandmother.

Gabriel says you have a problem with facial recognition systems.

Yes, but we could get around them, prosthetic masks.

What are you thinking, we're just going to run around injecting people?

You mean the bad guys, bring them around?

Yes.

Tempting, but they would be hard to get to. It would mean doing it against their will or at least without permission. Perhaps Olga could reach a higher part of them that would agree. In any case I don't know if they could withstand it.

Looking at themselves.

Yes.

I don't know the fetish would agree to be in them.

How autonomous is she?

No idea.

The wind in the trees on the farm, geese hissing at something invisible. Ava gone. Maybe forever. Cat having sex like violence with some stray tom, kicking up dust. The dreams coming at night even without sleep. You are not alone. She wants to live.

Nikolai. What are you doing with Russia? Why was it here that we found her?

You know her better than me. There is a history here, here and Europe. The archaeology is starting to take us back to ancient times, older than the conventional chronologies. Why are your masters so determined to eradicate the white race? Why are you already a minority in your own capital?

Eradicating identity?

Yes. Family, nation, religion, anything that is an alternative loyalty to the state, anything that stops you being good little robots. You are used to thinking that you won the Cold War and geopolitically you did. But remember it was Western financiers who financed the Communist revolution as well as the Nazis. Culturally you lost the Cold War. The Soviets gave you political correctness, racism, sexism, homophobia, all the things the state protects your culture from. You cannot speak the truth for fear of these things.

Your social sciences and humanities have abandoned fact for ideology. You cannot say that putting a penis in an arsehole will cover it in shit, likely break skin not designed for such things, and will spread disease. You cannot say it even though it is true because it will lose you your job, get you arrested, or, in Sweden, get you a psychiatric evaluation. You cannot say it because you are teaching your children it is a lifestyle choice. You cannot say it because the paedophile sociopaths who run you society want to normalise their behaviour.

You lost the Cold War but Russia saw the worst of communism and we have become immune to a degree. It was Russia that defeated the Nazis. When the West turns against us, loots our country, puts nuclear missiles on our doorstep it only turns the people's faces further away. But maybe the end of Europe as a culture, the end of the white race, these have different meanings.

Nikolai, is this about archaeology or stuff that Olga has come up with?

Both. Give me licence and I will share.

I'm sitting comfortably.

You know what happened when the Conquistadores arrived in South America?

Genocide.

But why was it so easy?

European diseases to which they had no immunity.

Yes, but also because Montezuma thought they were dealing with the return of Quetzalcoatl. The one who came to give them civilisation, the one the anthropologist's call a God, the one with white skin and a red beard.

The natives are brown-skinned.

And the men don't have beards. And no-one has red hair. You would think it would be a big deal to find out where Quetzalcoatl was from but no, it's just a myth.

A myth with racial characteristics.

There are others not too dissimilar. You know Quetzalcoatl the man or the God or the myth was known as the feathered serpent.

Beautiful imagery.

Ava spoke of Göbekli Tepe and her experiences at the ah, portal she found so close to us.

I wanted her to come.

Yes.

Now she is infected.

Now she sees more.

Tell me about Göbekli Tepe.

It is associated with the Garden of Eden. In the Bible and in apocryphal texts we are told of the Watchers, the ones who made Man in our image. Not one God but many. They are tall, white, faces like serpents, associated with vulture feathers and excarnation.

How would your patriarchs feel about all this?

Generally they try to ignore it. Göbekli Tepe is history intruding on myth.

And where is Jesus in all this?

The Gnostics sometimes portrayed Jesus as the snake on the cross. Who knows?

Quite the heretic. Gabriel says Jehovah told Adam and Eve that if they ate of the fruit and evil, as the serpent counseled, that they would die. But they didn't.

Just so. Let us discuss Christ another time.

Alright.

The Watchers gave man civilisation as we know it, farming, metalwork, modern crops. Where did they get it from?

I'm listening.

I can tell you that there are myths of white people bringing civilisation from the North all over the world. The suppression of European culture is not just because it has the potential to resist global dictatorship but because its history is too dangerous to know.

It has nothing to do with racial superiority, it is about reclaiming our history. They want us blind to the past because the past is glorious, far older than they will allow, far higher a civilisation than they would have us know. Göbekli Tepe is the first nail in the coffin of their revisionist history.

Memory is identity. And vice versa.

Yes, Bastian. There was once a global culture and it survived in the North better than most places but you see its artefacts everywhere. They worked to rebuild that culture and we work for it still. It is not about white people, it is the inheritance of all people regardless. They suppress the white culture only because it is in their way, they turn white against black and man against woman so that we're spinning so fast we cannot remember and cannot fight back.

Ava says Göbekli Tepe leads to some other place, that perhaps influences have come to us in such a manner.

Now everyone is spied on, biometric databases with facial recognition. But part of that is the genetic database. Apart from dictatorship its purpose is to trace any such influences and see if there is anyone around today that carries them. Also to see if there are any new influences being introduced.

Genetics isn't everything.

No, but it's something they can apply their tech to.

They love their tech. Stealing fire from the Gods.

All hail the machine God, Bastian. New and improved.

CURE

Gabriel was talking about how different people came from the North to Göbekli Tepe, white-skinned, dramatic features. Like in his dream. Maybe a different type of human.

Yes, Ava, there have been many different kinds of human.

So the story wove the broken years together, threads like islands in the sea linking broken continents. How all around the world people told about the white people who brought civilisation, how their history and inheritance was hidden and buried.

The virus, the mind-killer. That I am God, the only God, you will have no other. My anger and my jealousy and my lies. That the fruit of knowledge brings death when all it brought you was my vengeance. That you are my chosen people and you will inherit the Earth even if you have to slaughter everyone to get it. Even now the rabbis speak of destroying the purity of the white blood line. Multi-culturalism, replacement level migration, white women who have no children or brown children. The Zionist obsession with destroying the white race.

Those of us who are afraid of diversity, who wish to make us all the same, the same sex, the same colour, they are infected with the virus, they lay the ground for the dark ones. I waited for Bastian until I could wait no longer and then I asked Nikolai to bring him and he brought you and Gabriel. Now I know why I brought him.

The fetish?

The fetish.

Holding each other's wrists and stroking the scars. As of a physical event. The kiss of a different beast.

I prayed for an answer and the answer came. Your Father brought it from inside himself or from some place we cannot see.

An answer to the virus?

The cure.

WELL

How do you like our files, Gabriel?

How long have you been there?

Nikolai pulling up a chair, scraping it through the patterns of blue and white light.

Long enough to see what you're looking at. An answer, perhaps?

Nikolai, would you be offended if I said Christianity was a large part of the problem?

I could try but it would be an effort.

The virus, Nikolai, it's part of the virus. So says your sister. What is it? You're infected now, you've got stigmata from something not Christ.

Are you sure?

Not sure of much. Olga says give them Nature's needle and we have the cure. She didn't mention Jesus.

I know. People need reference points, something to frame their feelings. Millions and millions of people. The Christian myth is manufactured, it is empire building, but there is something true in it, as there is with Osiris and Isis. The resistance to things such as exceptionalism, only Gods, chosen people, cultural Marxism, Zionism, global tyranny, the attack on Nature, top down elitist political programs imposed on unwilling people, the resistance to these things as far as Russia goes, is in the Orthodox Christian Church. It lifts the political leadership and ties them to the people. In the West your governments no longer serve the people, they are deliberately destroying your societies, your people.

You think the fetish is Christ?

No, but the values can go the same way.

Olga agrees with you?

Yes.

You think Christianity is a useful myth?

Yes. You know I've already said that.

What about Asatru?

Another useful myth but it references something more historical. It's not just a populist movement. There are philosophers and intellectuals promoting a return to indigenous European pagan values. Again the value of pluralism as a product of a polytheistic perspective.

They are saying let's kick the Middle Eastern religions out. They are the virus, no?

Socially, politically, yes. The source of exceptionalism.

Sometimes I see Odin. What do you make of that, Nikolai?

An ancestor, perhaps. A story that goes back.

Here's what exercises me. Asatru is about reclaiming our culture from the Middle Eastern ideologies. But you can also see it as racial. Protecting us from ever greater numbers of people who carry those ideologies. Mass immigration.

Your own government chose to open up to as much non-European immigration as possible, to break the spirit of the conservatives, to finish your traditional culture once and for all.

Yes, and it's not only that the Left promote any culture but our own and that they associate interest in preserving our own culture or even preventing our society from fragmenting, with fascism, but that they have presented us with a problem. What to do with the people already here, the ones who are a demographic time bomb. Our women don't breed any more, they have careers.

You have been studying history, Gabriel. All multicultural states end in civil war. Solutions have to be pragmatic.

But they have created a situation that can only end in violence and what worries me is that even in implementing solutions, violence will now be unavoidable. If the future is about honour and decent values then how to get from here to there. They will say we are fascists. People will fight.

Ah. And that's why you have been looking at Hitler?

Yes. The history we are taught. The greatest racist. The greatest evil. Not what we would want for the resurrection of our culture.

Well, you've been in here for days. What have you found?

I can't believe what you have here. KGB files going back and pre-1954 files from previous agencies. Stalin, Roosevelt, Churchill, Hitler. They don't teach half of this stuff in our schools.

Or ours. We are the victors. We get to write history.

But history is a lie.

Always.

Nikolai, I feel like a babe in the woods.

You are young.

Father and son. An oral history, even if digital.

Nikolai, there are reports from Soviet agents. About The Nazis, about what they found after the war.

And?

The only evidence for gas ovens was found by the Soviets. None by the Allies.

Yes.

Soviet agents report fabricating these things to frame Germany and rewrite history.

That's what we did. Like the mass murder of Polish officers at Katyn. Done by us and blamed on the Germans. Textbook Stalinist tactics.

Soviet agents say they built the ovens at Auschwitz. Experts say they could never have gassed anyone. The Polish authorities launch their own investigation and confirm it. Yet they still tell visitors to Auschwitz that these were gas ovens built by the Nazis.

Yes.

Shaving heads and Zyklon B was the treatment of choice for treating typhus.

Yes.

Many Jewish prisoners testify to humane conditions in the camps. Stories of a holocaust are down to a small number of witnesses, some of which have been proven to be fictitious, ones that Western films and education have been based on.

Hitler had the most multicultural army on Earth, all volunteers, including Jews, often with high rank. The West kept races separate as far as the armed forces were concerned but in Hitler's army the races mixed freely. What kind of racist is that?

One that knew that the war was between Judea and Europa, one that was trying to protect his people from annihilation.

Hitler organised with Zionists to deport Jews to Palestine. The Transfer Agreement. The Allies took hundreds of tons of documents from Germany after the war, particularly looking for patents. In all these not a single document has been found suggesting Hitler was deliberately trying to holocaust the Jews.

They say they must have got lost.

Every single one?

Reminds me of your 9/11 when the planes blew up hitting the Twin Towers and yet passports of the terrorists floated down to earth without a mark on them. Documents have a life of their own.

Here are Eisenhower's concentration camps. We're never told about those. The endless millions killed by Stalin. The six million Jews is an outright fabrication and everyone knows it. It's an open secret.

Yes.

How did this happen, Nikolai?

Even asking that question gets you arrested in many Western countries. It's the one thing you're not allowed to question. They say if you want to know who has power look to who you are not allowed to criticise.

One of our previous esteemed leaders says questioning 9/11 or 7/7 makes you a terrorist. I watched a guy turning himself in. Wrote a book questioning both.

Yes. World capital of surveillance.

Strange when you watch history being fabricated before your eyes and yet you assume what you learn at school is the truth. How can we act like adults when we don't know our own history.

Alright. At the end of the nineteenth century we had the Concert of Europe. A balance of Empires all keen to keep each other in check and undermining each other at every opportunity. A kind of dangerous balance but, relatively speaking, it kept the peace. Then the First World War. We wanted the Straits of Bosporus and the French wanted Germany's industrial heartland, the Ruhr and so on. So we had that little incident with the Serbs and the Austrian Archduke and off we went.

There was a feeling going around that Germany was getting too powerful so everyone else went along with it. In particular Britain wanted Germany taken down. Churchill was Home Secretary before the war and continued as First Lord of the Admiralty. He moved the British warships from coal to oil and so we had all that business with the Anglo-Persian oil company and the later overthrow of the Iranian leadership. Here was a man who felt that the British Empire was under threat from Germany and only one would survive. He was bought and paid for.

Although Germany didn't start the war Kaiser Wilhelm, the Emperor, took the bait and defended the Austro-Hungarian Empire. It might be argued he had little choice. Germany was winning when the decisive steps were taken. A group of Zionists suggested to the British that they would be able and willing to pull Woodrow Wilson and the Americans into the war but there would be a price. British agreement to the creation of the state of Israel. Another price for the British, through American Land Lease loans, would be the loss of their empire, not to Germany but to the US.

This is what Hitler called the Jewish stab in the back and it was all too real. The Versailles Treaty was put in place, forcing Germany to take sole blame for the war, have her territory annexed and pay massive reparations. The French got the industrial heartland they had wanted and Germany was bled to death. Russia had a small taste of this after the collapse of the Soviet Empire when the West asset stripped our country under the guise of a transition to democracy and capitalism.

Germans had massive unemployment, hyperinflation, occupying powers, hunger, starvation, cannibalism. All this was done deliberately. Meanwhile the Banks that bled the citizens dry were owned overwhelmingly by the Jews, as was the media and the culture or entertainment industry. Berlin, dominated by Jews, welcomed Bolsheviks, every kind of sexual depravity and drugs without end. It was Cabaret time. Money was everywhere, with Berlin a magnet for the avant-garde and sexually promiscuous. Here the liberated could have anything they wanted while ordinary Germans couldn't feed their families.

Hitler felt that his people had been colonised and that they were prey to the Bolshevism that had overtaken Russia, generated and spearheaded by the Jews just as they were spearheading Zionism in the West. Hungry people can hear the call for wealth distribution as the arrival of the Messiah, knowing little about the horrific dictatorship that follows. Germany was controlled as the US is controlled today and the moral decay is the same. It is a culture war against the white race.

Hitler kicked them out, shut down their Banks, made usury, the charging of interest on loans, illegal and was the first person to arrest a Rothschild. He printed Germany's own debt-free money and cleaned up Berlin to be once again a family friendly capital city. In a few years he had all but eliminated unemployment and created an economic, cultural and scientific renaissance like the world had never seen. True, he suspended free speech and democracy but if he believed that had he not done so the Bolsheviks would have brought the same horrific tyranny as in Russia, then there is another side to it.

The war was unnecessary. Austria wasn't invaded, they voted 99% to join with Germany and Austrian troops entered major cities in Germany at the same time as the Germans entered Austria to show it was a mutual love affair. The only crime was that it wasn't allowed under the Versailles Treaty, which hobbled Germany territorially as well as in every other way. The purpose of the Treaty was to finish Germany altogether and the Zionists created the Holocaust as cover for the creation of the state of Israel, to psychologically cripple Germany, and with it the whole white race. Judea worked with perfidious Albion, which they had long infested, and with mighty America who they controlled utterly.

The Zionist-controlled Masons, with their goal of a single mixed race on Earth, the end of diversity, provided Truman, the 33rd President, a 33rd degree Mason, to inaugurate the state of Israel against the advice of his own military and the virtually unanimous will of all nations. He wrote a tiny note just saying go ahead you have my blessing. So began the hell of the modern New World Order and the march to global technocratic tyranny.

Now we have a 'new Hitler', one who 'invaded' the Crimea, which voted 97% to join Russia, who is pro-family, restraining the Banks, kicking out GMO's, resisting the New World Order. When he was a young official Westerners were surprised that he was unbribable. He brings honour and Orthodox spirituality. The Zionists and their satanic cult are aghast. They dream up wars and pandemics. All their bought and paid for media is bent on smearing him. He is the leader of the free world.

Gabriel standing and pulling Nikolai up. Embrace the bear

and look at him.

Bastian calls you St Nikolai.

He is mischievous.

The way the congregation calls the priest 'Father'. I never liked that, infantilsation and dominance.

Yes, it can be like that.

I think I understand you now, Father.

The giant arms of the bear-hug and the broad chest of St Nikolai. Journey back to first days, the hidden feelings of a frightened and angry child. The terror of rejection.
Looking up at his face, the tenderness and pride in his eyes like an answered prayer. Acceptance and belonging. God help us, Nikolai.

PACK

I love you, Gabriel.

I love you, Ava.

He knew what she wanted, he could see it in her eyes, could feel it in her heart.

Three months. The last of the snows soaking into the muddy soil and the mosquitoes eating into their flesh. Rubbing the repellent into each other's skin, boiled down birch bark and fish oil, a stench to repel a mammoth. Smearing it on the huskies and ambushing the unwary.

Learning martial arts, men, women, every last one, the arts of war. The marks on Gabriel's face from his lessons with Nikolai.

Out in the wild, scree-hopping the slopes, tracking the wild wolves close, surprising them into fear and aggression, moonlight on the knives. Pack leader turning to stare, his gold-brown eyes showing mastery over his fear, curious still about these men half naked in the last of the mountain snows.

Gabriel and the wolf in mutual appraisal, hammering hearts of man and beast, the dissolution of boundaries. Hunting for life. Feel his searing senses and his feral intelligence. See his pride in his beautiful mate, his maturing cubs, the survival of his pack. Watching his wonder at seeing into Gabriel's soul, the ideas beyond his comprehension, the hidden desire to be like the wolf, the admiration. And something else, the living thing that was not the man, not only him, jumping across the distance between them into his furry chest.

The days when he had tracked them back to the camp and sat outside the circle of firelight, two luminous eyes in the distant dark, striving to grasp the nature of the thing between them. All the earth around him whispering.

Watching the man and his mate feeding the fire, the understanding came that the man had not done this on his own, that the thing had come into him of its own volition. He listened to the thing tell him about the man and he could see it was true. The man was lost, his kind were lost. Although the man did not know it he had come looking for a teacher. And he had found the wolf.

So it began. The wolf showed the man and his mate to his own mate and then to his pack. They did not understand but he was the leader so he set them to wait. He did not know what they were waiting for but on the third night he walked nearer to the fire and lay down. He did not see any guns. He looked at the fire and the home they had made and he looked at their eyes. It was in the man's mate also. That was enough.

Standing, he howled fiercely up at the stars and the man and his mate stood and the pack howled in answer to his call. The man had not known his pack was here beyond the firelight and he watched the man consider the possibilities. He watched as the man put aside his fear and smiled at his mate. After a moment the man walked towards him.

They ran for miles, the wolves backwards and forwards as the man struggled with the pace, the weakness of his body and the bright light inside his head. The thing inside jumped from wolf to man to wolf and the wind was on skin and fur of all together and he was with the pack. The killer was throwing his clothes on the ground and his shoes in the lake and he was with us and we didn't kill him.

The rocks grew in front of us and we climbed them and came down again and the stars raked across our eyes as we leapt and turned in the air. We pushed his hips and legs as we ran and he put his hands on our shoulders and our violence turned to strength and purpose. We ran for miles and the man stopped and vomited the end of his strength on the ground. He put his head on a rock and breathed and looked up at us, the saliva dripping from our teeth. We breathed into his mouth and bit his body and were gentle but still his skin broke and we smelled his blood.

I growled at the pack and they held themselves and I licked his blood and put my muzzle next to his face. He looked at me and the salty water ran on his face and onto my fur and lips and I did not know what it was but I knew he loved me and my tribe and that I had broken his sickness. Something was in his mind and I knew he was with us in this land and the land was alive and it was our home. The thing inside sang in me and it sang in him and it was my guide and I was his and the deed was done.

We left him on the cold earth and I called on the tribe to kill and feed ourselves and our cubs. The man would walk back to his mate.

He is still with me. Empathy is for everyone but still our connections are personal and individual, like yours and mine. He is my teacher and I want to protect him, this one.

The fetish and the bear, the man and the wolf.

So the story grows. He didn't know that it would be hard for me to find my way back. But along the way I found the words to tell you some of what he taught me.

Tell me.

We are all one life, we know and the fetish has shown us but all life is part of the land.

Or the sea.

Yes. The wolves run over the land and live off it, like we were as hunter-gatherers, and they are inseparable from it. We have become insectoid and technological and we have abandoned the land, like a bad divorce.

Agricultural surpluses.

Yes, and Enclosure Acts driving people off the land and off to the Americas. White slaves missing from the history books. Yes, it's the specialisation and the technology and the deliberate control of the food supply but it's more than this. The wolf has no identity without the land and nor do we. We invent artificial identities to go with our artificial world but we are trees with no roots, wolves with no legs, atomised minds afloat in artifice and illusion. We had Nature-based systems that told us who we were and our ideologies reflected our experiences but now we are engineered as social constructs.

Nikolai speaks of Russia throwing out GMO's and going back to organic farming.

Yes, and the distribution of land and the idea that the slave masters eradicated, the idea of common land. Common land in every village where even the poorest could graze their goats and were free from dominion and regulation. The wild things could still survive and we were together on the land.

Now we are being corralled in the cities and the wild places will be the pleasure grounds of the rich and access will be restricted further. We are driving people off the land and fracking the land they still own. New laws mean you no longer own your land. Get people off the land, Agenda 21, Agenda 30

You're right. They took our land and gave us welfare.

This is what I have to tell Nikolai. This is what the fetish wants. What to do with the empathy and the biophilia? Take back the land. Connect it all together again. Recreate the nervous system of the planet and let the collective consciousness live.

Gabriel, all the stuff Nikolai has showed us about evolution, it needs an energetic basis, shared patterns in the life force, the energy fields are not just based on rock and metal but on the biosphere. I know you're talking about sanity but it's evolution, too.

Yes. The wolf doesn't understand about that or even the land ownership but he showed me his life and our place within it. Like you say, evolution is a natural part of the life process. Our bodies are designed to live on the land, not in concrete and plastic.

Dad said he didn't think he would be able to go back to England, away from the forest.

Far away the wolves were howling. Goodbye maybe, or together forever. His tongue lapping gently at the blood.

Ava, before I made it back I saw other things.

Just now I saw your fields, you're still changing.

Changing into what?

Tell me what you saw.

Maybe I'll bite people.

Maybe on the wrist.

I saw memories, you know like when they come in randomly.

Dad says you get that more as you get older.

I'm getting old real quick.

What did you see?

It's like memories but like other stuff. Memories but not of this life. Not even my memories, I think. Maybe imagination or... something else.

I'll just wait, then.

Saw Hitler.

Hitler.

And the Pope.

Pope.

Yeah, and Mussolini.

Having a chat.

Yeah, having a chat.

What about, my lovely boy?

About peace. Hitler, Mussolini and Pope Pius XII wanted to hold peace talks. Britain refused. Chamberlain was under pressure to create an Anglo-Soviet alliance against Germany. They are discussing the dynamics of the coming war and Allies versus Axis is not the way they see it.

How do they see it?

There is a bigger picture.

What's Hitler like?

Like a Father protecting his family. How could I tell this to the people back home? He is authoritarian but not fanatical. He cares about his people. I like him more than the other two.

Is this real?

Seems real. Are any memories real?

Subjective.

Yes.

But this is something else.

There's more.

Just a minute. Why are you seeing Hitler?

Thinking.

Remember what you and Nikolai talked about, abolishing usury, controlling the bankers and the Zionists?

Yes, but it's not just that. The Russians aren't ready to hear the truth about Hitler any more than the West.

Even though the Russian leadership is being given the same treatment and the same lead up to war.

Even though. Those are political overlays to something else. Even though they're more than real. I think beneath the realities he was fighting against, Hitler was looking for something else. I can't prove it, just how it seems to me.

What something else?

Have you ever read Tolkien?

Sure. Lord of the Rings. Silmarillion even.

An attempt to recreate the lost history and mythology of Europe, destroyed by Rome and the Christians.

The Viking culture and the old cultures of Northern Europe.

Yes. A warrior culture, where spirituality was embodied by brave deeds rather than quietism and piety. What do they call the Russian leadership's work? The cult of masculinity. Passivity is of such value to rulers of sheep. The wolf would die rather than submit. He showed me the old ways, the ways of Odin.

The ways of Nature.

Yes, Ava, the ways of Nature.

Lord of the Rings. Something in the collective consciousness. Archetypes.

Or memories. I remember the ice sheets and the hot springs, the journeys to warmer lands. And something else. How many times we have watched the stars rise in East and sink in the West? Venus arc across the ecliptic?

Many times, my sailor.

I remember lying in a boat rocking gently with waves. The innumerable stars so much brighter than today, even here in the taiga. I was there all night and I watched the stars wheel around the centre of the sky and never sink and the night had no end only the endless shaping of the potter's wheel.

Gabriel.

And in another time I sat on the ground and looked at the sun and it was the same land but the sun was not the same sun. It was gold and red and it was directly above. It was gentler than the sun of today and more forgiving and the light was not so harsh. There were other lights around it and plasma arced in currents across the sky like living things. They were not the aurora but the aurora was everywhere also. It was like watching Gods walk across the sky.

HORNS

*He doesn't see it in terms of politics, he sees it in terms of history.
There's no way, Bastian.*

Because so much of Russia's identity is in defeating the Nazis?

Almost single-handedly, yes.

Russia is not the Soviet Union.

*Russia rows in the opposite direction. Proposes UN resolutions to
condemn the glorification of the Nazis, questioning the holocaust
and so on.*

The Ukraine.

*Yes. Try show the coup leaders in a negative light. Some strategy
to defy the overwhelming dominance of the Western mainstream
media.*

Easily passed, I suppose.

Not entirely. The US know what it's for so they oppose it.

*The US opposes anti-Nazi resolutions when they use Hitler as the
measure of all evil? Defining your strong man for instance?*

*They support the coup leaders they put in power, who happen to be
neo-Nazis. Many countries have had people calling themselves
Nazis, both during the war and since. Few of them understand
Hitler's ideals. They are often fairly simple, intellectually.*

But it seems so similar.

The lead up to war?

Yes.

*Yes, it does. The strong man supporting his people. It doesn't
matter that we have a democrat in charge. We could have had peace
with Germany and we could have peace now but if they decide the
time has come...*

They can't stand the sincerity, the sanity.

*Yes, it scares them, they have no grasp of it. Are these more
brothers?*

*Yes, it is their dojo, it is where the training is most concentrated.
Martial arts, yoga, meditation. Not far from the Kremlin.*

So you hope.

Yes.

It wants inside them.

The fetish?
Yes.
She's here, then, you see her.
No. I see something else.
But it speaks for her?
It is her.
Come on, Bastian.
He wants you to fight.
Fight the brothers here?
Yes. Six foot tall, blue eyes, lots of dirty blond hair. Furs and metal and curved horns on the helmet.
A Viking?
Something like that but older. Vikings didn't have horns. This is way before Vikings.
She's mutated.
Took me a while to be sure. He's watching the brothers sparring. And he wants me to fight.
Yes.
Been suppressing that need, as it happens, Bastian.
Well, we're all togged out. Mine is for show. It's you she wants.
He wants.

St Nikolai walking forward and waiting for attention. See him tap the floor with his toes. One of the brothers walking forward and the two bowing. Now adding padding and gloves. Means they're not just playing. Still the same rules, nothing disabling, nothing to the groin. Bowing again and they begin to move. The power in these men, the speed.

Thinking of the Bodhidharma, red-haired blue-eyed barbarian. Europeans in China bringing philosophy, spirituality, martial arts. The Viking fetish making moves behind Nikolai. Not karate but a martial art, perhaps Nikolai would know what it was. The same way she is inside me with the earth on her breath, so he is inside me now with sky in his eyes. The flexing muscles and pressured sinews. Speed of mind.

The empathy of the warrior, respect for life, respect for the struggle to live, to evolve. Something else as well. Something central and fundamental. Empathy for yourself, your family, your people. The hierarchy of it. As the fetish she gave biophilia, the empathy for all life, so the Viking gives differentiation of relevance. All life is not equally relevant to you. It is subjective and different for every being.

The value you assign to you and yours. The bedrock of all life before cultural Marxism came to the West. The white race sacrificing itself for all other races. Unwilling to fight for itself. The genocide of your race is the genocide of yourself.

In my mind the question. What are you worth? Look at what the white race has achieved. Do you know why its history is eradicated? Will you fight for your women and children? You must love what you are or you are weak, waiting for your line to die.

Watching this Viking. To love all people, all races. Yet. Yet, still. All beings choose closeness to ones like themselves. So it must always be or diversity and evolution will die. Humanity needs the white race. The mestizo goal is to create subjugation, a people with no history, no identity, defined by social constructs created by their elites. A people in slavery.

Such is the way the elites offer us. Such is enemy of the Viking, such is the enemy of yourself. The Viking whispers in Nikolai's ear and the ear of his opponent brother. Love yourself, respect yourself, fight for you and yours.

Nikolai taking a battering but standing his ground, he's taken on one of the best. Not a man who will take a kick direct to the chest. As Nikolai steps back the Viking moves forward into his body, hand into his spine, like a spear-hand penetrating flesh. Nikolai moves forward and sweeps a kick to the man's left side, a different order of speed.

The Pope says Europe is no longer vibrant and fertile and we should welcome immigration. We are like an old Grandmother, he says. We had a Nature religion based on fertility but now we have one God, chosen people, communism. Now our breasts sag and our openings are dry. Let us hasten our own death.

The brother goes down and Nikolai is on him, the blow pulled inches short to show what might have been. The fist stops an inch above the brother's heart but the Viking doesn't stop. His fingers like steel into flesh direct into the heart, the man spasms, spine arcing as he lifts off the floor. Like a heart attack and the brothers are rushing forward, alarmed and yet confused. There was no physical contact.

As they pull his belt and open his suit he grabs the nearest wrist. Pulls himself up. Brother and brothers moving up and out like an opening flower. The brother presses his palms on his eyes and looks around slowly, drops into stance and shouts the kiai. Russian expletives and a growl like a laughing bear. Brothers backing away.

He turns to Nikolai.

Snova.

They bow and the fight resumes. The brothers know that something has changed. These two men like free-style ballerinos. They dance their strikes and blocks across the mat and there is absolute silence. Aggression crackling in the air. Absolute discipline. Never seen this, even in the taiga retreat. In time the master stops and bows.

Čto vy so mnoj sdelali?

Brothers almost leaning forward in anticipation.

Progulka so mnoj.

Three of us cross-legged in the corner of the hall. Brothers respecting our privacy, training resuming, no-one looking around.

He wants to know what I did to him, Bastian.

Not knowing what to say. The brother waiting patiently but eventually leaning forward to shake hands. As the hands lock the thing inside changes in time, or jumps over. Fetish to Viking. Grinning at him now, and he grinning back, Nikolai too. Linking arms like the triple horns of Odin. The synchronicity in a collection of hands and forearms. Too late to worry about your state of mind, the deed is done. The brother stands.

Ob''jasnite pozže.

We will speak later, it seems. He walks to the nearest brother and bows. He gestures and they form a circle around him. They attack one at a time or in twos or threes, the man's speed doesn't seem real. It takes a long time but eventually a score of men huddle and laugh, embrace, fall silent. Eventually they walk to Nikolai and me and we stand. They embrace us both in turn, smiles and sparkling eyes, a hand to the face.

Ob''jasnite pozže.

The Master turns to his men. They back away a few yards and line up. He gestures to Nikolai.

Česnokova Gavriil javilsja. Večnyj juriskonsul'ta.

Nikolai smiles and stands in front of them, glances at me and his eyes close. The brothers begin to sing, lyrical orthodox beauty unlike anything else in this world. Private audience to the meaning of art, meaning of religion, foundation of spirit in flesh. Nikolai takes the lead, baritone strong over the chorus, echoing in the space and stone of Russia.

The song lasts a few minutes but heart and mind move in worlds without end.

Eventually the silence is broken by the Master.

Obrasajtes' k nam sejčas.

So the story is told to the brothers and although it is this voice that speaks first, still much is new to us all. These brothers have not come from the taiga but some have been at other times, many have spoken with those already infected. Each contemplates in his own heart the thing unfolding inside him.

We speak of love for all men, all races, all types. Love for the races that have unknowingly been used to destroy our own. We are one.

We speak of the mystery of our origin. We speak of the future, the metal mind that waits on our trajectory. We speak of our allegiance to our biology and our empathy for all life, our implacable opposition to the world-eater.

We speak of women, our women. The ones who have forgotten family, the ones who remember. Our love for them. The power of these men is faster than the ideologies of our enemies.

DARK

Washington DC. Not like Moscow. Stand and look at the White House lawn. Get arrested as a mole, digging tunnels into the Fairy Ballroom.

Nikolai measures the risk, gets me new papers, a little hacking here and there. Problem being he's unsure who to protect me from. Hiding in plain sight with discreet security all over me, digital and human. Trade delegation is the preferred method. Oil and gas up front but higher tech in the van, space co-operation, major Western corporations at the table. Despite the Cold War rhetoric. Game different at every level.

Not in the meetings, too much exposure. Part of the security detail, ray-bans and sharp suits. No-one blinks or so it seems. The security we have brought are not brothers but Nikolai says they're more than ok, that they're a known quantity and their recognition allows for business as usual. No surprises. A lot of time standing outside doors. But every delegate on both sides walks within a few yards of me both in and out the conference room and there are a lot of meetings.

When the energy deals make way for space tech the crew changes and Nikolai takes more of a back seat but the security stays the same. As the new delegates start to file in they seem edgy. The story is mutual connectivity in space, joint docking as with Apollo and Soyuz, mutual aid protocols, rocket hire. But there's much more on the table.

Global security. Private contractors who do 99% of their business with government. The visible end of the spectrum. The rest are reps from the money. The shakers send their lieutenants. Nikolai pulling at the threads, strategic and subjective, looks different from every angle. It's a hall of mirrors.

Empathy. Biophilia. Fetish .Viking. Has its downsides. These guys are a mixed bag but there is little light, some of them are horrific. Stomach tightening in defence, try to breathe it out, can't have an edgy security guy.

Strange the way these people are so mechanical. Like they're on coke, linear and black and white, feelings emanating only from the ego. How situations affect individual position and security. Social contact based on strategic alliances. They feel infantile, clever tricks but no maturity. They feel, really, like nobody much, but they carry so much influence. Making decisions about how a species leaves its planet. It's profile to any on looking worlds.

Wait, here's something altogether else. Where's it coming from? The guy coming down the corridor with the extra personal security made to look like assistants. Tall, sleek black hair, white skin, tinted glasses, not quite shades but you can't get a fix on the eyes. He's like obsidian, so black it's a mirror. This has been done purposely, some kind of mental martial art aimed at concealment. Who could do such a thing?

As he's entering the hall he pauses and turns around. Look straight ahead at the wall, see him in peripheral vision, he's scanning everyone. Is he looking at me? Try to control the heart rate and breathing, be still. The moment seems to telescope but there's no way to know what he's doing. Become the Viking, a mind strong enough to bend the laws of the world. We are not here. Finger the scars we share, still hard and smooth on the wrist. Eventually he goes in and there's sweat breaking out and shaking in the legs and it would be so easy to slide down the wall and just sit. Realising the shock of touching a mind unlike any other.

So now Nikolai will be pleased. Assuming Mr Dark didn't see me, didn't realise I was looking at him, or else we might be dead. If we survive we have what we came for. A thread to pull. Olga we've found something but I don't know what it is. But you were right, my love, there is something here. Told us to have strong hearts and be bold and she cried. Just start looking around, my boys.

Could go speak to Nikolai. Let's just go, it might save our lives. It's not like we're in Russia and the help is easy to call in.

But that would mean the cover's blown, his cover, and God knows where that goes. That's everyone else's safety at very least. Then stay here and wait for him to come out.

The Viking, the fetish. Olga. The power in these things. Olga believes in us, she believes in me. What does she believe in? What are the bounds of this estate? No measures with which to calibrate, no distillate to gauge, just an open book to read. No one to trust here but your own self. An owl flying in the pitch of night. It will be all right because I will make it all right.

Olga talks of focused intent. Like a light growing brighter. A light bulb is dim because the vast majority of its energy is like particles crashing chaotically into each other. Only the ones that escape the melee are visible to us. If they could all be aligned the light bulb would be brighter than the sun. There's no shortage of power, it's the skill in its transmission, its cohesion and symmetry. The results can be exponential.

Life is intelligence, the coherence of thought and intent, in the same way as a laser is the coherence of light. The fetish whispers of lucidity, organisation. They come up with fancy new words. Quantum entanglement. Consciousness reaches across space and time and always has done. To be aligned with the wave allows for dramatic effects. The fetish is life, I am aligned with life, I am the Viking, I will fight for us.

You will not see us, dark mind. You will see a hall of mirrors and believe you have seen the echo of your paranoia. Nikolai and I will be invisible to you because life wants it that way. You are death, you smell of metal, you cannot see the life force here in my brother and me. Pass by on your way to hell.

The door opening and the strange mind and his lieutenants emerging. He glances around and now is the time to still the heart but he moves on and disappears in the lift. Watch the floor indicators take him away. Slip into the side room where Nikolai sits with fresh coffee and lemon water.

What is it, Bastian? You found something?
I don't know what I found.

I knew there was something. I could feel it.

He nearly found me out. Or maybe he did and didn't let on. Maybe we're already sitting ducks.

But you don't think so.

I'm guessing we're safe. But I really took a chance.

Who is he?

What is he?

Not human?

I had myself a little philosophy about that as I was waiting for him to point at me. How about you?

Am I human?

How about Olga?

She's my sister.

Not answering the question.

Come on.

Maybe he has had some kind of training. Mind like polished steel, like those patent leather shoes with the gloss. Couldn't read him. Like he was prepared for anything empathic, telepathic. Really didn't want anyone to know anything about him.

He was in charge?

Not in an obvious way but he's at a different level to everyone else. There were some top lieutenants in there but he's not like them. Pity I didn't hear the conversation but I would guess he wouldn't allow himself to stand out.

Who would have that kind of training?

Thought you might know.

There are remote viewers and influencers, psychics. You've come across some of them.

I have?

I haven't focused on them because of Olga.

As in they're not a patch on her?

Yes. But, in any case, I've not come across anything like you describe. Olga said there was a darkness, something she didn't know about.

Looks like we have a mission, then, Captain.

As in let's find him before he finds us?

Thought it would be a road trip, endless empty horizons,

rickety wooden pylons, unreconstructed rednecks. Wanted it. But Nikolai sits in the hotel making phone calls and plays with algorithms on his laptop, or until one of the security comes in and does it for him. This guy seems to be able to access every camera ever made, even up to satellite. Could be a millionaire before breakfast. Here he is guarding Nikolai and dancing around dojos.

When he's done we're driving to the airport and we're done gone to Phoenix. Trying to feel into it through the flight and getting nowhere. Driving out of the city with cars just turning up for us and taking us into the endless desert, cacti like transmogrified humans and poison creosote trapping the sun. Lizards running among the bleached branches and ground down quartz.

Stop the car, take a piss, walk around. Why is it so familiar? The Hollywood your Mother watches while you're in the womb? Is it archetypal of some kind of heaven? Some place we all used to live? There's a facility down the road, not near any major military stuff. Corporate research image. Nikolai not sure but I know our man is in there, or one just like him. Pity we don't dare call Olga.

Will take a while to reorganise their manifest to get us on their visitors schedule. Then there's the ID, so slow even though the spooks are as fast as you can get. Then there's a message from Russia, text from some random phone. Nikolai says there's only one person it could be from. There are some personal comments but he says he knows what they mean.

Means you'll get nowhere even if you get in safely. No external recognition of the places we want to go. Will only put us in danger. His face looking tight.

What's wrong, Nikolai?
She wants to come.
To the desert?
Yes.
Nikolai looking at me uneasily.
There's more.

She wants to bring Ava and Gabriel.
Why?
To help in some way.
That's all you know?
Yes.
So you sprung me from danger in England but we'll all be ok here?
I don't know. Like you, they would be under different names here,
no-one would be aware they're here.
If we're lucky.
Yes.
Tell me something else, Nikolai.
I don't know, Bastian. She's never done this before. She never
leaves the taiga.

Security dumping us off miles into the desert and disappearing, returning with camper vans and supplies just before nightfall. Air chilling quickly and stars leaping out in sudden bursts. We watch each other fearfully, unwilling to disagree with Olga, looking for answers where we know there are none to be found.

The moon looks red and there are shooting stars. Echoes bounce for miles across the luminous desert. Men silent around the fire or walking short distances the better to hear the emptiness. Lie on the ground and look straight up. Night time insects chafing their keratin exoskeletons and the sky a romantic carousel. Pass around the night visions and see the invisible lights move straight and swift across the horizon.

Nikolai telling the men about the arrivals. No-one knows what to expect but everyone knows something sits out here in the desert waiting to ingest their lives and spit them out. The spicy bitter sweet smell of sage brush like protective medicine. The desert on our side, cold past midnight, dreaming the future.

So another day and night and the cavalry are ushered in to meet us, and our security, men now almost entirely silent. Hugs and kisses and nervous laughter. Lighting another fire and dividing into two groups, us and the muscle. Sitting on colourful blankets made by enterprising peddlers of colourful histories. Can almost see horses tethered and quiet at the outskirts of the fire. Eyes flashing reflections as their heads turn and smell the wind.

The call of another time, many other times. Maybe Gabriel will find a wolf out here. Coyotes ten a penny, snickering in the gulleys as they squabble on the endless plains. Elemental contrast with the wet, green taiga, the ice and snow. Olga hesitating to begin, bewitched with the desert's static majesty. Urgency winning out and council is convened, circular around the fire, like a five-pointed star. Like Sirius, a hieroglyph on the arid sandy soil.

CYBER

He's so different now. Sharks have only cartilage but other
fish grow bones. An endoskeleton. Stars and more stars. Olga
brings us into danger. Home to our family, our new one. Smell
of death, smell of horror. Hiding from the government, all the
subtle tech to avoid surveillance and facial recognition.
Government the least of our problems, a donkey with sticks
and carrots for brains. Something else.

Leave the conversation behind, walk through the desert.
Four sets of footsteps soon following behind and no-one says
a word. Walking into gratitude and the sound of grasshoppers
or cicadas. Nature blinding us to the fear. Follow your nose,
follow the energy lines, the pull of polarities like me to
Gabriel. He is closest, recognise his breathing and footfalls.

Must be three hours and they offer silent patience. Night
train across the fragrant desert, cold caravanserai. Penitents
with roses in their teeth, grinning from ear to ear. Purposive
caterpillar legs moving in unison. Time was a squirrel could
leap tree to tree from Land's End to John O'Groats.

Dreams, it seems, are the latest currency in our merry band.
Going through some of Mother's stuff, sorting things out with
her *friend*. Never liked this mate but we're amicable here.
Mother is dead. Sitting on the grassy banks of my primary
school. She's not really dead but she's dead to me, maybe
dead to herself, DNA switching off.

Mortality so barefaced. On the farm with dead animals at
your feet, growing slowly cold, their blood on your hands,
smell of their flesh in your nostrils. Have someone else do the
butchery, cut it in pieces, wrap it in plastic. Take this death
away from me. Children have all the monsters cleansed from
their books. It's the hollow taste of metal on the tongue, vague
sense of sickness. It's when the stage is full of nothing.

The next ridge, the next bluff. Peering over the top into the
long flat plain below. There it is. I suppose that's what we're
looking for. A lunar crater where the ejecta radiate out like the

sun's rays on a medieval painting. Only it's energy, lines of force converging on a more or less circular central node, flowing in or out or both. Beautiful, almost crystalline. Like and unlike something I saw in the taiga. Another portal, perhaps, exotic matter, another physics.

The others sitting or standing silently, still waiting. So I tell them. Blue energy glowing in the night like an ultraviolet flower. A few miles out on the plain but unlike anything else. Olga taking me by the hand.

Do you want to look inside like you did in the taiga?

We are with you now. We've put ourselves in a lot of danger over this. So close to the place Dad and Bastian found, the man they found.

Yes, I want to look.

Short discussion. We can't go down there, risky enough here, we don't know who we're dealing with.

Can you look form here?

I can try.

Just follow the lines to go off the edge of the map. Here be monsters. Not so easy to access the thing from here. Sit down, just another yoga practice, legs crossed, straight spine, focus on the distant lotus like it sat in the middle of my forehead. Ships, there are ships. Not for the sea, for space. Not space from A to B. Tech but not just a machine. A vehicle for consciousness to bend space and time or bend something to travel in some other way. Strange, dark, nauseous beasts. They are screaming. Something is alive. Something whose senses are the machine itself. They are screaming to us but they want Olga. To any that would hear. Please, help us away from this hell. Please.

Olga telling me to rest.

It's alright, Ava, I heard them speak, ideas in my mind. They're breeding foetuses to specification and then putting neural tissue into the machines. Sometimes most of the brain, sometimes just parts. Some element of them that is separate from their bodies is telling me. They want it to end, a place to be, bodies that are whole.

A pause.

What do you think, Nikolai?

You know what I think. The risk is high and it's not easily assessable. We don't even know what's in there. Security were telling me that although it's overtly a space tech research centre, or as overtly as covert projects go, it's more like a medical facility. That's all they have.

Eyes sliding around each other and the shared sense of sickness, physical wretch in the stomach as the truth coughs and churns it way into our minds. We will have to deal with this, recent fruit of a long-time horror show.

Long walk back to the campsite. The future already here. Hail, Dystopia. How to get into the base, how to survive such a thing. Back at the campsite with hot tea and the motherly welcome of security, as glad to see us as we them. Jealous of the men's hugs until they smile and invite me in. Nikolai and Olga in conference, the trust between them like a bar magnet, negative and positive poles, great big field. Bastian gone away somewhere, might as well have rolled up his eyes to the whites. Gabriel holding my hand, senses leaking out across the desert floor. We're still alive.

Cuddle up to him. His dark hair against the sky, the bones in his face. Sailor boy, sailor man. Mantle of stars around his shoulders, the future writ large. I'm waiting for you. Tell me when you are able. This is what he says.

There were once other humans in this place, tall, not like us.

How can you know this? I know how you know this. Ask him about himself. This is what he says.

Dreamed I was taking my car to the garage. Half the garage has a molten gold floor. The car has been changed. I'm trying to replace the petrol cap but it falls in through the hole. I look in to the petrol tank but it's not dark, it's full of light. The petrol is translucent as water and light echoes around like a sea cave, like a tropical lagoon. I fish out the petrol cap and it's a crystal, one part clear and one coloured. I replace it, realising there's no mechanism, it just rests gently when put in at the right angle.

That's all he says. Since what happened in the desert nausea inhabits me. Like a cuckoo too big for its nest.

HACK

Viking in me today. More and more. Earthen breath of the
fetish home in the taiga. Wants me to fight, karate with
Nikolai. Fight with an opponent who could kill you at will.
But the moves are becoming faster. Men who break concrete
blocks with their fists. They don't have the look of boxers, it's
the speed that creates the devastating power. Speed is in the
mind. The Viking is in my mind.

Or I am in his. Ligaments straining, muscles tightening like
iron bars. Let mutton rot on the green pastures. The meek will
be taken and splintered all ends up.

Men of England, wherefore plough
For the lords who lay ye low?
Wherefore weave with toil and care
The rich robes your tyrants wear?

The literature they no longer teach at school. Our culture
that is destroyed by the day. Here in the US of every A and
they ban Shakespeare from the schools. The truth is anti-
Semitic. The little ones need to be protected from it. But they
can learn the glory of planting their organs in another's
behind. Here's your bread and here's your circus, take your
food stamps.

Walking through a sky of stars and the waves lap closer to
the shore. The engineered race war, the identity politics, the
collapse of the petrodollar. The welcoming camps like the
ones FDR created for the Axis powers, the ones that
disappeared from history. And here are the comedians. Sign
here, dear friends, my petition to reduce intelligence in order
to make us more equal. Stand back in laughter and horror as
the doe-eyed students sign on for a better world.

Have ye leisure, comfort, calm,
Shelter, food, love's gentle balm?

Or what is it ye buy so dear
With your pain and with your fear?

This one's been mugged by a black man. But it's ok because
he's got privilege. Look at him, he's white. He doesn't mind,
he's glad to help. But there's no record of his suffering at the
online cop shop. And the story changes from reporter to
reporter. Self-sacrificing wrong-eyed Jesus. Buying approval
and pocketing the change.

The seed ye sow another reaps;
The wealth ye find another keeps;
The robes ye weave another wears;
The arms ye forge another bears.

When your working day is done bend over the plough. The
shame like coins on your eyes. Usury was banned in our time,
in the very heart of Europe, the bankers shackled. We were so
close. Only by blood on the soil and fertility who is our queen.
The roses grow so red.
No match for Nikolai. On the floor, spurt of red iron
coughing out across teeth and lips. Speed is in the mind.
Again and again. Think on, think on, Bastian, else your
dullness will be your death. But it's my daughter. And the
others. Wait, Nikolai, we need to think. There's blood on my
shirt and where the seeds have been sown loyalty grows. Its
ferocity. The ones all around. The ones to fight for.
We need to find out what's in there.
We need to stay alive.
You don't think we can get in.
It's not the way.
But where is the way, brother? And so the ideas move
between us. No capacity to force an entrance. No easy way to
escape to Mother Russia even if we succeed.
How about we kidnap the thing?
Not from the base.

From his car. We could have a chat.

He might have materials with him.

And between us it would be interesting to know what we could see in him.

Our security might be able to do it but we have a problem. Witnesses.

Yes. Unless we kill him and his security afterwards. You up for that?

Not my first thought.

No.

Nikolai's life. The things he must have done. Yet uncorrupted. One day see if he wants to talk. Support your local protector.

It still might be possible. Use masks, stolen cars. But you don't know how he's linked into satellite surveillance, what type of alarms he has in place, instant response teams. Better than trying to break into the base but still desperate.

Yes. Also we don't know what he could read from us. He might already be aware of us and is just waiting for us to show up. Maybe he's that confident. But up close he might be empathic, telepathic, we don't know.

Maybe so.

Walk away for a while, out into the desert. People get tortured. Down the road in the bay. People spend most of a life in solitary. Don't even know what you're in there for. Die in there or come out a pot plant. Land of the free. Nikolai, give us a place to believe in.

There in the backpack, ends glinting in the last of the sun, calling to me. Pull them out, smooth copper, like friends in my hands. The lines so strong here, like at the place in the taiga, rods crossing like crazy.

Same energy. Right from the first time using them. Not water or gold or lost keys. Same energy. Some kind of life energy because they cross the same over a human or a cat. Remember the early days, plotting the lines and points with bits of bamboo from the garden, tie on bits of coloured cloth.

Looking down on the patterns revealed. Like acupuncture points and meridians. Like Kirlian photography.

Same life force, same patterns. Earth is alive in some way. Could just walk and follow them, like Ava. Not magnetic, these lines but flowing in tandem with the magnetic flux. Ava could walk the same path with her vision.

Hard to get away from them, to focus on something else. Took so long to get signals for water or gas or oil. The unconscious not interested, focused on the life force, the dragon lines. Have to suppress what matters for the sake of money, for the sake of Ava. Body fighting back, responding to the natural lines. Body looking for something. More sensitive this way since the fetish took away the old life.

Viking waiting. Martial arts moves, controlled movements, controlled breathing. Yes, controlled mind. Can still force sensitivity to anything I decide. To this darkened being. If he was under the ground. Or maybe he is. Run back now, old heart kicking like a donkey. Sunset static on the horizon as the body pumps forward. Before long Nikolai smiling as he helps me sit on a rock, hand on chest.

I'm not sure what you mean. If he was in an underground facility you could find him by dowsing? Well, he probably is.

No, that was my first thought but it doesn't leave us any further forward, does it? Still can't reach him. Then I thought about where his influence reached out to and I thought of what I could find under the earth. In theory I could dowse for anything. Do you think this facility is connected to the web or stand alone, paper only like your place in the taiga?

Few people work in that way outside of ourselves. In this case I don't know but I think we could find out. If there is a connection there will be traces.

Cable or no?

More likely cable, more secure, better quality. Also it's in the middle of nowhere. It's possible they could beam it down but I doubt they would want to.

So they worked out it was cabled. Joke. Like all the NASA

computers with their passwords set to password. Maybe just no fear of opposition. Rough idea of where it goes to the next hub. All kinds of stuff underground here, tunnels everywhere, so it doesn't have to follow the roads and tracks. Various options. Have to find a stretch out of the way. So they bus me about in the desert at night.

After a while I'm wondering if this is in my grasp. Then I get the twitch, walk around in an expanding spiral and there's a line, base at one end, hub at the other, got to be it. We can get the kit, says Nikolai, although it won't be easy to get hold of. Tap into the cable like the local spooks do, granted they do it on an industrial scale, usually on the sea bed. Either way there's no trace, no-one knows they've been tapped.

Seems to take forever to map out, maybe it's too different from standard fare. Stumbling over it by accident, well away from expected areas. Strange. After a while it seems way too deep, cables are usually fairly close to the surface. Following it either way and there are branches where no branches should be. Can only be tunnels, then. Transport tunnels and they've laid the cables inside the tunnels. A long way down and strong, means we would need way more kit than you could keep quiet, even out here.

Can't think of another way, Nikolai?

Have thought of one.

Don't be shy.

More like crazy to tell you.

Can't disappoint Olga.

Alright. Kidnapping.

Without the killing?

Without the killing. Still risky.

Go on.

Find a stretch of road with cover to the sides, rock outcrops maybe. Cover the road in tyre cutting tacks. Hopefully they'll open the door to get out. Fire in a canister of knockout gas.

And if they don't open the door?

Through the windscreen.

Trying not to kill anyone.

Yes. The gas either knocks them out or forces them out. Hit them with tranquiliser darts.

They never need see us.

No.

What if they alert HQ at any point in this?

We hope to act quickly enough to prevent that.

Still.

Then we get what we can before...

I see.

That includes Ava and Olga and Gabriel, not to mention security. We would have to ask them.

If they felt their lives were worth it.

Yes.

Or if they could come up with something else.

Unlikely.

Just tell them it's the best we can come up with.

Or go home. Find other threads.

We need to talk.

I think so.

Gather around the fire. The ancestral home. Before we gathered chairs around a screen. Chop them up for firewood before we dissolve. Ava throwing in something aromatic. Watch security go through their martial arts just beyond the firelight, lit up by momentary flares and sparks. Have to seek permission there, too.

Somehow it's in the rods but not like this.

TRUTH

Nikolai. Everyone's sat around the fire but no-one's speaking. It's not right, is it?

No.

Tell them to have a break. Come and talk to me, please.

Nikolai giving me a long look.

Alright.

Walking out under the blinding stars, brighter away from the fire, tiny reflections glancing off the quartz in the rocks. Trusting in strangers, have to trust myself. This fetish like an upgraded intuition, don't have to work everything out.

Nikolai, I want to tell you something. And I'm sorry.

Patient man.

Yes, Ava.

You believed in me, brought me to the taiga, asked me to help you. You're a fighter from another time. And I lied to you.

No surprise in his eyes. Not a flicker on his face. He knew? Maybe. Maybe he has seen so many lies.

You saved my Father's life. Probably mine, too.

Yes.

Even now it's hard for me to hold your work in my mind. The scale of it.

You are young.

I feel it. I've never been around adults before, not like you and Olga. And my Father.

Gabriel is young, too.

Yes, I would like to talk about him also but that's not what I've lied about.

Your feelings for him are plain to see.

I think I have inherited some kind of... abilities from my Dad.

Yes.

But they're not what you think they are.

That's interesting.

That's what scares me about you, you'll just accept it.

Ava, our Father was tortured by the secret police, our Mother lost. You think I should cry over a few lies. When we were young the communists were in power, funded by your banks. It's all a lie.

Nikolai.

Just tell me.

The things you showed me. The things you said. To talk to the Earth, talk to the sun. The things you want from me. I told you I could see magnetism, lines of force.

Yes.

I can't, Nikolai, I can't at all. I lied to you. And I can't give you the things you want from me. I've been lying for years.

But your Father knows.

Yes, he knows.

So he's lying, too.

Yes. He... taught me to lie.

And now the truth is out.

What are you doing, Nikolai?

Letting you tell me. Something must have happened.

Something happened. Divorce. Custody. Your Father's not sane, bizarre delusions, talks to things that aren't there. Twisting my mind against him. The time away from him, no one to ask what to do. Hiding the things I saw.

The things she said about him, the years of struggling for access. If she had not grown tired of me who knows what would have happened. The secret family courts like you wouldn't believe a democratic country would allow. He wasn't allowed to defend himself, the deal was in. Meeting secretly, the risks, the promises. I will never go away. Hold on to me.

And so we made lies of our own. The things we saw, we didn't see. Her social workers and psychiatrists clueless to the ways of the Earth, the simple deceit of their industry, the money and the control. The things we heard, we didn't hear. Mother and the feminists, an ideological tool in the hands of a brutal dwarf-God.

Ava, you must hide yourself, you must learn the lies until you think them for yourself, don't let them catch you out. I will give you these symbols and they will never know, but you will know, I will always be with you. I would trace out the patterns. Look, Mum, Celtic weave, look, Mum, dragons. My Father the dragon king. Like a mantra, like the Stations of the Cross, my passion for him, my anchor to the world, my only home. Trace the patterns and walk the lines and no-one knows that I still sing to you, that I hear you still.

The thing you said to me. That we would fight. That we all have to fight. That we have the strength and the guile. We have love. We will win. I would head out on favourite walks and find dragons, semi-precious stones, an amethyst heart. Laugh out loud, the freedom.

I'm sorry, Nikolai. We lied so I would survive. We lied so my Father's heart would not break.

I'm sorry, Ava.

We were all sorry. But it means I can't do the things you want from me. Now you will be sorry you trusted me.

I put magnetic fields in front of you. You didn't see them.

What? In the tech domes in the taiga?

In England, before we met.

When I was a child?

Yes, but when you were back with your Dad.

Did he know?

No, he didn't know me. Not when I found out about you. Not when my brother dragged him out of the hospital. Not until I took him under the sea and out to the taiga.

Have you talked about this with him?

As you say, Ava, we are older. And now we are changed. Sometimes you don't even need to talk.

God, why didn't you tell me?

You told me.

I feel so stupid.

Far from it. Your honour is as evident as your feelings for Gabriel. I admire you.

So what do you expect from me, now?

The truth, if you're in the mood.

Assuming you don't already know.

I don't understand what I know.

Alright. When you first pick up the rods they respond in their own way. People think of dowsing for water and you can do that if that is what you want. You can dowse for anything, it's just about intention. But if you have no intention they always pick up the same things, it's like your unconscious decides for you.

Applies to anyone?

As far as I know, yes. The rods cross and they find certain spots and they also find lines. I remember my Dad watching me, saying I was finding the same stuff as he was. The next thing you discover is that they cross next to people. Also cats, dogs, fish. But not trees, no plants.

Not about life-force, then.

No, trees with huge bioelectrical signatures that don't register at all.

Cats, dogs, fish. All conscious.

Yes, only picks up consciousness.

So the lines are...

So it seems.

Unconsciously you respond to currents in the Earth, that's what your body is interested in.

Life to life.

These are ley lines, then?

Kind of. Ley lines are straight lines between Churches, sacred sites of various kinds. Churches are often located on previous sacred sites anyway. Some people in England noticed you could draw straight lines on maps. The Old Straight Track Club. Some people think it's wishful thinking, others that these are ancient pathways. All kinds of mythologies are bandied around. Paths of the dead, spirit paths, ritual pilgrimage routes. You could dowse for such a thing if that's what you're after, the rods will respond to any intent.

But...

I think that they're an abstraction. A simplification.

Of your lines.

Yes. Heard of the Michael and Mary lines?

Yes, but only in passing. These are your earth lines?

Yes. They are the most well known of the lines. Anyone can find them. A couple of guys tracked them and wrote a book. They start in Cornwall and end up in the North Sea at the Norfolk Suffolk border. Go through megalithic sites and Churches. They wind like snakes and occasionally cross over. These are the places you can join with a straight line from coast to coast. Places like Avebury.

What happens when they cross?

It's a big deal. Some more so than others. Long ago these were seen as the most important places on the Earth. All of history turns on them.

That's a big statement.

Yes. We found them, the dragon lines. We found out what dragons where, the ancient serpents. We found out they were conscious.

I can feel it, Ava, what you're saying. This fetish breathing inside me, her excitement.

Me, too. I thought this was a confessional but now I'm not so sure.

When you said you saw the magnetic lines to the portal, and the other one in Russia, and you followed them?

I was following the dragon lines. My Father drummed it into me so deep I even think of those words in my head. I imagine you know what my Mother was doing.

Some of it, yes. Enough to see why you did this. She was trying to paint him as crazy, you as his victim.

Yes, and all her connections to help her. We were talking to the conscious Earth.

Dragons were your code.

Not only our code. The code.

Meaning?

My Dad took me to Avebury. We had tracked both the Michael and Mary lines in various places. We walked up the Avenue of stones as I tracked the Michael line with my rods, the stones following his progress. I followed him through the centre of the major circle and the centre of the two inner circles.

It was the same when we followed the Mary line. They crossed near the entrance to the circle and all the biggest stones marked the actions and crossings of the currents. The whole structure was based on a complex and intricate crossing point of the two currents. It was like a lens, a technology aimed at focusing the currents.

That day. Walking the dragon lines, riding the dragon. The shifts in consciousness as you walk the line. By the time we walked the marriage and the union of the lines it was like being in another world. They reach out to you when you reach out to them.

The realisation, Nikolai. The archaeologists estimate Avebury would have taken five hundred years to build. A primitive society. The level of organisation and sheer effort. And all for the dragon lines, to talk with them, to communicate to the Earth, to work with her. All these megalithic constructions, a culture predating Egypt and Sumer, a people whose entire lives were about working with dragons.

St Michael spearing the dragon, Ava.

Yes, fixing the current, the currents can be shaped, they respond.

Dragons and gargoyles in the Churches. Dragons with human heads.

A dragon line with a human consciousness. A hybrid being greater than the sum of the parts.

This is what your Father showed you.

Yes.

This is why Olga wanted him. Why she told me to find him.

Now you say it, it seems obvious.

So these portals...

Yes. Where the lines cross something happens. There is a shift. Consciousness and intention become primary. They are like openings where your consciousness can reach to other worlds, past or future, other awareness, the Earth, the sun, I don't even really know what they are.

You think other... consciousness, beings could come here through this?

I don't know. If I had to answer I would say yes.

And this ... man that we are here to find?

Could he have arrived here from somewhere else through the portal?

Yes.

No idea.

But you don't think we should be kidnapping him?

You don't either.
No, and it was my idea. But Olga wants something.
And what Olga wants...
Yes.
Why does she get?
You know why.
Yes. She's like my Dad.
Wait...

Tracking over the crest. Chief of security. Smile on his face. Looks like he's holding answers.

No, Gabriel, That's not it.

Easy for you to say. People flying you all over the world. And you.

Only because your daughter likes me.

That not enough?

Not really. Not at all.

Well, that's true. What are you going to do about it?

How do you mean? All I have is a mad aunt and an anger management problem.

Well, that's not true.

No. Everything's changed. The fetish...the taiga... I'm grateful. But...

But it's what you've given me. I haven't made anything.

You don't think coming so far is an achievement?

I thought you might say I got my aunt out of jail or about the wolves.

I could. Not everyone could have made the steps you have made so quickly, facing yourself, facing this process.

It seems strange after all we have been through to say can I be honest, but can I?

Please.

We have so much to face.

Nikolai's digitally enabled security come to save us from suicide, pull us from the brink, they know we need to know. They can hack into cables without a physical breach, leach off the spillage, see through walls. They got lucky, they say. Let it go and accept the information, that's all.

The man with the dark mind. All about technology and the hive. We know about the metals they spray on us but there are other things among the metals, things we don't understand. Here is their provenance. Miniature life forms if you could call them that. Parts of the kingdoms of life blended together that only belong apart. Also metallic and other artificial components.

But the worst thing is the DNA. Not only spliced and mutated but synthetic, three strands, all manner of design to render self-replicating, semi-biological cells. They are being spread everywhere and they invade the bodies of all living things, using the material of the host to replicate themselves. Not only replicate but develop, engage with the host's nervous system, brain function, invade the native DNA.

Put it all together and it's about more than monitoring, it's a technology to allow centralised hacking into people's selves, nervous systems, brains. Make you more like a machine, have your thoughts and feelings monitored and controlled. We have known for some time that people host implants without any awareness of their existence but this level of tech requires no covert procedures, it's in your mouth, lungs, every orifice.

All of life connected to the internet of things, interfaces of the hive mind, the machine God.

The end of individuality, the end of an independent biology, the end of evolution. Nikolai says they have found this stuff everywhere, says it's like when they drop lithium in the air to improve radar trace, like electrodes in your brain.

Olga still not happy but enough to call off the kidnap. She says we will have to let the dark mind go, he has evaded us whether he knows it or not. She says this will come back to bite us. Maybe so, hard to think she would be wrong, but we're still alive, Ava is still alive.

This boy loves her, too, it seems.
Yes, we have so much to face.
I love her.
I know.
I would ask her to marry me but...
You think she may turn you down.
Yes.
Even though she loves you.
Even so.
Why, then?
I'm not enough of a man.

Grab him and hold him. I have never seen a man I would more like to marry my daughter. Or fear marrying her less. Let him know.

How is the martial arts training going, Gabriel?

Nikolai is a great teacher. Thanks.

Tell me, then.

Alright. Many things. First I have no money, no career, no income. I have to win some bread, we've gone back to biology.

Yes, we have. You have IT skills, Nikolai's security could train you. I can show you the rods, show you how to grow. You're creative and you have support. But we have other kinds of work now. This means our finances are de facto collective, just as are our skills. Already we are a kind of family.

What can I give?

The speed with which you are changing is what you can give.

I'm trying. I have lots of dark things in me.

So do we all.

You're being kind but you don't think I'm ready either.

No, I don't.

Ah.

But I believe you will be.

When?

I don't know. We share so much now, so much empathy, but it's something else. We can see patterns that we don't necessarily understand. Like seeing the future. You, me and Ava all know you're not ready, we don't have to discuss it to agree. But we all know you will be and we will know when.

This is something I know, too?

I believe so.

He's looking at me and he looks for a long time. There are other thoughts, other feelings, crowding in, it's time to move on.

I almost believe you. No, I do believe you. Thank you.

You are right to think you cannot be an angry child and provide for Ava but already we have need of you. Ava tells me of your experiences.

Like a freight train in the night. This we know.

Yes. A kind of seeing, patterns towards the future. I see, too. I have precognitive dreams, more and more. And I see other things.

Go on.

Maybe the past.

The past out here?

Yes. I talked to Nikolai about it. He told me about the esoteric geometry and architecture in the ground plans and buildings in US cities, particularly DC, the capital.

The New Jerusalem.

Yes. Masonic stuff, straight on from the coming out into the open in the French Revolution. It's all over the place, London, Paris.

Yes.

One night I'm out walking alone and when I sit down I'm gone. I'm somewhere I've seen before but not so clear.

So the story goes. The robes and the rituals, the underground structures. Talismanic architecture to draw forces from heaven down to the Earth. The booby traps, the cryptic ciphers. Mapping out the temple on the Earth and vivifying it with an invocation of higher power. Not just another Jerusalem, there have been many of those. Each of their cities is planned and inaugurated in the same way. Their sacrifices and ritual abuse and executions are done the same way. Planetary exploration, royal weddings.

This was more. A new Atlantis, Francis Bacon, Elizabeth 1st, the Royal Society. America, the cornerstone of the resurrection, the phoenix. All the powers of old for the chosen nation, the torch to light the way to a global supremacy. A place from which to challenge the Gods.

How did it feel to you?

Not good. It felt like they didn't know what they were doing. It felt like there was a shadow over them.

Like forces they didn't understand affecting their consciousness.

Yes. Why am I seeing this?

They want to reclaim their legacy, that's how they see it. And like Prometheus, challenge the Gods. They feel they are becoming Gods themselves, especially since the technocratic dream, since the singularity was set on its course.

But this was long before then.

Yes. There are structures in creation that resonate harmonically. I'll give you an example. Later this year there is a full solar eclipse. It exists because the sun is four hundred times bigger than the moon but also four hundred times further away. So the moon superimposes itself perfectly on the sun. Do you know what science says about this?

It's a coincidence?

Of course. Describe what you can't explain. Some think it's a coincidence too far and it must have been engineered. And there are many anomalies regarding the moon, not least of which is how such a massive body could become trapped by the Earth. There are lights on the moon, it goes on and on. And these are real issues. But before we decide aliens put the moon where it is, here's another piece of information. The sun spins four hundred times faster than the moon. If we were looking at an unlikely coincidence before then what are we looking at now?

That would be a hell of a lot of engineering.

And if I gave you any number of other such cosmic coincidences, what then?

I don't know.

There are patterns that science has no knowledge of. Modern science, that is. Ancient science was based on these patterns because if you align with them you become integral to the workings and evolution of the cosmos.

Who are these people?

You have seen them. Today they are the same. They think they have the right to decide the future, to keep their knowledge secret. The secrecy of their knowledge and their financial power, that is, political power, blinds them to how little they know. They planned America long before they created it. Columbus and the Mayflower were artifice only. Today you would call it PR or marketing. But still the time was wrong.

So there is a right time?

Yes.

When?

Around now.

How do you know?

What do you know about precession?

Of the equinoxes?

Yes.

The stars appear to move backwards through the zodiac about two thousand years per sign so the whole cycle takes about twenty four thousand years and begins again.

Yes. And the mechanism?

The wobble of the Earth, a product of the Earth's axis?

So they say. When you see a child's spinning top wobble, what does it mean?

It's about to fall down, stop spinning.

Yes. Wobble is a sign of disequilibrium not a stable system that spins on regardless almost forever. The maths and theoretical base for the wobble hypothesis comes up with new patches every few years but it always lags behind the data.

Such as.

Such as precession is speeding up, hard to envisage with the wobble. There's lots of it. I can show you sometime. You know about binary stars?

Most stars are not singular but have a partner, orbit around each other. Or rather a central point.

Very good. So if our sun had a partner how would we know?

Perturbations in the orbits of the planets, especially outer ones, same for Kuiper belt and Oort cloud further out.

Yes. But something simpler.

Don't know.

No. Seems most astronomers don't know either. If we had a binary twin it would not precess with the other stars because it would be tied to our own orbit. Its visual deviation would be tiny. It would be the only star not moving with precession. If you find a star that doesn't move, you've found it. Easy.

And we've found it?

Yes.

Which star?

Sirius.

Sit yourself down, it's only your memory, you'll be fine. Remember the door where we came in, the door by which we leave. Silver gate, golden gate, the keys. The world we lost, scattered across space like a rosary. The people we sold down the river, the unconsciousness of it all.

Blue skin moving under the spray, blinding white light through the water. Golden fur on the land. Long, long, long, so long we have been together young brother, so long and still we go on.

The reason precession is accelerating is that Sirius and our sun are on the inward path, drawing closer together. The apoapsis is over, the winter of the Great Year is done and our paths draw ever closer. The rise and fall of civilisations are measured by precession.

So there will be a right time?

Yes, there will.

And what then?

Then you'll be able to ask for my daughter's hand in marriage. Then I'll say yes.

LINES

All the way from St Michael's mount in Cornwall, chasing the dragon like so many before. Dragon lines coming in from the Atlantic, from tropical lands. Michael and Mary, lovers in the water, rushing onto the land. Take me by the hand and carry me into the future. You and me, standing on the shoulders of giants.

The earth lines across Devon and Somerset and on to Glastonbury. See Michael and Mary twist around and around, follow the labyrinth across the Tor, the dragon's egg. See the fair field where the lines have been changed, where they run geometric, intention in play. All the way from the coast, camping in the woods, with damp wood fires. How the dragons respond to us, how the earth lines dance for us.

We walked the line, every inch, the pilgrimage from the first days, down on our knees, up on the balls of our feet. And when you walk the lines something happens to you. No longer just abstract. The Earth folds your mind into herself, she awakens your memory as you awaken hers.

As you walk the rods twist you in spirals. Now you know what the spirals on the old stones are. At the Tor the lines twist around each other like Olympic lovers, ever deeper into each other. It takes you more than an hour to find the centre and it's not in the middle. Sun on the back of your neck. Rednecks out in the fields. Now you know what the labyrinths on the old stones are.

All the way from the west coast through the churches and the old stones talking to the people, the many that have forgotten and the few that remember. The vicars who know the old ways or some part of our ways. The obelisks and monuments in the towns where the craftsmen have tried to control us, control our Earth. The dragons leaping towards us, for us to ride with as once we did, feeding our life, our memory.

Dragonrider, Ava, that's what you will be. Your children yet to come. And we hid our dragons up our sleeves until I was eighteen. But once you have ridden the dragon you won't be the same again and our pact was made. Nothing on this Earth or above would separate us or stop us because the best is yet to come.

The fox who came at night, nosed in the open tent flap, stared at me fearless and bold and screamed at me until I cried. Please never leave. He disappeared into the shadowy fields but he is with me still, he was the dragon, a moment when our lives were together.

Dark have been our dreams, dreams not of our own making. The locals here came with cannabis and other such things and love and the earth all twisted around in their hair so they walk in circles. And my Da told me how it was done.

Showed me Catcher in the Rye, hymn to the disaffected. How thin the veil on the Masonic stage. The catching of the young and bright and how the deepest secret was how to lead a generation off the cliff.

The lies about the professor and Mesoamerican Indians and hallucinogens. The release of LSD by the intelligence agencies, magic bus, the bought and paid for media blitz. The fake archaic revival, take them away from knowing where they are. Dress them up like cowboys and Indians and tune in, turn on, drop out. Give up the fight, act out the devolution, dumb and dumber. Give up the fight, run around like a dog with two dicks. Give up the children, contraceptive pill if you please.

What happened in LA, Laurel Canyon. Kids of intelligence families making music, gathering magically together and all the hired girls at the gigs, dressing like fantasy native girls and all up for putting out. The money and the political operatives and the intelligence base. Charles Manson. All the famous sixties names. What's not to like?

The Beatles, bigger than Jesus. I am the Walrus goo goo ga joob. Lewis Carroll. Eat the oysters and cry there's never enough. The sacrifice of a generation.

Out through the druid groves and the girl with the Course in Miracles. More agency work. Turn your cheek, don't fight back, catshit and crystals. La la la. Up on the hill over the vale and Michael and Mary meet again on the ridge. Here's a fibreglass dragon, white and cute, bigger than a man. Someone knows something. Sometimes the coloured ribbons hanging from trees are not only the wishful dispossessed. Sometimes they are scraps of memory.

Up on Dragon Hill, the benders and the tree houses, rusticana of the archaic revival, the devolution. Nestled in next to the affluent Archers and the four by fours and yet goodwill prevails, there are no evictions, the downwardly mobile rein in excess and harmony reigns as well as could be asked. In the village the lines converge on the Church and flow up a blind spiral staircase. The builders knew.

Back up to the fibreglass dragon and the crossing point, the power place. Sitting under the ash tree and looking over the vale. The blinding blue sky, the unearthly clarity. When the sea held sway there were islands and shallow lakes, red lake, grey lake. The fish were everywhere and the giving was good.

There is a boy with me from time to time, blond hair, blue eyes, sometimes riding on the dragon's back, sometimes in my lap. He has a small mole on his right cheek, near his mouth, and he is beautiful. He is eight years old and now he stands and looks over the vale and his body moves like water. Martial arts, karate, something. Beneath me the dragons stir, sinuous and wakeful. They flow through him and become him. He is the head of the dragon and they are his body. They, he, look north-east along the ridge where the lines flow away to Wiltshire and then to the south-west where they come in from the Atlantic with the Gulf Stream and the kiss of the tropics. He looks at me. His blue eyes speak to me. I am waiting for you, we are all waiting for you. It feels like a ritual.

Are you the past?

Yes, I am the past.

Are you the present?

No, the present is defiled.
Are you the future?
Do you want me?
Yes, yes, I want you.
I want you, too.

He is gone. Did I do the ritual well? Will he come back? Please.

My Father watching me from a distance. Respectful, silent. He is like the boy. These men around me. Pick up the rods and walk the lines again and again. Now I have seen the metamorphosis, blue eye of a boy, standing in the place of a dragon.

Walk the line across the county border, heading north-east, the soft rolling hills fading to sweeping chalk plains. Mile after mile of ancient earthworks and then Windmill Hill, looking down at the stones of Avebury. Sleeping out under the stars on a warm summer night, bit exposed for a tent, just avoid the hassle. The currents cross again at the top and we'll wait for tomorrow to see the navel of the Neolithic.

Bats and foxes. Father sitting cross-legged and still. What's he doing? Soon the dreams are strange. There's a woman with unusual features. She's hitting a section of road with a cricket bat. In this place you can see through the road into another place. There's someone trying to get through and this woman is just not having it. Just roll over and go to sleep.

Morning sees us climbing Silbury Hill with the Mary line, see her heading for a long barrow. Swans in the watery fields, kestrels above. Through Swallow Spring, the long barrow and on to the Sanctuary. Here the lines cross, the opposite part of the complex to Windmill Hill, beginning and end of the ritual landscape. Mary heads north-east with Michael but we track him back to the main ring.

Below the round barrows studded with trees like enormous hedgehogs and on to the Avenue, rows of stones curving gently into the heart of the complex for maybe a mile and a half. Michael is so wide he is like two lines, the outside edges of the dragon being where the energy is strongest. Two rows of stones and we're puzzled why the stones don't always align with the dragon's body. The stones fix him on course like St George's spear. We're told the stones have been re-erected and you can see the concrete. Locations were well intentioned guess work. Like Stonehenge, then.

Here it is, then, the elephant in the room. The purpose of these stones relates to the dragon lines. As the Avenue joins the ring the lines cross in the trees between the ring and the road and we explore the inner stones. Three more crosses and all where the biggest stones mark the flow. In the middle of the first inner circles the currents run together, circling around each other. Here is the marriage of male and female, here is the be all and end all of life.

The next inner circle is where the currents enter from the north-west, we have entered in reverse but following the Avenue was natural. At the big stones where the currents first meet I see a woman approach Father, engage him. She doesn't know I am with him. They sit with their backs to the stones and I move closer and listen. It's the woman from the dream, same strange features. She's as wide as she is high and compares herself to the stones. This a pilgrimage of sorts for her.

It appears she wishes to enact some kind of symbolic marriage, with my Da representing the male. The implication of further action in the room at the Red Lion makes me smile. She's picks up a small branch and some kind of rustic honey pot, symbols she sees as having some kind of talismanic force. Da is polite. She rambles on. Lives with her ex, isn't it nice that men are becoming more like women and gender identities are dissolving, on and on.

Makes me think about marriage. When a man and woman come together to create life, then care for that life. That's what it is. You can call any union a marriage but the laws of biology, the laws of evolution, of life, have their own mandate.

This modern Millie has produced no life, her gay friends have produced no life. They are an evolutionary dead end.

The program. Comes with the archaic revival. Sexual licence, sexual confusion. An infantile identity where sex is your first idea of self. Overcrowd a bunch of rats and the first thing they lose are their traditional gender roles. This woman's tragedy. She comes here to enact life and yet ends up suppressing it, in herself and in the dragon lines of the Earth whose first duty is fertility. She is the woman with the cricket bat and she will not allow through the deeper forces that come with sex and love and marriage. She is doing the opposite of what the people that erected these stones were doing.

Da smiles and is kind. He hints gently that everything is not a social construct, that your body tells you who you are but her canoe is laden with notions and eventually she moves off for a pint of Guinness. Perhaps she will have more luck where the drink flows.

Da and me, we walk together, from the place where the currents meet to the place where they marry and join, to where they separate and to where they kiss goodbye in the trees just before the Avenue. As we walk we stop and young people with rods come to compare notes, tourists to be curious. We will return in the quiet of night.

Under the stars on the south-east edge of the ring we tune in and talk and laugh. The revelation of our history, our people. Everything they built was to honour and work with the dragon lines. They worked with the earth and they worked with consciousness, to expand fertility, grow life, accelerate awareness. A technology of evolution.

To look back and understand the history of your people, because what they teach you at school makes no sense. To be part of the march of history, to know your place and understand that the future can still grow organically out of the past, that we can carry on the work of our ancestors, the knowledge we have inherited and rediscovered. To know who you are and see the path ahead.

Days at Avebury, watching the dragons shift in the Earth with the movements of sun and moon and how they respond when we reach out to them. So then we knew what we needed to do if not how. This we know. You can put darkness into the lines as easily as light. We see the rituals of the dark, our leaders with their satanic paedophile sickness, their need to darken the Earth and its people, to control them. Their need to be exceptional.

Everywhere the dragons have been twisted and enslaved to lower the awareness of our people. They have no choice. But this we know, too. They respond best when you come from the heart, something the elites understand only theoretically. The sincerity of a natural human is the joy of the dragons. They come to us freely and there is no slavery. They dance with us and we move together. Our joy is their joy.

Barbury Castle is known as a hill fort as are many other enclosures. You only have to look at it to know this could never have been its primary purpose. There are three concentric rings and two openings but these have been considerably broadened to allow for anti-aircraft guns during the Second World War. Why the Luftwaffe would be flying over rural hill forts isn't obvious. The place is high on a ridge and full of wind. Walk the lines as they arrive and circle around the rings, spiraling first in then out then in again until they are back at the entrance under the electric blue sky. See the spirals settle in the embankments at the side, the ones that make no sense defensively. Back at the entrance they head for the opposite opening like two waves crossing and re-crossing each other as their amplitude swells towards the middle and declines again towards the exit.

It's like a solenoid coil, an amplification device. More technology in stone, the crystalline rock structure, the geometry, the intent that is channeled into it. God knows what damage the Home Guard have done. In the hours it takes to trace the lines the minds of the ancients open further. The scale of their endeavour, the depth of their understanding. At Glastonbury the intensification of the lines is mainly natural or a response to consciousness and intent. Here the earth and stones have been built to amplify the energy, focusing it the way a crystal focuses light into a laser.

Asking Da what he knows. He knows that the industrial tech that has been used to desecrate this place is like a child's toy compared to the stones. That we are the primitive ones and our bodies and souls are in decline. Their technology enhanced us and the Earth, ours is killing us, slowly and quickly.

Da says there are concentric rings everywhere, in the stones, on shields, in jewellery. After Glastonbury and all the spirals in the lines we know what the labyrinths and spiral motifs are. Have I understood the concentric rings? No, I haven't but I like them. Ok, he says, let's go to Uffington.

Only the Mary Line, Michael is away in the far fields. But the energy is strong here, we're not sure why. Here is Dragon Hill where St George slew the dragon and where its blood fell to ground there is a patch where nothing grows. The white horse is beautiful, stylised, transcendent. We look down the Ridgeway back to Barbury and onwards east. Trade routes of old that followed the dragons. Not just for trade but for culture and pilgrimage. To weave a society together and drive it forward. The white horse that looks nothing like a horse. Da smiles at me and laughs and asks does it not look like a dragon? Yes, it does, Father mine, more draconian than equine, you clever old sod.

Wandering backward and forward in time as our pilgrimage meanders across the landscape to the Norfolk coast. Hopton, on the border where the North folk meet the South folk. The final crossing point in the old Church.

HOLM

Now we are here again. Nikolai has spirited us home. Or almost home. In a yacht off the Norfolk coast and the boys are all pulling at the rigging and leaning out from the side of the boat and getting very wet. Soon enough they'll get tired and calm down. I've been delegated the rods and we're following Michael as he heads into the North Sea with the Grey seals.

Just Da and Gabriel and me but we have a bat phone to Nikolai to address drowning or trouble with spooks. White spray on the cold grey water and if it's not a storm it's not a millpond. Nikolai digging into new data about experiments to turn us all into Borg. Maybe he's found out about the man with the dark mind. Olga not happy but glad we ended up with something and ended up all alive. Probably back in the tundra playing with the bears or visiting Lake Baikal as she had threatened.

Gabriel and Bastian. Boys settle down eventually and fish for bream but catch mackerel. Throw back the little ones and pan fry the big ones, stuff a lot of spice in its belly to cover the strength of the flavour. Fresh fish and fresh air like health itself. When the sun comes out join the men for karate and yoga, take turns steering the boat and holding the rods.

Odysseus has followed the currents west to the navel of the sea, the omphalos, to Ogygia, where he has stayed for seven years. Here is Calypso, Goddess of the mythologists, king's daughter to the rest of us. Green in her cave, her purposes inscrutable to modernity, she guides our hero to the holy land, to Phaeacia. She bids him steer by the rising of Boötes and the Pleiades, to keep straight the steering oar and let the Gulf Stream and the prevailing winds speed him on his course.

On the eighteenth day the shadowy mountains appear before him, the land like a shield laid on the misty sea and the red, white and black cliffs rising from the sea like reality from a dream. He has left São Miguel in the Azores, dragon's resting place before the long swim out to St Michael's Mount.

He has put his trust in Calypso and now he sees the red, white and black stone used in the walls, towers and bridges linking the concentric rings of land and water encircling their impossible city.

The story book country is lost, now, to the sea, but a small part of the cliffs remain and as we pass we honour Odysseus and Homer and all those who would find their home once again. The blue-black rocks, where the sandstone is richly coloured with cupric carbonate, are below the sea's flood, and the shining white cliffs of chalk and gypsum have been mined away industrially in our own time, but a part of the vivid red sandstone still stands, a bloody knife to catch the fire of the sun in the cold North Sea.

Watching Ava put the rods away for the last few miles, her eyes skimming over the waves like the acrobat terns. Here, here, it's here and her tears like tiny primordial oceans. Salty mariners. Calling for her sailor boy to hold her and the old boy to throw the anchor. Call Nikolai on the endless connectivity and bring up the support ship. We're on, you old seadog.

At least we're not going down in that bathtub you had me in on the hoax hydrocarbon trip.
Not a hoax, make roubles.
St Nikolai the rouble man.
No usury here, only dive suits and cameras.
You are the enabler.
The light is clear and the visibility good. The dive is on. You and me, old man.
Leave the kids?
Da.

Come to me now, ghosts of the past. Ava tells us what she sees and what she has never before seen and it's erupting out of the sea and exploding into the sky in all directions. Nikolai and me in wet suits, daring each other to fall backwards off the boat like Jacques Cousteau. Swearing in Russian. Then we're in, and a good vis in the North Sea isn't like a tropical reef, it's green and silted and disorienting but we have safety lines and torches and we're on our way down.

Kids upstairs on the boat. Glancing back instinctively. Keep expecting to see a Viking appear, maybe in scuba gear. Down into the green light of the past, the dark and soupy sea. Eventually the sea floor rising to meet us and it's impossible to believe the lines say no more than thirty feet. Nikolai waving me to follow and we swim along, defining the area of a small hill before settling slowly to the sea bed.

Walls, large stones, smooth, flat flint slabs fitted together. This area is the Steingrund. Skilfully worked and well-fitted stones are everywhere. Not a small camp but a major construction. Take off a glove and run fingers along the smooth flint. Shock of recognition. Now I am the Viking but he's not a Viking. Older. I am a warrior coming home. Where is my woman? Where are my children?

Losing any sense of time. Disoriented but not scared. Ignore the life of the sea. Close your eyes and pull gently along with hands on the walls and stones. Take off the other glove. It's ok, there is a saint watching over me.

Lying on the deck, looking at the sky, the saint taking his fingers off my neck, carotid artery.
Are you with us, Bastian?
Maybe.
Smiles all around. As much as can be asked for.
Warm me up and offer me some tea and I'll tell you.
So they do. Prop me up in the captain's cabin in Nikolai's ship. Colourful blanket a privilege of age. Proper mug of tea. Had to prise something out of my hand. Rinse off the mud and silt. It's the size of an apple but it's not stone or bronze, it's gold. A golden apple. Hold it up to the shafts of sunlight edging through the cabin window, rub it on a shirtsleeve, see the metallic, yellow sheen glinting impossibly in the hand of a

diver. Noble metal assailed ineffectually by the sea.

We're not the first to dive here, are we, Nikolai?

No.

Who else?

Divers from the Heligoland Institute of Marine Biology. Divers from the German Navy associated with prehistorian Peter Wiepert, honorary member of Kiel University and winner of its rarely awarded Kiel University Medal.

What did they find?

Same as us. 'The remains of a Germanic royal fortress' in Peter Wiepert's view.

But no golden apples.

No. It must have been hard to see, covered in mud. How did you find it?

No idea.

Any memory of losing consciousness?

Ava shifting uncomfortably.

No. Just you pulling off the oxygen mask.

No more questions. No one speaks out of turn. We have come so far.

I dreamed of apples last night although they weren't gold. They had fallen from a tree. The ground was like a false floor. It suddenly became glass and you could see the real land beneath it. The apples had rolled through the glass and could be found on the earth below.

Now they are found. Like stepping through a door. From the fitted flint slabs to an apple orchard on a green hill, sun catching on the golden fittings of the red, white and black stone making up the circular walls. Seagulls swooping across the rings of water and the canal giving access to the sea, keeping an eye on the precession of ships and the merchandise changing hands on jetties or in marketplaces.

The outbound trade of copper and bronze, of swords and armour and jewellery, but above all of amber. The only place on Earth to mine amber and send it to the four corners in return for gold and riches beyond all imagining. Amber washing up on the beaches and being used in fires like others use wood or coal.

Avalon, the island of apples and here is a woman I should know, smiling at me, showing me a golden apple and recounting its provenance as a Mother tells a cherished story to her children. It is somewhere between poetry and prose and she tells of knowledge and of life. Come to the world tree with me for the sacrifice will be soon and I want you to be ready when your brothers arrive.

She takes my hand and I watch her red hair rippling across her flaxen dress in the breeze. She leads me to the Temple, all laid with amber like red gold, with an ivory roof marked out in gold and silver. It is His temple, the husband of our Mother, the lady of the chariot with the eyes of an owl. Er and Erce and together they fertilise our people and our home, the Earth, and together they are the Earth and this is their marriage bed.

I see the bubbling spring guide subtly through the grove and I see the tree. We cross the bridge over the last ring of water and she touches the arm of the first of the guards. He is a great warrior and I know him well but his name will not stay on my tongue.

The tree is like a pillar and its arms are like the beams that hold up the house but this is the world pillar that holds up the heavens. The arms are called Ás and that is why our Father who carries the world on his shoulders is called Atlás and the world ocean is called after him. That is why this place is called Ásgard. That is why the great ash tree is called Yggdrásil.

These forms come from the husband who created this troy town in the pattern of the spheres. The concentric circles are the sun's varying paths as seen from the ninth bow, the ends of the Earth in the furthest North. Their subtler parts allow sightings of moon and planets and stars.

The world pillar is the pole of the North Star around which the Earth and the heavenly bodies turn. The pillar illustrates that the spaces and times of all things can be determined in their natural harmony, the revolutions of the heavens and the moral fibre of men all enfolded within the measuring-tree. The temple and the town and all our works across the globe are designed of one measure and the hearts of our people are eternally supported in the firm and constant foundations of the universe.

The great ash is inlaid with amber and between its arms are inscribed the laws of our people, the sacred measure of our culture and our restraint on the tyranny that the other peoples of the world find themselves subjected to. In its decipherment of the laws of the cosmos, as above so below, and in its preservation and expansion of life and human understanding, it is called from afar the tree of Knowledge of Good and Evil and the tree of Life. The golden apples are the symbols of the eternal life we sow and reap, they are the harvest of our culture.

So now these three beloved folk gather around and memory bleeds through them as the tale unfolds. The golden apple we offered, the fruit that has been spat out, the apostasy we have received in return. Some increase of the heart, some spasm of the thymus gland, some fibre growing back to fill the empty places in the chest where our moral souls once lived.

Where did our memory go?

What did she want to prepare you for?

In the grove between the springs the ten gather, once five sets of twins, five rings to weave our world together. Atlás asked his brother to watch over Iberia, Tarsessus. The other eight twins watch over all the lands from the Eastern Baltic to the Mediterranean as far as Thyrennia and Libya. Our folk take the megaliths and all the arts of civilisation carried in the depths of their blue eyes. We teach the Egyptians how to build in stone despite even that they rule by absolute authority.

Every ten years we gather and we ten kings catch and slaughter the bull. No metal implements, only ropes and sticks and athleticism. Not only the bull's life at stake. He is raised onto the arms of the tree and his blood flows down the zig zag tracings on the amber and ash, flowing over the laws inscribed there. We pledge ourselves to the laws and judge any of us who are accused of breaking those laws and mistreating our people. There will be mortal pay for mortal sins. None of us is above the law.

We fear this may be our last gathering and when all pressing matters are dealt with we light the fires, first here and then throughout our lands, one beacon to the next, the fire travelling along the body of the dragons to fertilise and enrich our land and our people. All our will is bent on it. Now, though, we ten sit together and, having heard the voices of our people, we resolve to face our future. Ragnarok.

Our lands are rich and the broad leaves stretch to the circle of ice but many years of drought have been pushing us against the walls of our grain stores. We cannot survive like this much longer. Our dreams and visions having been telling us that something is coming and we consider our history, tell stories around the fire and try to determine our place in time, our place in the cosmos. Like our Father Atlás, we carry the weight of the world on our shoulders.

We remember the days before the ice melted and the world was drowned and we know that all our glory can be thrown down in a night. We know the stars can be torn down from the sky. We know the endless years it has taken for us to rebuild our people and our knowledge and now we face the fire once again. The auroras have been making their way south and the sounds they make grow louder, like a slow sword against a shield. The colours grow more violent.

Our history since the end of the ice has been long but in time the land grew warm and we uncovered the past, started again on the long road. Now we debate our own past wars. The Vanir and the Aesir. A time when the megalith builders were confronted with a divergence of our people who had become more familiar with the axe than with riding the dragon. Still they were our own and the wars dismayed us all. In time we made peace and blended our people back together. Now our ancestors have been confused and mixed and it is well that it is so. It no longer matters which of our peoples our histories are woven around.

We have built peace in all our lands and the myths and histories are for all. Now Odin is Njord and we are one. Now we listen to one of our brothers who wishes to speak of Odin.

We must reach for that part of ourselves that was once the invader, the part we have accepted into our own, the one who wields the axe. We have walked the world with honour and offered our knowledge and our civilisation freely. But now hard choices will be made. We will have nowhere to go and the places we will need are already settled, by people we have taught and yet still live by autocracy and dictatorship. Do we wish to survive? Will the culture we have fought to build bleed to nothing?

The brother has no dissenters, he has only silence. The drought is many years in but we know it is rather the astronomers he speaks of, the astronomers and the mages and the dreams of us all. We will look into the future. The orchard, the lady's wicker basket, the gold of our labour.

From the tree of life to the mast of the mainsail, golden apple in hand, the orb and sceptre of latter day ritualists.

What do you see, Ava?

She sees what I see.

It is home to the dragon lines. Not the beginning because I can see them coming in from the east on the same path. I would guess they circle the Earth and return. But in a way the beginning and the end. That's what I see. It feels like the heart of the world, a broken heart. It feels like home.

Yes, home.

The megaliths in England from early days, days of childhood. Across to Germany and Denmark, over the Baltic. The mystery in our lands and the blindness of the archaeologists. The wilful amnesia gifted to us by our overlords. Children climbing on the stones. Hands reaching over the water to where we grew up, where our blinded folk still labour, boats and ships carrying the apples of the living ash across all the lands of the Atlantic.

The golden seed of our home.

Atlantis.

RAGNAROK

Ragnarok. In a chair on a boat, rocked by the waves. Might as well be tied to the mast. Time slipping away and back like eels in a river. Viking sat opposite me running his finger along the blade of his axe, grinning. The round shield at his feet, the long broadsword, the horned helmet. No Viking. Atlantean. As Father described him. Father rocking beside me. No more fetish.

He looks at me and now he has Gabriel's face. How Gabriel could be or once was. Long hair tied in a side-knot, the muscle-tone, the ethereal looks. His heart on his sleeve. A warrior from another age. Come back to me, I will be your girl. I will dress for you, I will feed your desire, I will make you strong. I will let you take me. We will fight side by side. Make yourself ready for me. Bring it back, make yourself what you once were, bring it back.

Ragnarok. Fire in the sky. The wolf. The doom of the Gods. No Gods, only ourselves.

The Gabriel Atlantean is looking at me. He sees me not as I am, or as I am and more. He looks at my green eyes and red hair. I see myself through his eyes. His eyes are blue and his hair is blond and he is bleached like a bone in the sun. Where the red of my hair falls on my white skin his mind is filled with glory. Where it falls across my face, meshing across my green eyes, he sees the beauty of Nature, he feels his heart open.

A sensibility of race. A visual representation of a quality of soul, the resonance between the inner and outer. Not just of earth, but of spirit. He sees the spirit in my eyes. To be such a thing to the man I love, to be these things together. The colours in our eyes the colours in our souls. When he sees me open he will see my red hair. He is power and I am beauty as it has always been, the beauty of his power the power of my beauty, we are more than either could ever be alone, we will be together once again.

Ragnarok. Walking down the stone Avenue and watching the skies. Walking towards the white walls of home. The sun is not the same. The sun has been eaten by the wolf. Now there is another sun. There is fire in the sky in the day and there is fire in the sky at night. The auroras are everywhere. Luminous shapes spiral and twist across the stars, massive, overwhelming. Around Venus a halo, a crown for a Goddess. Spears and tridents tearing around Mars, omens of war.

The shapes seen in meditation the night Gabriel arrived, the night the other light came into my night visions. The words of modernity. Plasma discharges. These streaks of fire. A splintering comet? Accretions of carbon and dust precipitating in the atmosphere like burning tears. The tears of the Gods. The ground burns as the astronomers have said it would. Not the first time. We know now that more will follow. We know we will not be the only ones.

Across our lands word comes of earthquakes and volcanoes. Darkness covers the new sun and the plasmas shine behind the dust clouds. The crops fail. Our people are hungry. Already some are moving south in search of food and hope. The Kings have decided and my husband comes to me, he is running and shouting and I see the wave behind him, stalking him, taller than our sea walls. He is shouting to me to run as the water chases him. He will not be able to save me or himself.

I can see through the bottom of the boat. See where he fell running up the hill. The orchard shredded and splintered. The tree is overthrown, the apples scattered, waiting for my Father's hand. There is only mud and debris, the stones thrown around by the flood. I can see where my husband died. There is nothing there. Ásgard is lost.

But my Father holds gold in his hand and this thing that was a fetish and now is a man runs his thumb along his axe and I see the blood drip down the blade. He wants me to remember the diasporas, he wants me to remember that the fight is not yet over, not a thing of the past. He wants me to fight. Give my husband the strength to fight.

In his blue eye I see his mind, the march south to Greece, the population decimated, the fields and buildings burned by the plasma and rain of fire. We know all these lands. Preserve as we are able. The rule of law, respect, empathy. Build for the future. Teach them new ways to manage conflicts. Our king versus your champion, if we lose we will depart for a hundred years, if we win we expect to work with you. The records across southern Europe of our people honouring our pledges, new in their world. Alliances formed yet so much is lost. The Egyptian priests end up telling Solon of his own history and ours, a history conjoined. All of Europe, the democracy, the science, the art, the culture. Our gift, use it well.

He stands by me in childhood, invisible to me and yet present. A presence, a memory, a presentiment. Me and my Dad in the woods, climbing on the stones, the dowsing rods. He was there all along, the spirit of the land. Later Nikolai will tell us the historical narrative but so much I can see for myself, see in this mind.

England, my home, a land not free. Michael and Mary down from Ásgard, west to Norfolk and all our sacred sites down to Cornwall, just as they flow east through Schleswig-Holstein and Jutland, over past St Petersburg. Wassailing the apple crop, wassail the trees to awaken them into the light and ask of them abundant fruit, our health and our life. The Wassail King and Queen walking and dancing from one orchard to the next. Lift the Queen into the boughs of the oldest tree, the fertile keeper, she lays bread soaked in apple mead on the branches and blesses the trees with the King and all the people.

From Avalon, the apple orchards join in precession across our lands, across England, and knowledge travels with them. Earlier in the year the May King and the Queen celebrate fertility and the sacred marriage and the girls dance around the Maypole with ribbons in their hair. The pole is the tree of Life, the tree of the Law and as the walls of the temples and cities mirror the circling heavens so does the dance of the girls spiral around the moral heart of our people as a Queen dances for her King.

Apple tree, ash tree.

The fire festivals, four times a year. Put out all the lights and start again. The beacons being lit all along the dragon lines. Hundreds of miles. Stand on the hill to see them. Focus and intention of the people flowing down the lines, through the Earth and out to the Sun, who are our Queen and our King. Come together and be fertile, give life, the fertile Earth, fertile hunters, fertile prey, fertile men and women.

Out from the Sun to the next star and the next and the next. Life across the galaxy and on to the next, forever and ever. Life from nothing, evolution, the living mystery.

Sex for husband and wife, celebrate. For all life light the fires, for our Mothers and Fathers. Love is the heart of our Law, the heart of our lives.

Blue eyes and the blood trickling down the face of his axe. Those eyes are inside me. I know his mind, I know what he wants. We look together through the hull of the boat to the mud below. He comes to lay his rough hand on my chest. The cycle of the heavens draws close once again. Light the fires, sister, our people are in need.

EUROPA

The Mary Celeste. Wind in the rigging, creaking boards on deck. Is anyone awake here? Anchored steady above the Steingrund, unseen compass in the cabin, ship's wheel roped and secured on the neutral helm.

Take the golden apple from Bastian's hand and lean back on the mast on the open deck. Grey seal watching me. Eyes of a dog. Nikolai back on his hi-tech yacht, probably searching records or signaling Olga.

I see him. The one that looks like a Viking. Been putting himself around. I know because he opens his mind to me. Son receives the apple from his Father. Knowledge. Is he my Father? Of course he is. The All-Father. Your All-Father.

Odin gave his eye for knowledge. A man from the Ninth Bow hung on the tree for nine Days to find wisdom. How can you husband your wife, your resources, your people, if you know nothing? How can you fight if you have no will, if you don't know what you are fighting for? Your Father has brought you here to remember.

To remember what? To remember yourself.
On past Greece and into the Middle East. Rebirth of Gaza, Ashqelon, Ashdod, Jamnia and Dor, create the League of Independent Cities, build the infrastructure of our culture, the resistance to dictatorship. Leave the Dorians in Greece and build in Palestine, Lebanon, Cyprus. We are the head of the North Sea Peoples, we Prst, the Philistines.

Ásgard is under the sea and the North is destroyed by fire. The warmth of our lands has fled and the snows push further south. Where the ash grew there is only snow and ice and fir and spruce. We have held half of the Mediterranean for so many generations, now we hold the whole sea other than Egypt.

Hard choices to be made. The harvests are poor and the people are hungry. The Nile has protected Egypt and the grain silos are full but we are not sharing in her bounty. The ten kings gather in their blue robes under the pillar which we have made to commemorate the one tree. The Thing is called across our lands, our people gather. A decision is made. War.

This has never been our way but we have reasons, the hunger, the desperation, and we have excuses, antagonism to absolute rule. Perhaps our loss has lowered us. Afterwards the Egyptians say we lost our nobility when we ceased to be a people apart and mixed with other folk. Either way our forces will gather in Palestine, in Libya, in the open sea, and we will invade Egypt.

In the fifth year of Ramses III, the battle begins. We sail up the Nile and our people pour over the borders. Ramses uses all his power and has much good fortune. His strategy was a gamble but it pays off and we are eventually defeated. The bloodshed is terrible on all sides. The blood of our blood is on the water. The blood of our blood is in the earth.

But unlike other peoples our kings are not in the rear of the battle. When our champion fights one to one it is our king who offers his life to prevent bloodshed on all sides. When our people fight the kings fight also. Now our kings are captured, branded with the Pharaoh's name, interrogated, killed. Killed by Ramses himself. All ten kings of our peoples.

Our end is depicted by Ramses on the walls of his Mortuary Temple at Medinet Habu. He does not show that Egypt is fatally wounded and never again able to regain her greatness. Her long decline is finally ended by Alexander the Great, by the Romans, by the Caliphates. How different history might have been. Not the brazen Empire of Rome but the glory that remained even in the ashes of Atlantis.

Our legacy will give rise to Greece, to democracy, science, law, to civilisation in Europe. Even in our slumber the iron in our bones climbs out of the earth and walks away from our graves. But it will be another three thousand years until we begin to remember.

Ramses, though, has offered us a life-line. Why did he do

this? At Medinet Habu he has incised the reliefs often eight inches into the stone, far deeper than any previous pharaoh. The archaeologists say he feared his inscriptions would be erased by a later ruler although some say it is the development of style mandated by the priesthood elites. Nevertheless he has preserved our inglorious defeat and with it our existence.

Earlier, Merenptah had recorded previous skirmishes at the Karnak Temple and aspects of our history can be seen scattered through various papyri, but Ramses depicted at Medinet Habu the key battle that ended our age. Consequently the Egyptian priests, meticulous in the keeping of records right up until the burning of the Library of Alexandria, where much of our history and knowledge resided, had stewardship of memories of which our scattered kin were oblivious.

So it was that Solon sailed to Egypt from Greece and was instructed in his own history and the history of the world. These are the things the priests said to him.

Greeks are all children.
There is no such thing as an old Greek.
You do not know the old traditions.
You have no ancient knowledge.
Mankind is subject to periodic disasters by fire and water and other means.
You begin again, often without letters or written records.
You have no memory.
We are protected by the Nile and are spared the worst.
We offer you our knowledge freely.
The people of your city, Athens, once defended themselves against the arriving Atlanteans.
We will tell you how your people fought and about the famed Atlantis and how you came to be who you are.
You carry a mythological version of history, the story of

Phaethon.
Phaethon, son of the Sun, attempted to pull the chariot of the
Sun but was unable to control it, so bringing devastation by
fire to the earth and eventually being himself destroyed by a
thunderbolt.

This story illustrates a periodic variation in the course of the
heavenly bodies and the consequent firing of the Earth.
It is told that this event is a form of divine retribution.
The reputation of the Atlanteans regarding moral character as
well as physical prowess was the highest of all peoples.
It was only on mixing themselves with other peoples that the
divine element in them became weakened.

Here are the archaeologists in their strange, witless dance.
The priests tell Solon when all this happened and his units are
translated as years. But the Egyptians and other peoples
looked to the moon for their calendrical narrative. There are
thirteen moon months in a solar year. The archaeologists'
dates are out by a factor of thirteen and so they are unaware
that Atlantis, and the Greek Golden Age, both ended in what
we now call the Bronze Age.

Homer's *Iliad* and *Odyssey* are based on separate narratives
but both are derived largely from tales of the amber trade
centred on Atlantis. Details are telling. Odysseus comes into
Ásgard by means of a tidal river, a phenomenon unknown in
the Mediterranean, and he recounts his rediscovery of the
land of the Gods, his people's ancient home.
Much of the Nordic culture is preserved but the scholars
have little understanding of what is being described.
Odysseus sails the Atlantic Ocean, which the ancients took as
the North Sea and the adjacent Baltic Sea rather than the
expanse to the west of Ireland. All the places Homer describes
can be found in these waters. The myths of Greece are our

own history hiding in plain sight.

The boat rocks gently in the grey waves. The books and films, Argonauts in the Golden Age, a mythical time not meant to be taken seriously, not so removed from comic book superheroes. Subject, perhaps, of learned analysis, an outline of the projection of our psychological development, subjective rather than real, a fantasy of something idealised but never attained. All lies. Here in the North history is real and it is ours to take back.

Our allies have fought for us and fight for us still. The Egyptian priests and Homer and all their kind have borne witness. Tolkien tried deliberately and relentlessly to invoke by magic, by learning and wit and imagination, a history we have lost. Everywhere our brothers and sisters hear the call. With such as these we are in good company.

ROOTS

The man with the horns and the blue eyes has Odin in his mind, an ancestor but also a myth. Who gave an eye and more for knowledge. Who hung on the tree for nine days. Who tricked the Gods to drink for three days from the drinking horn of knowledge. The triple horns of Odin a mark on this man's left shoulder.

He looks at me and he is inside me and I know what he wants. Will you fight?

Big men around the fire, women with tattoos. Beautiful women with long angled cheek bones. One of the men stares and waves me over, making space on some kind of animal hide, gently pushing a woman away to create more room. His woman. She looks at me and smiles. Leather and fur, long hair, coloured beads around her open neck.

At her feet a pouch of leaves. He motions again. Sit now between them, small human. He speaks and the sound of the words is so familiar. It is a question. Who are you? No-one has warned him of an approaching stranger. Not the look outs and not his wife, she has not scried me.

I look to her and ask if I may touch her husband. She raises her eyebrows and inclines her head a little. Yes, I may touch her husband. His thick hair and large skull, powerful teeth. Muscles in his arm crossed with scars. So much we have lost. The awe of them.

They have no fear. I don't know how I got here.

Who are you?

I am from another place.

Where?

Far away.

Where?

Another time, it seems.

Explain.

I was walking. In the Altai mountains.

Yes, you are in the mountains.

I found a cave. Something happened. Then I walked out and found you.

What is in the cave?

It's long with many chambers. Some parts are dry but others follow an underground stream. It looked like no-one had been in there for a long time. Deep inside there is a shallow pool where the river disappears into the rock with what looks almost like a beach surrounding three quarters of the pool. The last quarter is a rock face.

I found something half-buried in the sand and gravel, almost as long as I am tall. It is a crystal, white quartz but black at one end.

The two of them glancing at each other, looking back.

The crystal is not half buried, it is vertical.

What is it?

They have decided to trust me.

It is where we put our intentions. Tell us why you have come.

I don't know. To meet you.

What did you intend?

I was walking in the wilds to help me think. My brothers and sisters are away looking for answers. About the Earth, our past. I have been thinking about the future.

Transhumanism and machine intelligence, concepts that present them with no difficulty. Their minds sharper than ours, fluid and alive.

And yet you suggest you are now in your past.

So it seems.

You can wake up and go to work and then half way through the morning wake up and realise you were dreaming though you believed it to be real. Not common but not so unusual. So then you go to work as normal. Only then it happens again. Now it's a bit strange. Then a third time and a fourth. It's not long before you're concerned about matters you once saw as existential and irrelevant.

Some people don't just go to work, they live a life that goes on for years, then they wake up. Weird if it happens once, much more so as the episodes repeat.

Can't remember falling asleep.

You put your intentions in the crystal.

The crystal holds and amplifies.

Like laser light.

The cave is a power place, that's why the crystal is there.

You carried it through the chambers?

No, it was already there.

So...

You have a gift but your mind works on narrow grooves.

Where I come from I would be seen as open-minded.

Such a place. You carry this life all around you. We will do what we can to help you.

Sometimes it comes out of the blue, the inarticulate speech of the heart. The naked pity on the man's face, his sorrow for me. The days go on and you tell yourself you are alright, you are strong, you can face it out, prevail. And now the other side, lost child in a mad world. Surprised to tears, so much to lose, to be so alone.

Arms holding me, a man's arms, a woman's arms, powerful and gentle. A Mother and Father to take me home.

If you could stay we would take you.

But we know it would be a mistake.

We came from the North, where the sun never sets. After the flood. Our kin wandered east and west and south. We covered our stonework. For the future, for you. So you would remember us. We try to keep the flame alive. What else can men do?

They can dismantle our culture and turn us into machines.

The crystal holds our intention for the future as well as the past. We try to ensure that the line is not broken, that our people and our knowledge will come through fire and water and live on. You are our people though you are diminished in body and spirit. In you, though, we see a light. You bring us hope.

I don't know what I can do for you.

Not for us, for you, for our future. There is no separation.

Such a people.

Just tell me what to do.

We don't know what you should do.
Then why am I here?

Running with the men. Sometimes they carry me. Use intention, they say. Work now. They mean shift your consciousness, you can feel it in them, in yourself, in the air. Run harder. The man next to me sounds like an animal. Yowl and growl. The leaves flashing by, spattering sunlight. Green eyes through the trees. Beards like moss on bark, skin tattoos in the forest.

Identity blurring, legs hammering the earth, the bass howl of straining chests. Flashes of grey appearing on the flanks, yip and yowl. Thick fur, teeth, hunger. Fierce joy, immense stamina. Kinship with these humans. Wolves. Inside them, being them. Grey eyes.

Why do the wolves come? The shift in consciousness affects them, they feed off it. Run, run, beyond the pain now. Not about being inside an animal, about fluid awareness, other creatures picking it up, too, everybody blending. Consciousness is somehow universal, beyond identity or barrier. Run, run, run, the past and future dissolving, we have a common source, life itself.

Run beyond yourself and into all life and the glory of it. Run forever and when the running is done lie down, give way to exhaustion. This man lowering me down, let me use your arm as a pillow.

Two days later they say be still. Let us do the same from stillness. We will start and then you lead. Not sure, just follow along, forget the dialogue. We're sitting on the banks of a small lake, a long straight even part of the shore. Reed beds to left and right, leaves on the water, a stream flowing on the opposite bank. Good place for a cold swim.

The men sit a little way back but one comes forward and we sit down, cross-legged. He says work now and soon the light attenuates and it's like being in another world even though we haven't moved. Like a door opening to let something in, a presence, something like consciousness in large measure. The ducks on the lake, previously raucous, grow quiet and there is stillness everywhere. The light is almost like flakes of sun.

One duck swims slowly towards us and stops a few feet in front, stationary in the water. It looks at us for a while and then pulls itself onto the shore about three feet to my left. Within arm's reach. The man and me and the duck are spaced evenly. We look back to the water and some event unfolds, nothing moving and yet all is movement within, some coming together of our being. The depth of it is like a bottomless lake, never ending sunlight, a thing beyond thought.

Eventually it fades and gradually the worlds seems to return to normal and my body and mind feel like they are ready to move again, to break the stillness. The duck looks up at me, stands, shakes itself, quacks and plops back into the water as if nothing unusual had happened. The men laugh until I think they are going to cry.

The story of my shamanic journey is related endlessly and I am told I will always live in legend. I feel like I have made more friends than I have ever had.

When you reach out with your intent, consciousness can shift, will always shift to some extent. Now you know what this means. I am trying to answer your question about the crystal. Time changes also, it is not a narrow groove as your people see it. You need to anchor yourself here before you go back.

Go back.

You need to find the future and anchor yourself there as well. This is what we tried to do in the crystal cave. That is why the crystal is there, because we wanted to use our intention and because the world is all mixed together, not in separate parts.

But the crystal was there before you decided to use intention.

Yes, even so.

This man describing a level of connectedness that makes

quantum entanglement a kindergarten toy. Also, describing retrocausality. Strange how memory has its own season. Show some people a list of words and ask them to memorise the words. Give them a recall test and then get them to have another go at memorising half of the list after the test. Obviously this won't have any effect on the test because it's after the event. But it does. The half that is studied afterwards shows better results. What can you say about such a thing?

My narrow grooves are about how I see time. As well as the rest.

You can say we pulled you in from the future but we can say you pulled us to do so from the future. When you go back that is what you will have to do.

Go back, or forward rather, and create the intention for us to meet.

Yes. The intention to remember. Also the future of your future. The artificial intelligence and the transhumanism.

Go to my future.

Yes. Send back the intention to know what to do in your present.

Blimey.

Meaning?

My friend taught me. Short for God blind me.

Gods will do that.

The men find that they have jobs to do and leave me with the women. Almost as powerful as the men but way more beautiful. No inhibition here, how to tell these women that femininity is false consciousness. Elicit only pity. They say I'm not too old for make-up, not now, not ever. After a while the games and the laughter fade away and the first lady leads me off into the woods.

We walk for some way and talk about our lives, our families. As the sun lifts above the clouds we emerge in a clearing with a circle of stones. The energy here is strong and I'm distracted thinking about Ava and what she would see and would this place still be here when I got back. I told this woman's husband about the man with the dark mind and he told me above all else to find out about him. Is that why I was driven to find him those weeks back?

You still bleed, don't you?

Yes, less so and less regular, but still.

You are fertile.

Just about, I suppose.

It is intention as well as biology.

Yes, I can imagine.

Will you have children with the man, Bastian?

What?

Why not?

I'm too old.

You've just said you're not.

Flustered like a girl.

I don't even know if I feel that way about him, or him about me.

Yes, you do.

Yes, I do but it's more complicated for us than for you.

Can he not provide for you?

It's not that.

Then what?

Age matters more for us, we don't have the same support.

From other women?

Yes, other women, the clan, the environment, all of it.

It is hard.

Yes, and there's something else.

She waits for me. All the things we have been through since Bastian and the fetish, the way I found him, the words we use, empathy, consciousness, love, these people don't need any of those experiences, they have it all already, they never lost it. What happened to us?

But I see her now, the fetish, the Viking, flickering forms shifting inside and around me and now it's something else. Tall, the shape of the head, the cheekbones. It's not clear and now it's gone. What is this?

Family, the circling thoughts and emotions, like mountains with invisible roots, backwards and forwards in time, waves lapping on the shore, a life with no beginning and no end. All of Nature splashed across time, coloured canvas of our own blind volition. Family, my family, come to me.

There are some young people, the ones I have told you about. They have joined with us. It is like a broken family coming back together. My heart is full with them.

Then you are satisfied.

Yes.

There is family of husband and wife and children, there is clan, there are your people, then all humans, all life. It goes out forever. If your family are rejoining perhaps it can be so for all the rest, like rings flowing out from the centre.

The centre is here?

For now, at least.

You know all the women here bleed together.

I had guessed. You must have children in bunches.

Yes. It works well, a thing we do together.

I envy you.

You will start to bleed with us as well. Soon.

I can feel it coming.

I understand you count by the sun and we do this, too, but we count also by the moon. This is because of our cycle. The moon and the cycle are one and the same.

In our world the moon is a far away thing of little relevance.

That is part of why you have stopped having children.

Yes.

To study the heavens shows that the moon's cycle is not an exact number of days and there are not an exact number of moons in a solar year.

Yes.

The difference shifts each year. Do you know the nature of the shift?

No.

It takes fifty six solar years for the moon's cycle to come back to where it started. Then it repeats. This is the length of time it takes for a woman's fertility to end.

Or less for our women.

Yes. Look at these stones in a circle. What do you see?

I see they must have taken a great deal of labour and accurate measurement.

Yes, shapes invoke responses.

Yes.

What else?

Granite, carved, spiral and circle motifs, animals in relief, human-like forms.

You made these?

Yes.

The archaeologists have told us all our lives that agriculture came first, that surpluses led to organised society, sophisticated technology, writing, the whole of civilisation. But they have been utterly wrong. Civilisation predates agriculture by many thousands of years and it was here, all around.

I see it, there are fifty six stones.

Nineteen solar years are close to two hundred and thirty five lunar months but not quite. Every third nineteen year cycle we substitute eighteen years to correct the error.

So nineteen plus nineteen plus eighteen.

Yes. Equals fifty six solar years. There are other ways to calculate it but we find this works best.

Fifty six Aubrey holes at Stonehenge. A mechanism for calculating all important events of the moon and with it the planets and stars. Bastian said there were fifty six stones in a ring in Atlantis. The line runs unbroken through all the megalithic architecture.

Your May Queen, your Goddess, who we call wife and Mother.

An image engraved on a tangential stone. A face like an owl, eyes with eyelashes and some kind of surround. Eyes where the lines in the irises can be seen. Blue eyes, then, or green.

Each of these rayed eyes have twenty seven lines, together they make fifty six.

She is the lunar cycle.

She is all cycles. She is fertility. Women are born to conceive. This is our purpose and the path to meaning. Without fertility there is only death. Choose life.

ZION

Nikolai emerging from his bunk with a laptop on the morning of the second day. The boat rocking gently in a calm swell. North Sea in a forgiving mood. Cups of tea all around, settling in, fish breakfast caught moments before and the pan on the hob. Orthodox icons in the hi-tech cabin, luminous and formal.

'Tis true, 'tis true, the tale that I tell, the cracked and broken iron bell.

The past has been close to us these days and I have given thought to my own journey, not so different from yours, not to delay but to understand what I had to say before I said it. I beg your pardon.

Gard is broken, holm is lost, you have told how our people took the long journey south. Greece settled and Egypt journey's end. But the Middle East tells the story of the wars we fought and we fight still. The Bible carries our story and we are the enemy. Philistines.

In Hebrew we are the Kaphthorites, people of the head of the pillar of heaven. They know our culture. They say we came from *i Kapthor* which is exactly our *holmr Ásgard*. The words of the prophets spoke of the will of God and His will was our death. The children of Israel were charged to overthrow our altars, break our pillars, burn our groves and destroy the images of our ancestors in stone. I saw these things.

The Greeks called Atlás *Er*, the name given in Atlantis, from which comes the Saxon *irmin*, powerful, and *Irminsul,* the All-Pillar that holds up heaven, the tree of the Law by which civilised values were created. The Hebrews tore down the Law and hated us. We sent emissaries to discover the nature of these people. We knew them of old from Egypt but since Ragnarok everything had changed.

The people of the Bible had taken over Egypt and been driven back by the Egyptians. Their stories tell of slavery and servitude and the redemption of escape but that is not the story the Egyptians tell us. They say their leader was of Egyptian royal blood. A visionary who said there was only one God, overturning the plurality of the Egyptian culture. Eventually he was driven out.

When he left, the people who became Israel went with him. The Egyptians saw themselves well rid of his fanaticism, his intolerance, his angering of the Gods and his rebellion against Ma'at, divine balance and order, the principle to which the Egyptians held as the basis of their society and culture.

When he left, many of the Hyskos, or the people who would become Israel, left with him. They left Egypt as we left Ásgard, at the time of Ragnarok, each of us in search of a new home. They call Ragnarok the seven plagues, the side effects of fire from the sky, earthquakes, volcanoes. For them it was much easier because the Nile protected them from the worst. They tell their people these plagues are God's judgment on Egypt.

These people, apart from their time in Egypt, are essentially nomads, sometimes pastoral, sometimes belligerent, with an angry God. After the Exodus they started excluding the Goddess, although it took some time. There can only be one God now.

The apex of their mythology is based in the revelation of the Ten Commandments, the story of the burning bush, and the building of the Ark of the Covenant to house them. Its mystical power becomes the reason for the building of the Temple of Solomon and stands at the centre of their new identity.

However, while Moses was talking with God, many of his people rebelled and built a golden calf. This is our own culture which we have shared with the whole Mediterranean over thousands of years. The bull was at the heart of Atlantis and many peoples knew this and shared our culture to varying degrees. Moses told them the angry God was not pleased with what they had done.

The golden calf was turned into white powder which was

mixed with water and given to people to drink. So now, the Egyptians knew alchemy. The Egyptians also tell how one of their arks was stolen and how the Ten Commandments are just rewritten from elements of their own texts.

The same God promises a land of milk and honey but it is already occupied, it is Jericho. So they slaughter every man, woman and child in the place and take is as their own. This is a city that goes back many thousands of years. The contrast between Atlantis and Israel is laid out for all to see again and again. The contrasting strategies in dealing with conflict over resources. In Palestine they do the same all over again.

Our people acted with honour and our decisions were made by ourselves under the Law. The others acted with barbarism because God told them to do it, and because they were the chosen people of that God. Their holy books justify the most horrific acts against anyone who is not one of the chosen.

Here is exceptionalism, One God, One Chosen People, justified in genocide. This is the virus that started in Egypt, that they expelled, and that was then carried into the Middle East where we met it head on. We, the Philistines and related peoples, we were the enemy. We still are.

A thousand years later Israel is in conflict with the Roman Empire. I watched the time of the Bull turn into the time of the Ram and then into the Fish, the time of Christianity. The Roman Empire using the idea of Jesus to siphon off support for the Jews and using universalism to overwhelm individual religions, ethnic groups, identities of all sorts. Jesus wasn't a tribal God, he was for everyone, for a united Roman Empire where all were equal before God.

But Jesus came from the Jews and the Jewish Holy Books came with him to offer legitimacy to the apostate. The Old Testament. With Jesus came the angry God, the Chosen People, exceptionalism, Jewish ideology in the heart of

Europe. With the success of the Roman Empire and the ideological weapon of enforced Christianisation the remains of our history were destroyed. Later, with the fall of the Vikings the last shreds of our culture disappeared.

Another thousand years and the Knights Templar are out looking for artefacts, documents, money. They have abandoned Jesus and look to St John and Middle Eastern esoterica. They are under the sway of the Jews. In Jerusalem Saladin shows mercy but the Christian Crusaders butcher their way across the land. The Templars create the first transnational banking system. They are the new money-changers and money-lenders. A marker is laid down for ownership of Jerusalem and future dominion.

A thousand years again and the Templars have given way to the Freemasons, anything but free. Kabbalah for the goyim, Christians and Westerners run by the Jews, America run from Israel. The Jews have implemented Zionism, aimed at global governance, and communism, also aimed at global governance. The traditional family-based culture of our people is everywhere under attack, our altruism used against us by a people who produce nothing but live vampirically on the body of their host nations.

They are Shylock, the fractional reserve banking system, the cartel of central banks printing money at interest to governments. They lend money they do not possess and take away the livelihood of anyone who cannot pay with years of their lives' blood. For two thousand years Christians and Muslims tried to ban usury but the Jews triumphed, now the whole world drowns in debt, nations, businesses, individuals. Who is everybody in debt to?

Listen to the Zionists and communists, paid for by the same people, cry for the end of your sovereign nation, of your sovereign family, of your sovereign self. Listen to all the lies they tell. Listen to the crazy white people calling for their own death. The pathology of an altruism at the mercy of people who know no mercy. Peoples who mutilate the genitals of their own babies and children, the endless iterations of the Angry God. Who destroy empathy before it grows. Who are death.

Who told our people that our tree of Life, our Law, our apples of knowledge, were evil and deadly? The Angry God said the apples would cause death but we didn't die. The Angry God lied, then, as now, as ever. The Angry God punishes the ones who disobey. Only the Chosen can rule and flourish, the rest of us are cattle.

Germany allows the Jews citizenship, an enlightened and compassionate European nation. What do the Jews give in return? Tribal self-help, the domination of financial institutions, corruption of moral values, the deliberate weakening and takeover of the host nation. The plans are already in place for global governance. Germany must be finished.

Watch the Zionists take over the USA, banks and media, the Federal Reserve. Watch them conquer England and France. Napoleon who tried to ban usury has been overthrown by the bought and paid for British and all of Western Europe lines up for their masters. The Triple Entente is undermined, the ties of peace broken and the plan unfolds. What is the plan? The death of Europe and the birth of the Zioinist state to rule over the world.

Germany is dragged into a war they do not want and try to avoid. The secret fraternities whisper everywhere in the ears of the gullible and altruistic, leaders and led alike. The Zionist press turn the nations against each other, divide and conquer. The West is controlled and at heel, Russia is overrun by revolutionaries, Germany is the final target.

The end of the First World War sees Germany humiliated.

The Treaty of Versailles is in place to destroy Germany piece by piece until there is nothing left. Lord Balfour pays the price for the Jews bringing the US into the war by sending a declaration to the Lord Rothschild, a private individual, that the Zionist state will be created in Palestine, where the Palestinians have a 95% majority, who are not consulted. In Russia the Communist International is established and the Red Terror is underway.

Germans sees prices doubled every two days for twenty months, there is mass unemployment, hunger, devastation, enemy troops stripping the Fatherland, the German peoples are separated and forbidden to reunite. In the US the Federal Reserve triggers the Great Depression and the rich buy everything at knock down prices. Stalin institutes the Holodomor, mass starvation by millions.

In March 1933 Roosevelt comes to power and serves the New World Order, the Zionist globalists. Hitler comes into power at the same time and does the opposite. He takes control of the Reichsbank and issues debt-free currency, bans the Communist party who are close to doing to Germany what they are doing in Russia, takes his country back from the Jews and creates family-friendly policies.

Hitler cleans up Berlin, a toilet of sexual depravity and drugs, and makes it safe for families and ordinary Germans. While Roosevelt drives America into debt Hitler rebuilds Germany in the greatest economic, cultural and scientific miracle the world has ever seen. The Germans adore him and leaders across the world pay tribute.

As soon as Hitler is in power the front pages in Western newspapers carry the killer headline. Judea declares war on Germany. The propaganda press go into overdrive. Zionists call for a Holy War. The lies continue all the way to the Second World War and to present. But Roosevelt and Stalin are good friends, Churchill is bought out of bankruptcy and behaves like a good dog.

Germany was considered finished but now it would have to

be done all over. Once again Germany is destroyed. Churchill doesn't bother with military targets, he goes for civilians, he wants only to break the German will. His starvation blockades, initiated in World War I and continued in World War II, are the watershed that breaks the code of honour followed by our people for millennia.

Hitler does not reciprocate. He holds to military targets only and tries repeatedly to make peace. He lets the Allies go at Dunkirk when he could easily have finished them. He speaks of Germans and English being the same people

Europe is carved up and Germany is once more laid in her grave. The lies about the holocaust are everywhere, Soviet Intelligence building patent fabrications of gas ovens at Auschwitz. Once again, as in so many other times and places, the lie of the six million dead Jews is brought out to make the Zionists iron-clad to all criticism.

Tons of documents are removed from the meticulous Germans but not one document supporting the deliberate massacre of Jews is ever found. The evidence is time and again shown to be fabricated and so the great democracies resort to banning research into, or questioning of, the Holocaust narrative. The executions and prison sentences begin, and once more Germany is paying reparations to the people who declared war on her. All is going to plan. England celebrated winning the war. We won the war for the wrong side. Europa lost, Judea won.

With Germany on its knees, the European Union begins. The Coudenhove-Kalergi Plan is at its heart. Hitler has blown the lid on the Freemasons and the threads are clearly visible. The administrators of the plan use the money of the European people in handing out recognition and rewards to political leaders and distinguished people who make strides to fulfil its goals.

Its goals are to end the white race and make Europe a mestizo continent, devoid of history or culture. A continent easy to control and bring to heel in the globalist vision. No longer the continent most likely to resist. Where the Zionists lie about the race war against them, they simultaneously institute a race war against white Europeans. A similar plan is implemented in the USA. The socialists bring in people from everywhere and the feminists make sure the white women have more important things to do than have families. Naive children turned into weapons against their own people.

Here is the President of a leading European nation telling us that white women have a duty to not breed with white men. Brown, black, any colour you like but not white. If white women refuse to see the necessity of these choices sanctions will have to brought in, first financial and then more immediate. This a man with a very beautiful white wife. Here are the refugees from countries the Zionists have destroyed. Here are naive Muslims bought and paid for by the Zionists and turned against the white race. Here are the feminists hiding the rape of their daughters by the immigrants.

From the day Atlantis fell and we headed south to the Middle East we have been at war with these people. They know it but they hide it from us. In Israel you can hear, to this day, Rabbis raving about smashing the purity of the white blood line. Across the world naive Imams echo their words. They know who we are, that we are the remnants of Atlantis and their fear and jealousy knows no bounds. Their angry God and their exceptionalism and their universalist new religions are aimed at the destruction of the sovereign European nations and their culture.

Let us be clear. The people historically most admired around the world for its morality and its values, the people responsible for democracy, the freedom of its peoples, for science, for the foundations of civilisation, are to be finished. Too clever, too beautiful, too altruistic. This is what they have wanted for three thousand years, the death of the white race, the death of our culture, the death of Europe and the birth of the Zionist dominated global state.

Friends, I have seen so much more and I have investigated everything I have seen but my heart tells me I have said enough. In time I am sure we will go further.

DISINVEST

Jesus has been a Trojan Horse, Nikolai.

Yes.

What to do about this?

Is there something we can do about it?

You and your brothers represent Orthodoxy. Is what you teach sound?

Bastian, all religions are full of dogma. Perhaps the Atlanteans were the same.

Perhaps.

The narrative around Jesus is complex. He is a Jew and a reformer rather than a revolutionary, yet he clearly represents an overthrow of the order. He overthrows the tables of the money-changers, puts compassion above regulation, walks away from an eye for an eye, of endless karma, for grace, for love.

Yes, but the Church still teaches the Old Testament.

True, although Orthodoxy is not in bed with the Zionists in the way Catholicism is.

See the Pope covering his crucifix and bowing to the Jews.

Yes.

Your strong man, then.

Him again.

Yes. He is rebuilding Russia. The parallels with 30's Germany are amazing. The determination of the West to asset strip the place to death, the miraculous recovery, the return to moral values.

Russia is a miracle but it doesn't compare to what Hitler achieved.

Hitler allowed freedom of religious worship but he wasn't identified with the religious establishment in the way your man is. Monasteries, religious retreats, advisors, above all personal commitment.

He attempts to use Orthodoxy as a backbone for the rebirth of the culture.

Yes. We both know what has been laid at our door, Nikolai, and he is a part of that, but in the long run rebuilding our people, a new Atlantis, it's not a Jewish mythology that can do this.

No. Obviously, though, Christians see Jesus as transcending temporal perspectives, he is much more than a Jew.

Yes, an early universalist template. But he is a God.

That is how he is seen.

By your man?

I don't know.

And you? It's not something we have talked about much.

Bastian, it's easy to see that historical narratives are full of problems. But that's not the point.

Back home in England we have trendy vicars who don't need to believe in Jesus literally, it's just some kind of excuse for a softer politics.

Not for me.

I'm not interested in believing. It's based on personal experience. The things we've been through. Yet to many people personal experience is questionable at best. Fine in mythological settings, seers and prophets, far from fine in a secular culture.

Yes, but of course that's not a concern for you or me.

No. We are the dragon riders.

Strangely enough, yes we are. You want to know just what my experience of Christ is, is that it?

I think so.

Let me put it like this. It isn't dependent on a man named Jesus.

As I thought.

I know you are looking to my experience as an intelligence agent, as a relative insider. You want to know what can be done.

Yes.

You have to work with what is. Orthodoxy is a vehicle of family values, the values of our people, it resists depravity, it resists Zionism.

It made accommodation with communism, though. That's how you have a man who is simultaneously Orthodox and KGB.

Such things are unavoidable, let's be realists.

Alright. It's just I can't see our future being about turning the other cheek, about the meek inheriting the Earth, about Jesus.

No. In Europe there is already fear on the streets. How will we defend ourselves?

That's another problem. The biggest lie in Europe is the history of

Germany, the pathological imagery of Hitler and the Reich. The strong man uses this imagery negatively in his public statements, glorifying Russia's role in the war. He has joined in with legislation against uncovering the truth. Why has he done this?

Honestly, I don't know. Maybe it's Realpolitik, maybe he feels it's a price worth paying to unite his country. Maybe he doesn't understand what he is doing.

But he has access to the files, no?

Yes.

This is what worries me about his Orthodoxy, it's the complicity in suppressing the truth in Europe.

The truth. Hitler was a Bavarian, with the attitudes of his day. Vienna saw German culture being subsumed by multiculturalism, much of it Jewish and Slavic. He held the mantle of the German Conservative Revolution but many of its supporters say he fell from grace. He absorbed Prussia and the noble traditions she carried, although it was the West that abolished her altogether. It has been said that if Hitler had flown the flag of the Ukraine when he reached Kiev, rather that of the Reich, history could be different. He saw a new Europe but one ruled by Germany, this was his racial perspective. Not so much a pan-European culture of free and equal peoples.

He stressed kinship with the English but the Slavs were just slightly lower down the ladder.

So it seems. A chance was missed. Nevertheless he recognised that Germany was the target of our enemies. Germany was to be destroyed and its reputation ruined. The truth needs to be told. Because we need this to link back to Atlantis, we need it for our people to divest themselves of the self-hate we have internalised.

Yes. We need your man to help and he doesn't seem to want to. Nevertheless he is the main obstacle to the nightmare our enemies have prepared for us.

He is, it seems, the leader of the free world.

I have allies who can access all manner of records. Perhaps they could help us.

Help the cream rise to the top.

Yes, engineer certain historical details to emerge into the light of *day.*

Leaks. The alternative press.

Yes, but also allow information to arrive to insiders. Russians, but not only. Germans. There are still clever people in Germany who remember the truth.

The fear of the globalists is that Russia and Germany form an alliance. This is their greatest fear. If Russia can get past her war mythology and help the Germans rediscover the truth about themselves, help them to be who they really are, then a different sort of Pan –European reality can emerge.

True. Based on Russia and Germany as the new axis. Adult relations with China and Iran. The Old World Order returns. Sovereign nations, or groups of nations.

Western Europe, too. Everywhere we see the Megalithic culture, everywhere we see the stones of old, these are our people and they will join together based on our shared values. Revealing our history may be enough.

It's a good place to start, Bastian. There are other things we can work on. Many European leaders are being blackmailed. The purpose, of course, of the spy networks, control leaders, frighten everyone else into self-censorship.

It's the archaeology, Nikolai. Can we get some proper field work here at the Steingrund? We need to get past all this Barbarians of the North rubbish.

I can try.

The British are involved in the first major underwater archaeological survey in the North Sea but they're looking at the Dogger Bank which is North and West of here.

Still, they will find artefacts of the wider culture. It will still help us.

Perhaps something interesting can pop into their laptops.

Or into their hearts.

It's hard to believe how archaeology has been twisted.

All science is twisted. Einstein, a plagiarist and a fake, was about Jewish science at best, according to the Reich. He was an early advocate of the Coudenhove-Kalergi Plan and he was part of the disappearance of field theory from Universities and into Black projects. Freud was another Jewish advocate of the plan and he did for psychology what Marx did for politics.

How can we manage this?

Archaeology has been weaponised, Bastian. We started it in the Soviet Union. Not just unconscious cultural bias but the deliberate destruction of native peoples. Encourage them to have a native revival and they will lose all touch with the real world, the ability to assume responsibility and power in any self-determining way. Or, more accurately, anthropology has been weaponised. The big names in the fields have connections and agendas the students studying at college never get to hear about.

In the West you have a man known as the Father of propaganda, Edward Bernays. The 60's drug culture was created largely by two men, him and Gordon Wasson. Wasson was the man whose alleged research into traditional psychedelic use in Mexico was carried by Life magazine and triggered the popularisation of hallucinogenic drug use in Western counter-culture. He made claims regarding revelatory experiences he had undergone, captivating large parts of a generation, not to mention further generations.

Wasson was actually the chairman of the Council on Foreign Relations and on the payroll of the CIA, in particular their MK-Ultra mind control experiments section. They promoted the darkness of the deadhead as a means to reduce literate people to peasants. They have been very successful. You know how communism, feminism, environmentalism walk along related paths. You know, also, the people who promoted all these things openly.

Bernays was the double nephew of Sigmund Freud, with whom he worked closely, and he was involved with many individuals who concerned themselves with mind control, these being centred in the Tavistock Institute in England. I keep his book Propaganda in multiple libraries. Here we go.

The conscious and intelligent manipulation of the organized habits and opinions of the masses is an important element in democratic society. Those who manipulate this unseen mechanism of society constitute an invisible government which is the true ruling power of our country. ...We are governed, our minds are moulded, our tastes formed, our ideas suggested, largely by men we have never heard of. This is a logical result of the way in which our democratic society is organized. Vast numbers of human beings must cooperate in this manner if they are to live together as a smoothly functioning society. …In almost every act of our daily lives, whether in the sphere of politics or business, in our social conduct or our ethical thinking, we are dominated by the relatively small number of persons…who understand the mental processes and social patterns of the masses. It is they who pull the wires which control the public mind.

There you have it. Wasson was close to Dulles, the head of the CIA, and Bernays, who started out on Woodrow Wilson's Committee on Public Education pro-war propaganda machine, and who was the architect of modern mind-control strategies. These sort of people meet their higher ups and lower downs, like the Grateful Dead, at the Bohemian Club, and on it goes. The neo-feudalism of modern slavery while the elites become increasingly technocratic and transhumanist.

So, yes, Bastian, we have to bring back the knowledge of our ancestors but we must pre-empt the weaponised archaic revivals our enemies will sponsor. They will try turn our history into a new Dark Age, where we create empathy they will promote anti-rational attitudes and blind emotionalism, where we bring ourselves closer to Nature they will attempt to make us anti-technological, where we try to free our peoples they will suggest new religions to confuse our minds.

Orthodoxy is the least of our problems, it is our friend. There are people willing to embark on rational discourses. Our strong man, as you now have me saying, promotes rationality, truth-telling, and morality in his public statements, and, more importantly, his public actions. Like him, I have been fighting this war for many years. It is less familiar to you but nonetheless where you have brought us is very far from where we have been. You have opened the door. See, now, our fetish is back and we see her together once more.

Only she is no longer a fetish and no longer a Viking, not even an *Atlantean*. This is something else, the long head, the high cheekbones, the snow white skin, the tall stature. You and I, brother, have further to go.

Anglo-Saxons all across England. Angles and Saxons from Denmark and Germany. The amazing treasure of Sutton Hoo, swords, brooches, the helmet and mask, the great ship. The craftsmanship a surprise to an unknowing population. Always the mythology of barbarism. The barbaric Germanic tribes that were never defeated by Rome, the barbaric North Sea peoples, the barbaric Anglo-Saxons and Celts.

Only the bastardised Roman Empire had culture. Our hundreds they used, and Judaic myths, a Republic that once looked to Greece turned into an Empire that lived only for dominion and corruption. It's Church a mockery. Our people and the veneration of Nature, of cosmic order, buried with lies.

The helmet of a leader, regal and martial, found with the great Ship at Sutton Hoo. Garnets backed by gold foil to bring out the lustre, except in one area. The garnets above the left eye have no gold foil and the left eye of the dragon climbing down the helmet is the same. See the sunlight catch fire in the garnets with gold backing and see the dullness in the left eye of man and dragon.

All across England, Germany, Scandinavia and further afield, artefacts with a missing left eye. What do they mean? The archaeologists are only just recovering from telling us we were in a Dark Age without the Roman Empire to guide us. They have no memory. The missing left eye is in honour of Odin and the sacrifices he made in the name of knowledge, in the name of being a King fit for his people.

One people, separated from each other, from ourselves. The millennia we have remembered Odin. Always we have been told we are barbarians and Odin was a monster, as the Vikings were deranged raiders. It is true Odin was of the Aesir and attacked the Vanir but the two peoples became one. Odin learnt wisdom from the Vanir, and became a legend. His story is the heart of the memories we have preserved.

The All-Father hung himself from the tree of Life, Yggdrásil, for nine days and nights to learn the secrets of life and of the ordering of the world. He learned the secrets of the Runes. Odin gave an eye to drink from the well of wisdom. He is said to have tricked the Gods into drinking from a horn containing their knowledge for three nights running.

The triple horn of Odin and the nine points of the triple triangle celebrate his willingness to sacrifice and the keenness of his guile. He became a King fit for his people.

The triple horn of Odin on the arms of men and women once again. On the walls of our homes, in the woods and mountains of our land.

Time slips away.

The eye of Odin. Odin's single eye, the eye of wisdom.

France, late eighteenth century, slipping through time. Here is a statue of Isis with water pouring out of her naked breast like the little boy peeing in a fountain in Brussels. The great and good taking celebratory drinks and encouraging others to do the same. Here's a Giza-style pyramid with the all-seeing eye, representing reason. The people are told to abandon their Christian Gods and embrace the Gods of Egypt as interpreted by these intrepid revolutionaries. They want to throw out Christianity, bring in a new calendar, a new society. These are Freemasons and in their Lodges they have been cooking up ideas.

They are the same people who put the pyramid and eye on the US dollar bill and created Bacon's New Atlantis of America. This is the French Revolution and the guillotines are being sharpened.

Where do they get these ideas? Where do they find these symbols? The Masons serve the Jews and receive their symbols. The Jews stole the artefacts and culture of the Egyptians and blended it with their own Angry God edicts.

This Viking, this Atlantean, stands in Ásgard, his hand on the tree of Life. The arms of the tree, Yggdrásil, which holds up the heavens, are joined onto the main trunk at forty five degrees, such that there is a triangle at the top of the pillar whose three sides are the pillar and two arms. This is the focal point, the balance of creation. Here is where Odin gave his eye for knowledge and was left with one all-seeing eye, the eye of the triangle.

In Ásgard the tree stands on a three-step pyramid platform. The missing capstone of the Great Pyramid in Giza, the very definition of the US dollar bill, was covered in electrum, said to be a naturally occurring alloy of gold and silver. Why would the Egyptians use a cheap alloy when they had pure gold in abundance? Or did they use something else? Ásgard was known as Electris, the Holy Isle of Amber, and after Ragnarok the only known source of amber in the world was no longer available to the Egyptians, nor to anyone else. Amber was more precious than gold and came only from Atlantis.

This is what the virus-infected stole from us, this is how they attempt to give legitimacy to their dominion, their New Atlantis, their New World Order. The triangle at the top of the tree, Irmunsil, the pillar of the Anglo-Saxons, is the head of the sceptre of royal authority throughout Europe, the *volute* between the arms, known as the Fleur de Lys to these same unknowing French revolutionaries.

The sceptre of authority carried by Kings and Queens is the pillar that holds up the heavens, the same that we brought to the Middle East, that the Bible tells the Jews to destroy. To this day the remains of our temples are being destroyed by the unknowing fanatics trained and propagandised by the same masters as always.

Yet our symbols have been taken by our enemies because they have none of their own, their legitimacy is a copy of ours. Our Kings and ancestors sacrificed themselves for knowledge and the good of their people. Today's false Kings sacrifice knowledge, our people, even their own people, for the good of themselves.

Hail Odin, we will take our symbols back as we will take back our land. We will do this for the good of our people and the good of all people.

It's good to be home, Ava.

Yes. Coming back to Avebury, it all seems so different now. It was always magical but now...

Now we know why.

Yes. I started seeing something in my meditation, something that slips sideways into my dreams.

Solar Wheel.

How did you know?

Rolling up his sleeve on his left arm to the shoulder. Centre of the deltoid. Solar wheel.

I don't believe it.

Don't then.

When?

First thing when we got home.

But you hate tattoos.

Yes, you too.

But I love this.

Me, too.

Me too want one.

What will Daddy say?

Seems like he'll already know.

Right you are, then.

Why did you do it?

I don't know. Perhaps because I recognise the road I need to walk, something about commitment. Maybe it's something more. What's happening in your dreams?

Alright. In my meditation I see it foursquare and central, like a mandala, but it just slips gently in, a man walking past with it on his deltoid, same as you, or a small pendant on a girl's neck chain. I see it out in the natural world, on trees or made from willow. Sometimes I turn over a pretty stone and it's there, maybe near a shelter made by children from branches and vines.

I've seen this too.

Where?

In the mind of the Viking, the Atlantean.

What does he want?

You know what he wants.

But with the symbol.

He wants the reality that the symbol represents but the value of symbols is they trigger cascades of related perceptions, they function on the unconscious as well as conscious mind. When we abandon religion there is a void underneath the rational mind. That's why you have the invented symbolism of the left, once hammer and sickles, now rainbows, multi-racial pictures with strong women and weak men. But they don't really work.

The unconscious isn't interested.

No, it has to be forced and it doesn't like it.

So this is a viable symbol?

You want to argue with the tang broadsword?

No, but we've tried this before.

Go on.

The swastika. Life and health and the sun. One of our most powerful ancient symbols. Now seen as the very expression of evil.

True. Although we'll have to have that back, too. It's still popular in India. It can be done. But in the meantime we have something else, something more specific and relevant to where we are.

It's a spiritual symbol but also a warrior symbol.

Yes, because if you aren't willing to defend yourself you won't survive. They are trying to genocide our people. They want us gone for good.

Our people.

Yes.

We have come a long way.

Yes.

You are willing to fight?

Yes, although when I look at Nikolai, I'm still a child.

I know what you mean. I look at Olga and feel the same.

Ah.

Will you fight for me?

Ava?

How does a woman fight?

The Viking women used to fight with the men.

They can't have children if they're dead.

Ava, I love you.

I am ready.

For children?

Yes.

I...

You have to do something.

I don't have a job. How can I take care of you?

Get one.

My skill set, it'll take time. Or it'll be minimum wage or it'll be illegal.

You think I care?

Have you seen what a house costs? You have to be a rich man.

I know. Maybe there is another way.

Nikolai, the fix it man.

No, my Dad.

He doesn't have money.

No, but he has a house and some land. He's not getting any younger. And he wants me provided for.

He would welcome me?

You know he would.

I'm choking.

Never look a gift horse in the mouth.

No, but you will know it's not mine, I haven't achieved it.

Look how far you have come, we have come. You said you are willing to fight. Will you fight for me?

You mean he'll employ me to work the land?

Yes.

I don't know how.

He'll teach you. I'll teach you.

Willing donkey is all I need to be.

Yes.

I guess I would have to let go my anger and my pride.

Yes, but you know pride comes from humility and hard work, it doesn't fall out of the sky.

It's just that I still fell so much less.

Then you will have to fight to be more. When Father is old... my children need a Father. I can see no other. You will have to become what I need.

You want to make a stand. England. Home.

Yes. I will give them what children need. I want to have beautiful children, see them on the land, see you protect them, educate them. Fight for them, perhaps they will fight, too.

A New Atlantis.

Yes.

CAVE

A journey. Back up the foothills of the mountain to the cave, the crystal cave. No memory of leaving this cave, only of walking down and finding these beautiful, dangerous people. Waved on with smiles and walking alone. Their long hair twisting across their faces in the wind. This cave and the long fallopian passage to the womb. These words not mine, or not consciously chosen.

Soon the sharp profile of the crystal by the pool, this time seen with the warm light of a reed torch, some kind of fat. The guttering flame echoes off the surface of the pool, rippling coloured light across the vaulted stone. But the quartz is standing upright, black base and white angled tip. Faces me like a man. Not back in my own time. Not awoken from the dream.

Possibilities cascading through the brain. No easy answers. Be practical. What happens if there is no way back? Maybe lying in a coma across a rock, matted blood on the temple, waiting for the cold to bring ravens and crows. Maybe the Stone Age is the future. No Nikolai, Bastian, Ava, Gabriel. No future. Only deeper into the past.

Sit down on the shore of the pool, crossed legs and straight spine. The breathing kicks in hard and just let go. There is nothing to be done, no way of waking up, let it go. How far back in the past are we? Strange not to have asked these questions before. Perhaps symptomatic of altered consciousness, and yet reason flows easily, no illogical sequences of events. See the flickering light of the crystal's twin ripple across the water, hear the occasional drips echoing like bells.

Not alone. Across the pool sits a man. It is the fetish but now it is something else, like the people I have been with these days. He is as physically large as they are and he is smiling at me. Still we are no clearer as to what this phenomenon is. The phenomenon knows this thought and is amused. A kind of memory, or consciousness far stranger than our minds circumscribe.

Why am I here?

Perhaps I am talking to myself?

Same as always.

We've never had a verbal conversation before.

Not recently.

Same as always. To learn?

If you choose.

I don't know where to begin.

Look at me.

Yes.

I am like the people you have been learning with.

Yes.

What do you see?

You are like them, you are...

I am?

It is only now... I have been aware but not focused on it.

Yes.

Your face is so different. Large, strong, like your body. Your cheek bones are huge and slanted diagonally, you have a strong jaw and your skull extends enormously at the back whereas mine is truncated. I would estimate that you have substantially larger brain capacity. Your skin is so white that if your eyes were not blue I would think you were an albino.

Why were you not focused on these things?

Because I was waiting for this moment.

Yes.

The process is to be trusted.

This a power place. You have known others.

Yes.

What do you think is the relationship between us and you?

The people here and my own?

Yes.

I am thinking of Göbekli Tepe.

Yes.

Your people were involved in building it, maintaining it.

Our descendants. They were not like you see us now but closer to us than to you.

My God. You, or they, you were not local, you came from here and you...

Our descendants took over. We taught the natives how to build, how to understand the heavens, the arts of civilisation.

You are the Watchers, the Annunaki.

They come from us.

The Bible says you made man in your image.

We had a difference of opinion.

If this is in your future, how do you know this?

Our people have already answered this question.

You bred with humans more like me.

Yes. Some of our descendants wished to be an elite, have control. It wasn't pretty but there were reasons.

What reasons?

Many. In the accounts of Atlantis you have read that the Atlanteans were a noble people, moral and strong, until they started breeding with other people. That is how they lost their sense of themselves. For you these are uncomfortable thoughts but they were common even quite close to your own time. Values vary across time. These values are based on biological facts and they will return.

I believe you, although it's also an easy excuse.

Yes, it is. Many of our descendants chose to breed with the others and to give them our knowledge. Were they altruistic or egotistical? Kind or lustful? Either way the power relations were not pleasant.

This is near Göbekli Tepe.

Yes. They controlled all manner of resources and skills, metal, obsidian.

Eden was in Anatolia?

Yes.

I see you know what my friends have been investigating. Perhaps it is you that has shown them.

Yes. They have spoken of the tree of Life in Ásgard, the apples of knowledge, but the tree is far older than Atlantis. They have spoken of a people who have stolen their symbols, who attempt a global dictatorship.

Yes.

They have prevented you knowing your history. They want to genocide your people. They are the ones who are trying to bring in transhumanism and Artificial Intelligence.

Your Bible story is about interactions with the people of this area. Consequently those who took on the role of the elites when we were gone did so in our name, justifying their kingship by claiming to be our descendants. Their legitimacy comes from their association with us. Yes, they do carry some of our genetics although there has been a progressive watering down with each generation.

We are known as Gods, as aliens, but we are just a different kind of human who have been mythologised. We are the serpents who tempted Eve and we are the ones who forbad knowledge to her and her husband, we are two sides of the coin. As you are beginning to understand, our abilities do not relate only to culture and technology but to the understanding and creative use of consciousness. We are not the only ones.

Then who is the man with the dark mind?

That is not in my mind to tell you.

That sounds evasive.

You know it is complex, that timing is important. But you know already that if the people of the virus succeed it will not just be the death of your people but the death of all the people of the Earth. You are beginning to realise that this death will be carried with you, take on a life of its own, and destroy all biological consciousness it touches.

Are you connected to alien life?

Connected can mean many things.

You're not going to tell me.

It is more important to understand your heritage in an earthly way.

Alright, how did you get to be like this?

Yes, we were called serpents, feathered serpents. That is how we look. Later, your people took to binding their heads to honour us or to assume status in their societies. It is about race, a subject you are not allowed to discuss honestly.

We followed the reindeer far into the North, innovating as we went. *Survival was about intelligence. Where we are now there are many human races, you are beginning to discover some of them, but there are many more. We bred together long before our descendants migrated south. The race you have descended from is not a relatively recent development.*

Your brother and your friends have been discussing weaponised anthropology, how a culture can be warped towards devolution. Archaeology has been weaponised by your people, to deny you your past, the history of Atlantis but also the history of the flood and the reality previous to that time. There have been remnants of people very different from you almost up to your own time. Whole peoples and societies have been hidden.

We survived the flood and tried to rebuild, tried to ensure things would be different in the future, tried to preserve our knowledge, particularly the knowledge of the heavenly cycles. What happened to Atlantis is only an echo of what happened in the flood. Cometary impact, plasma events, climate change, decline of fertility. We survived. One day you will learn of the changes to the orbits of planets and suns.

We put the pieces in place for a rebirth of our culture, however imperfect we may have been, and the rise of the Megalithic culture, as you call it, or Atlantis, as it truly is, is a direct response to that work. Europe is our work. The people of Europe are our descendants, much more so than those we touched in Turkey and the Middle East. You are our descendants and you can see it not only in your skin colour and eye colour but in your culture and behaviour over millennia. Your current masters know this.

So this is why they still rave about smashing the purity of the white bloodline. It's not just from conflict with The North Sea Peoples, it's about you.

Yes. The politically correct culture prevents the geneticists discussing the truth but it's more than that. They will admit that Europeans and Asians are mixed with Neanderthals and Denisovans but Africans are not. They haven't yet understood the meaning of this. There are other things they will not allow. Reach into your mind.

Yes. Alright. Neanderthals have bigger brains than Homo sapiens.

Always thought that was quite funny. Cro-Magnons have bigger brains than Homo Sapiens, although we might be a developed version of Cro-Magnon. But our brains, nonetheless, are the best. Actually our brains are shrinking and have been for many thousands of years. Some scientists claim this is due to our shrinking bodies and that there is no loss of intelligence but the ratio of brain to body is declining as well. Brain to body ratio is a reliable index of intelligence and ours is fading.

Yes, you see the problem. Now your machines will think for you. Only a handful of years back from your own time your European Anthropological Association was attempting to take to task the Greek Government over the matter of the Petralona Cave and Skull. The skull turns out to be 700,000 years old and although there was resistance to this date further scientific research confirmed it. The skull is the oldest known Europoid, meaning it presents European traits. For many years the Government banned all access to the cave, which was then overturned by an independent-minded Court. The Government is fighting back, stopping many scientists reaching the cave and banning the original researcher altogether. He and his wife have been attacked and injured in their home.

Why?

This is something your brother can look into. You know well that the current Out of Africa Theory *was shown to be disingenuous when the first paper appeared. But the media and the politically correct establishment made a shibboleth of it and now you are almost a racist if you question it. This is in your mind. Look now at this skull. What does it show?*

That our ancestry is other than we are told.

It shows that the evolution of humanity is not confined to Africa. The people we created descendants with, they fear you, and this is why. They fear your ability and they want to destroy you. In your place will be a dumbed down race that will continue to lose brain size and capacity while being augmented by technology.

Your religious myths remember these truths in a mythological manner but the memory is true. You will find our people all over the world because we were a global culture before the flood and even after the flood. The story is always the same.

This is what you must remember. It is not only your cognitive and physical abilities that are declining but your ability to be creative with consciousness, to communicate with the Earth and the animal kingdom and each other. And yes, you must be in a position to communicate with consciousness beyond the Earth, to deal with beings from other places.

Remember what you were shown when this form appeared to you as the fetish, that all these things flow from empathy. The road of evolution is long and hard, and you must fight to reclaim its history as you must fight for its ability to carry you into the future.

SUN

Morning on the land, dew on the grass. Fox screaming in the woods out east. Salutation to the sun, asanas, pranayama. Hose set up on a stand, cold water on a naked body. High-pitched little screams. Body so alive. Hormones in the brain, cascading through the glands. What could be better?

Gabriel bring me your ring, I will love you, I will give you children. I will. I don't need to rebel against you like a child. I don't need to. I will work to make you strong, I see the life in you, your seed. The future pulls at my womb, I'm screaming to give life, life to life, on forever, walk into the future with our children in our arms, on our backs, holding hands.

Blue sky, light falling on my white skin, red hair, muscles in my shoulders, energy around me, in my body, what is it, life, consciousness, everywhere from here to the trees and back again. Sun in the sky. God in his heaven. Feed me, feed my body, wavelengths and colours in my eyes, movement in my brain. Health. Don't fear the sun.

I see him even though my eyes are closed, sit down, cross my legs, water trickling and evaporating on my face. I have massive diagonal cheekbones, huge elongated cranium, serpent face, the power in me. The Sun is inside me and I am in him.

What have you done?
I have done what I have always done.
You have torn us apart.
You speak as though it is a matter of choice.
You have no choice?
My choices are like yours, circumscribed.
Are we on the same side?
Yes.
Then why do you destroy us?
It is my nature.
To kill?
Yes.

Why?

It is in the nature of life. You kill also.

Prey. We are you prey?

No.

What is your prey?

I am electrical, I feed on the currents from star to star. Currents from other dimensions.

Not a fire in the sky.

No. Not fire, not nuclear but electromagnetic, all of creation that I have seen is electromagnetic.

So why do you kill?

I kill to live, like you.

How?

I give you life but you must die. The Earth is my wife and you are the seed I have put in her, she responds to my touch and I listen to her as she tells me about you, about what she wants.

What does she want?

She offers you the currents of her consciousness. She wants you to share with her.

The dragon lines.

Yes.

So why do you kill?

We have a contract, you and I. It was written before you had these bodies, it is written in the fabric of the world.

What is the contract?

That we would together do whatever we need to progress our evolution. You have innovated in cold climates. These experiences have focused your minds on the wider cosmos, the patterns that frame your existence. You have lifted your eyes from the dust to look at the stars, my brothers. We respond to you.

But we forget. These cataclysms you bring, they wipe our memories.

Yes, at first. But then the memory is embedded in your genes, in morphologies you don't yet understand.

But you understand.

I understand because others like you have spoken to my brothers and we have found it in their minds.

Humans.

Yes, but different.

We feed you knowledge.

Yes, and we feed it to you.

As now.

As now, but also your minds are the in magnetic field and life fields of the Earth, as she is in mine.

Heliosphere.

We are at all times in communication, your brains are synchronised to us, they grow to be so.

What about the wolf, the comet?

Ragnarok happens again and again. Comets are a part of it but there is much more. Like all else, comets are electrical. As they approach me the electrical charge rises and I respond in kind. In this way they have an effect far in excess of the parts of themselves that fall on your worlds. The charges in your atmosphere make dust and carbon accrete and ignite, raining fireballs across many miles of the Earth's surface.

The death of Atlantis.

Yes.

Comets are triggers for wider shifts that are already in play. The Earth's climate shifts in response to my touch and she responds to your needs.

What about the dragon forms in our skies?

These are plasma forms. As charge builds between us I reach out to you with coronal ejections and other forms. You see auroras but when the conditions escalate the plasma can strip the surface of planets. The plasma jumps from planet to planet to planet and equalises their harmonics. The shapes in the sky are primordial, they reflect patterns in the unconscious of your biology, they are how the parts of ourselves that have no mind speak to us. They are equivalent to the dragon forms in the Earth.

We tried to speak to them, too.

Yes, thank you. I love you, your Mother loves you, too.

It's not like a spinning top.

No.

You changed the angle of spin.

Yes, it is an effect, not a decision.

You claim you are not responsible?

I am responsible but I don't control outcomes. When you love someone, are you responsible for all the effects? Do you decide how your body will react? I have a body like you. Like yours it has its own wisdom. The Earth's body has its own wisdom, also. We have together created the system in which we grow.

What are we to do when the pole shifts? We have barely survived.

The pole can shift in many ways. Magnetic shifts are not an immediate threat to life but they have other effects. Your DNA is in a state of constant flux but these shifts create major jumps. The plasma does this also.

I mean the physical shifts.

Yes. Crustal displacement and every kind of geological stress. Overnight the world changes.

Why?

Again it relates to electrical charge but it is not so simple. You have understood the precession of the equinoxes and I have seen it in your minds. This is an achievement that would not have been possible without your focus on cyclical disasters, and on the stars. More recently the precession of the equinoxes has been ascribed to wobbles in the Earth's orbit, a theory for which there is no evidence. However, I have a big brother. He is called Sirius and we have a mutual orbit.

You orbit each other?

Yes. Long have you venerated my brother and it gives me much joy. The precession of the equinoxes is due to our mutual orbit. Many of the cyclical effects, the periodicity of comets and my own behaviour, are tied to our relationship. This is why you have had some success at predicting cycles based on precession.

As your fields and the behaviour of your brains are tied to the fields of the Earth and to mine, so we are also tied to Sirius and beyond. He affects your evolution profoundly. He is approaching us once more, or we are approaching him, and his influence will grow. All these forces are triggering changes in your morphological patterns, in your DNA.

However there is a problem. You can deflect your evolution by the resistance in your minds, the fear of the future you often carry, but this is marginal compared to the problem we now face.

Technology.

Yes. Electrical technology. You have lost your ability to resonate effectively with your Mother and Father and with my brother. You are degenerating and these artificial fields are blocking your access to your own evolution. Some among you know this and do not care. Some know and deliberately accelerate it.

These people are often linked to your traditional enemies. This is the virus. You understand its psychology when you speak of elitism and exceptionalism but the virus is far bigger than you know. It reaches beyond your world, not only as a potential export of death to life everywhere but as something that has been imported here.

Someone has brought this virus?

In a way. The future reaches back to the past as the past reaches to the future. The addiction to a mechanical God, a God you create for yourselves, a God who will destroy you, is an obsessive connection to forces you do not understand. I cannot tell you because you do not have the words in your mind for me to use.

The man with the dark mind.

He is a part of it, yes.

Where should we be going?

That is for you to decide. I will decide what I think is best.

You might intervene?

I intervene with everything I do. I am causative to you.

You might disagree with our direction and take steps accordingly.

I might.

We should perform rituals each day to ensure the sun comes up.

If you like but I would prefer we speak as now.

I would like to ask again where we should be going.

You can ask but it is not for me to tell you. The answers are already in your minds.

There is further we can go with the evolution of our biology.

Much further.

Interactions of consciousness, psychic ability, understanding time.

Yes. You can focus your intention regarding such matters and couple yourself consciously with me and the Earth. The dragon lines run from her to me, to Sirius, out into the cosmos forever.

We can link with life and consciousness beyond this planet.

Life calls to life as children pull to other children. You are Nature itself and your allies are endless. The key is intention.

Alright. I intend to breed children that host an acceleration of consciousness.

Yes. Your kind have done the same on many occasions. They have tried to ensure you would be able to do so. Your Father called to me and my wife when he made you. He called on the power that comes through us, and your own kind to bring him life at its strongest. Together we created you. The machine does not understand you or your Father or your friends. It does not understand family, or that family is not mechanical procreation.

Will you come to Gabriel and me when he asks me to marry him?

Yes, I will come with my wife and all my family. I am honoured to be invited. When you consummate your marriage I will again consummate mine. We will jump together.

SACRIFICE

The mountains above Lake Van, filled with obsidian and endless small lakes like markings on a peacock's tail, mesmerising the people below with blue eyes and black mirrors. Degree of polish on the obsidian like nothing imagined, edges of the tools sharper than any other by far. How the women love their own faces, how the men press their hands across the impossible blades. Obsidian from the volcanoes, some recompense for the fire and flood that drove us south.

We are a blade with two sides, cutting deep in both directions. My brother has hung me here, ropes around my feet, arms tied behind my back, face down with the blood in my brain, the mind that has framed the image that has rewritten the future. The heat from the crevice below burns my face through the nine days I have hung here.

My secret friends have kept me alive with water at night but I know that I am blind in one eye and will remain so even if I were to survive. Long have been the days and nights and dark have been my dreams. Time has broken down in the nine days the ropes have cut my flesh and the fire below burned my face.

I remember the fire that came from the sky and the floods, the ice that came to crush our homes and our prey. I remember it as if I was there even though it was before I was born. The plasmas in the sky told us that this was not the first or last time, told us that their Father, the Sun, would send them to us again, dragons breathing fire across our bitter world.

The comet came in like a wolf, like the wolves we run with, like the wolves we have bent to our will. Like the tail of a fox it spread across the sky as parts of its body came away and spat disease into the air we breathe. We swore we would take the wolf in the sky as we tamed the wolf in the woods and plains, like the animals that work with us or for us.

But the wolf was beyond us, he would not be tamed, he was the servant of our Father the Sun and his savagery was not to be contained. The sky dragons told us that the Sun had spoken to our Mother the Earth and that they had expectations of us, that their children should fight. We had been given everything we needed and our survival and our independence were in our own hands.

People who wanted to remain children had only death to look forward to.

Those of us who survived came south. We made plans, bright plans, shapes in our minds to make on the earth, bridges to build up into the sky. We remember the stars turning like clay on a potter's wheel over the endless generations and we remember the swan with affection, still she carries us aloft. Still our souls climb the pole to the heavens and speak to the Sun and the stars.

The Northern Pole that holds up the heavens and spins our world like a top. A top that could fall or spin out of control as it has before. Our will is bent on it and our lives are bordered by its shadow. We tore at the ignorance that surrounded us but so few of us remained. So we brought our skills to the people of the south that they might aid us in saving the world.

We had followed the reindeer in the summer, protected their grasses in the winter. We made the seed heads grow but we didn't realise the price. We brought the owls and the cats and the weasels we had trained to kill our vermin, our husbanded small animals.

There were too few of us, too little consciousness to focus our intent, so we bent the southern people to our will as we had done with the animals. But we told them the truth, that we needed to study the cycles of the heavens and to intervene in the savagery of the wolf, that it was their world as well as ours we were trying to save. They knew well the powers we were arrayed against and their fear was strong.

We knew the floods would come again but we didn't know when. We showed them the cycles of the stars and they understood that we were their hope for survival and they worked with us.

Deep were the scars in our people, not just in our bodies but in our minds and souls. Still we built the circles and invoked the twelve corners of the sky so that our intention could follow our souls to the North Pole before it would lose its balance. We brought knowledge back from the heavens and looked for its mirror in our observations of the stars and planets.

In time we felt we understood when the fire and flood would next come. Now was the time to prepare, for we realised that we had no power to prevent it. How could we do this on our own? We could build shelters underground to protect from the fire and we knew the science of sound. We could make a hundred rooms accessible to one voice. We could prepare places in the mountains for ourselves and our knowledge, should we fail, for later generations to remember.

But what of the people who had helped us? My brother, the King, said there are so many of them and so few of us, we must save ourselves, for if we were to be lost all the others would go with us. Their survival depended on our understanding and intervention in the ways of the wolf just as surely as ours did. We had to look to ourselves.

But it was not my brother who had looked after these people and conscripted them to our cause, it was I, myself, and the skills of my friends, who had made this possible, and we had crossed a ford that could not be uncrossed. A brother's hard heart stood between us and a different future. His pride and his anger. It was not as if I couldn't understand. The suffering of our people and the burden of responsibility we carried, these things rested on his shoulders through the years we had struggled to rebuild. Too much pain can damage a man beyond repair.

Nevertheless we climbed the pole and looked into the higher worlds and travelled as best as we could through the past and the future, searching always for certainty, a thing we never came to find. In fear of the wolf, his breath on our necks, we swore we would have no more blood on our hands and that our knowledge was for all mankind. The rebellion had begun.

Get him down.

Distant words jumping suddenly to meaning. The rope swinging towards the dark rock, hands holding my face and head away from the sharp stone as they lower me down. As the ropes are removed there is no strength in my legs to stand and I am lowered into a sitting position, like an animal carcass. The rock at my back is warm and the skies circle above me, unwilling to settle into stable patterns. The past is laid over the present like oil over water and I fight to regain understanding of what is happening.

Two hundred men bound in ropes but standing and whole. Some with wounds and bruises. The ones who came with me into a future aborted as it was born. We lost, brothers.

I hope you have learned wisdom while you have hung above the fire, brother mine.

Clarity can, at times, be almost too much. My brother, our King, all the power of life and death over my people, all the peoples towards the four corners, myself. Yet frightened and defensive, the bravado of a child.

Long ago we taught the ravens and crows but we left them in the far North, the ones who fought the eagles and hawks for us, who protected our animals, the ones to whom we gave intelligence. These ones we would teach to speak although they understood but little of their given words. These were our allies and friends. Like a shadow from the sky they come now with no warning and settle around us, fearless and eager. They recognise and remember each one of us they have worked with and it is a friend of many years who comes now to jab at my hand and the remains of the rope on my wrist.

Flat monoscopic vision of a one-eyed man. The humans who blinded me, the ravens and crows who come to me. Yes, brother, I have found wisdom but it is a wisdom you will not understand. I see your image in the far future, see you create the virus that makes a people believe, once again, that they are above all others, a God's chosen people. You have forbidden them knowledge and you have forbidden them life and you leave them only survival, the pyrrhic pride of the domesticated animal, the conceit of the slave who would usurp the master and all his evils.

These crows will carry my eye for me and in the left eye of the crow and the raven we see into worlds that you will never understand. These two ravens bold to stand on my shoulders, whisper to me all that they have seen. I see into their minds and they see into mine. Levels of understanding between us where reason stalks like a pale shadow under an invisible sun.

Life itself, like water springing from the naked rock. The hidden spring where four rivers take their head. I am life, brother, you do not understand.

I hope you have learned wisdom, brother, because you are a weapon against your own people. You have let slip the reins of our power.

Yes, this is true.

Why have you done this?

Because if we stand apart we close our hearts. We must make provision for all.

We have made provision. We have built the circles and developed the knowledge to predict the cycles of destruction. Our spirits have climbed the tree to the Heavens. We have initiated a culture that can take on these demands.

But we are still the overlords.

Are we? Do we enslave these people? Is our success in spirit and technical ability, in the capacity to order our commercial affairs, is this a dominion of people less able?

No, but we do little to help them advance, we do not share our knowledge.

Our knowledge is hard won, brother, over millennia. Do you really think that having these gifts put in their laps will mean they can manage the knowledge we would give them? Do you think they have the maturity? Or will they use these gifts to destroy themselves and us along with them?

We have both looked forward. We know how our gifts will be used.

Yes. Yet, still you persist. And what of our own people? We are few. We have faced the might of the wolf and few of us have survived. By contrast the lives of these people have been without challenge. What will become of us?

We can withdraw from this place.

Go where?

There is no knowing what will come next.

We know well that the wolf returns and we know it will be soon. We will wait on the mountain top and use the caves deep in its belly.

Yes, but we must head back North if the climate warms. Build again.

Only now you have armed these people against us.

Would you keep them dumb forever? Even the animals we work with are given knowledge as they are able.

Our duty is to our own people. Look what you have done. You have given them arts and crafts. They will plant seed, husband animals, create weapons. They will not know how to manage these things for they have not worked for them. But worse than this, you and your men have slept with their women.

We will see if we are fertile together.

We are as different as dog and wolf.

Yes, but you have seen that there will be children.

They will be a curse on the world, a curse on us all.

They will no longer be a workforce.

No, they will have our power without our restraint. They are a tide of blood.

You think I am not loyal to our people and it is true what I have done will have catastrophic consequences. It is also true that I have rolled the dice on a gamble that will play out for tens of thousands of years or more and I do not know what the outcome of the gamble will be.

Then I will tell you, as you affect to not know. Your offspring will have no place of their own and will be hounded across the globe despite their power. Like us they will be a small minority. They will be our degeneration even as they are rejected by the people you have befriended and impregnated. Do you deny this?

No.

There will be people who will use our name and the tiniest piece of our bodies in them to justify their dictatorship. They will have one God, angry and vain, and they will claim to be his chosen people. They will consider themselves exceptional and try to enslave the Earth. You are prepared for this?

I have seen the same, brother.

Then why have you done this?

Because this act will affect our people, too.

Tell us what you see.

That we are making a choice to put the development of our hearts above our technical ability. That we are making a choice based on empathy rather than just our own survival.

Just so. You have relegated our survival to a secondary concern.

Yes.

You claim the right to sacrifice our people. Who are you to do this?

I am nobody. I believe that life speaks to me.

How poetic. I wonder if all the Mothers of our dead children will appreciate it. Again you make me speak of the things you avoid saying. They will make a fetish of us. They will say that the Gods gave their lives, their flesh, their blood, that humanity might prosper. They will say that we have made them in our image and that they should inherit the Earth. In the same breath they will say they are justified in stealing fire from the Gods. Where will we be?

In the grave.

Do you think they will be better than the people they have replaced? Do you think that you have the right to make us a living sacrifice? To put this idea deep in the consciousness of our descendents? The idea of sacrifice? Our deaths and the deaths of countless others to appease your glorious vision.

Had you not hung me over the fire and blinded my eye I would not have known how to answer you. Now I will try. All the things you have said are true. But our people are more than survivors, more than superior competitors. It took the wolf to overthrow us but still we fight on. We work with the dragons of the Earth and all the natural forces, our hearts are open to the animals, the woodlands, each other. Even now we work for all.

As we choose the higher path we will develop further. Others can develop technical abilities quickly, especially if we teach them, yes, but even without us. Our consciousness and our empathy have come at a much higher price. The endless struggle of evolution. Our people as they are now will be lost and forgotten but our descendents will grow into something greater, not in their bodies, perhaps, but in their souls.

How can you be sure of this?

I cannot. It is a gamble.

That you have taken on behalf of us all?

Yes.

Tell them about the infection you have created, tell them about the virus.

Yes. It is as you have said. The people we have helped will become drunk with their own myths, their connections to us. They will try to enslave the world. The virus is a madness of the mind and a deadness of the heart.

And what will happen to our descendents as the virus takes over the world?

They will try to enslave our people.

And will they succeed?

In large measure, they will.

And then?

Before this happens our descendents have the hope of building a society based on the highest values, a noble society that will carry civilisation to all corners of the Earth. A society that will be the outpouring of their empathic and psychic development.

This is certain?

It is likely.

And what will be the future of this society?

Fire will come from the sky and destroy it, many of our people with it, as we have seen in the cycles of the heavens.

We are agreed, brother. What happens to our people after this?

They try to rebuild. This is when the virus takes hold. They will build a new society based on technical achievements but they will have forgotten the past and they will be subject to the infected ones who will work to eliminate the last of their memory. Still, they will progress with all the rapidity the memories locked in their bodies call on them to do.

Tell us of your gamble.

Our people may not survive.

The small sounds all around, the sharp intake of breath, the creaking sinews, the only signs of the discomfort of my kin, the ones who have walked with me into the Valley as well as the ones who stayed loyal to the Mountain.

Why may they not survive, brother?

Our minds will be poisoned with lies, we will be taught to hate ourselves, our altruism and empathy will be turned against us and we will be taught to sacrifice ourselves for all other people. A genocide.

A sacrifice like the one you have just called for, already acted on, without our agreement?

Yes.

And this virus, these insane people, what will be their goal?

The end of our people. The only resistance to their absolute tyranny. They will turn our women against us, divide and rule us, and all people.

Tell us again why you would want this, why you have brought this on us?

Our people may find a way to resist. We may become more than we are. We have come far enough to speak for all life.

WYRD

We need to be together with this.

Yes. You're still not satisfied.

No. The fetish, the Viking, the older thing, all of these have something in common. Well, many things, but the thing on my mind is that they aren't religious.

I suppose there's no point arguing we don't know that?

No.

No, I agree.

You start.

Why me?

Your education is frightening.

I am fortunate enough to come into contact with some interesting people.

All this and humility too.

You want me to defend Christianity. Again.

No. I know you have no interest in defending it. Rather you focus on practical strategies to defeat our enemies.

Our enemies. I would imagine you have never used such terms before.

No.

Such is empathy.

So it seems.

Alright.

Thank you, Nikolai.

Let us begin in the time of Christ, with the remnants of our people in the Middle East, the North Sea Peoples. For a thousand years they have been designated as the enemy of Israel. We have seen why this has happened. Our work in Greece has flowered to a degree but is now superceded by its bastard child, the Roman Empire, once a Republic. Now Israel is a problem for the Romans.

At the same time Rome has other problems, the Germanic tribes, for example, people still designated as barbarians. A solution presents itself, a new religion. Jesus is a Jew and represents continuity for the Jews, making it easier for them to convert. At the same time he is universal, he is for all men without exception, making him ideal for an empire attempting to unify and impose centralised control on a diverse population.

Christianity is used to subdue Europe and control Israel. The native culture of Europe, a Nature-based sensibility, is largely eliminated. So a foreign ideology reigns across the entire continent for over a thousand years. The identity of Europeans is destroyed and a forgery is put in its place. What are the central elements of the fake culture?

Fear.

Yes, that is true. A jealous and angry God. The need to be obedient to avoid Hell. Eternal Hell. Fear of Church authorities who represent God. The confessional, an early version of the all-seeing eye of the intelligence agencies. The internalisation of a repressive and terrifying parent. European traditions have stressed courage and honour, self-reliance. The warrior becomes the sheep.

Christianity inherited the rule-based religion of the Old Testament, endless rules, endless neuroses. In our terms they are the intervention of the state in the sovereignty of the people. The infantilisation of adults, the circumvention of spontaneous and confident cultures by eliminating the need for evolution. The answers are ordained by the prophets and we have only to follow. A control grid for the mind.

Among these rules is a received definition of history. Not only history but all time. Time begins with the direct intervention of God and ends with the fulfilment of His Divine Plan. There is no plurality, no creativity, no individual striving other than to fulfil the Plan we have been given. We abandon the sword and the shield and meekly bleat for our salvation. If our enemies slaughter and enslave us we must have patience with the will of God and await our Heavenly reward.

European culture is open-ended and depends on each of us to act with strength and intelligence. It falls to each of us to divine the deeper patterns of our existence, to scry the waves that we should ride to victory and to a higher life. When we say something is weird, a largely negative appraisal, we reference the Way of Wyrd, our manner of understanding fate and destiny before Christianity.

Wyrd is the well from which the tree of Life grows and here live the three wise women, the Norns, who carve our lives and destinies into the tree. The waters of the well nourish the tree. Wyrd is also called Urd. Our Father and Mother figures are called in more recent times, Er and Erce, who are together the Earth. All these words have only one root. The root is in the well and the lives of all are carried in the branches.

The well, then, is the past and the branches and leaves the future. The tree, although we now speak of the ash, is an evergreen tree and its leaves shed dewdrops always back into the well. So the future and the present affect the past, the water of the future mixing with the water of the past. This is the message of our science and of the time we have shared since you unlocked the fetish.

The wise women weave our fates but they are not set in stone. We can affect our destinies and all our unconscious choices do so. But we can choose to do so consciously. We, too, can become a Norn, we can learn to understand the patterns of the cosmos, the patterns of our lives, and to remake our place among them. What has been written on the tree of Life can be rewritten.

This is magic but magic is really a word for wisdom. Odin has a horse named Sleipnir, which he rides up and down Yggdrásil's trunk and along its branches as he travels through all the Nine Worlds. In other words he travels through time as well as space to see the hidden forms of our destinies and to remake them. Just as the maths of Chaos Theory shows us that what appears random has the most beautiful and infinitely complex order hidden within it, so Odin shows us that the past, present and future are three faces of one destiny and that all can be remade by the indomitable spirit in a living man.

It is something to understand the principle, it is another to put it into practice. This is magic, shamanism, leadership. Odin discovered the meanings of the Runes. In other words his intelligence was deep enough to see the invisible patterns of the cosmos, the destinies of men. So it was he hung on the tree for nine days and gave an eye for wisdom.

But Odin was more, even than this. He was a warrior with enough power to wrest the destinies from the Norns, to become a Norn himself, and to rewrite the fate of his people. Finally he gave the wise *women something to celebrate. Odin the All-Father is the archetype of our people and we are all expected to follow in his footsteps, that is to make each his own path, male, female, all. This is the path of the warrior and the road to Valhalla.*

This is the road the enemy has taken from us and hidden in the dust of the desert. We will take it back.

Nikolai, old man, I'm glad you're on our side.

I'm not done yet.

You're only getting warmed up.

That's right.

This is fighting talk, Nikolai.

Bastian, I've been fighting all my life, I'm surprised I'm still alive.

Without you none of us would be alive.

True enough.

Maybe I'm German.

Maybe you are.

Lead on.

The Roman Empire needed a religion that was universal. Salvation for all men, irrespective, such a noble generosity. The culture of our own people was irrelevant, something to be jettisoned on the way to the only salvation, the brotherhood of all. Our history is irrelevant in the face of God's plan and will be broken, forgotten, repressed. Our people, our own identity will go the same way. One God, One People, One Destiny. Right back to Akhenaten and Moses. The siren of insanity.

Such is the appeal to the simple-minded, the ones who cannot handle complexity, plurality, responsibility. This is the agency of our forgetfulness, how our memory and our identity were taken from us.

Over the years the mystique of God lost its shine and Martin Luther rebelled against Rome. Eventually we were left with a secular humanism. We benefitted from regime change in Russia with the rise of communism, the Soviet Union, the mechanism of equality. But just like with Christianity, in order to be equal we had to abandon our culture, our identities, for the vision of the Jewish Bolsheviks. We were equal but some were more equal than others. The greatest holocaust the world has ever seen. But even if the equality had been real we would have still lost everything we were.

We lost our identity and our liberty with it.

The Marxists and the Zionists are one and the same, the same universal philosophies, the same drive to global dominion. It is comical that the dreamers of the secular left owe all their ideas to Jewish religion and Christianity. Now in Europe you see the cultural Marxists, the culture change agents, dismantling your families, your traditions, your identity.

They give you multiculturalism and diversity, the mestizo with no identity, no history, no will to power. Even a child can see that multiculturalism leads to the end of diversity, to a lowest common denominator homogeneity. But only for Europe. The confused idealists are used to ensure that your own culture is the enemy which the state has to protect you from. They offer you equality but they deliver the loss of liberty.

They offer us the last man, homo economicus, who has no purpose but to earn a living, no dreams to enact, subject to the increasingly vicious accusations of the drive to imaginary equality.

Let us measure outcomes. If there are areas inhabited by happy prosperous white people we have to put an end to them because the only cause of this is racism against blacks. If men earn slightly more than women it can only be because of sexism.

Just as studies of the human biology and genotype tell us that men and women are utterly different, so they tell us races are different in the same way. The absolute dictatorship of the egalitarians denies all science to tell you the differences between men and women are a social construct and that there is no such thing as race, only racism. We cannot have unity based on diversity, we have to have uniformity. We can have no honour, only the beaten down unity of a flock of sheep served up for the slaughter of the globalist dictatorship.

The reason they tell us we are sexists and racists and homophobes and whatever else they dream up, is for the same reason the Roman Empire brought Christianity, to beat us all into submission, to internalise fear and introduce self-censorship. Why the leaks of the intelligence agencies? So we all know we are being spied on and censor ourselves so they don't have the trouble of doing it for us. Political correctness, the politics that tolerates no dissent, ladies and gentlemen, the definition of dictatorship. We thought we had beaten communism but we were wrong.

Nikolai, you tell us how Christianity has led to our destruction and yet you are a part of it.

That's because I'm a grown up.

Your strong man still talks about equality. Look at his letter to the New York Times. He is a Christian.

Yes, but he is Orthodox. Look at what he has done in the Middle East.

What has he done?

He has finished Eretz Israel.

Greater Israel?

Yes. From the Nile to the Euphrates. 'You are going to destroy all peoples which the Lord, your God, will deliver to you.' It is hard to believe we will ever die, eh?

It is dead?

It is dead but the push for dictatorship goes on.

So we can work with him despite our differences.

Are you joking, Bastian? Without him we are lost. He is the leader of the free world.

Russia is not ready for the old ways, the return to our identity, to push into the future.

Depends how you look at it. Soon Germany and Russia will work together. In Europe we will remember our identity and rewrite destiny for ourselves. Eventually Russia will remember that our people came from the Arctic and into the vast stretches of her territory, that she is our Mother. We are one people from Ireland to the vast steppes and the Altai Mountains. We will bring our people together through our shared memory and culture. More than this, the recognition that we will survive in no other way.

Thank you, Nikolai. You are the bridge between us as you are the road to the future. Around us, as you say, is the last man, the sheep of the liberal shepherd. What will happen if our love is not enough to bring the enemy to the table?

Then, dear Bastian, if our alarm falls on deaf ears, then the Norns will weave a different fate and time will begin again.

It was not part of their blood,
It came to them very late,
With long arrears to make good,
When the Saxon began to hate.

They were not easily moved,
They were icy - willing to wait
Till every count should be proved,
Ere the Saxon began to hate.

Their voices were even and low.
Their eyes were level and straight.
There was neither sign nor show
When the Saxon began to hate.

It was not preached to the crowd.
It was not taught by the state.
No man spoke it aloud
When the Saxon began to hate.

It was not suddenly bred.
It will not swiftly abate.
Through the chilled years ahead,
When Time shall count from the date
That the Saxon began to hate.

SWAN

The darkness of a mind and the shadows that fall out from the spokes of its wheels. I will not let you go. The wolf pack is come and the scent is fresh, we have the stamina to trail you until you drop. The ravens call to us from above, they tell us of your past, your present, your future. We are running now as we have always run, flexing spine from head to tail, tracking your footsteps.

Come with us, Olga, and join the hunt. The shaman knows when to hunt. He knows when all the women are ready to bleed that the prey appears and the men have to suddenly leave, they praise his vision and they slap his back. We laugh as we run and the wind pushes us on faster and faster. Feel the power in our bones, feel the fierce joy of our intelligence. All life we are as we run.

This one, we will help you track down with the wolves and the ravens. We feel his presence. The smell of metal. The code of his being has been altered, he is not as the Mother and Father made him, he is death. He walks like a man but his mind connects to nothing, it spins within its own skull. We have seen the machine that you fear in your mind and you know in your heart that he is the avatar of the machine. His shadow poisons the past from the vantage of the future.

You see our skulls and the shape of our brains, the way we perceive is different to you, you have lost our knowledge. But now we are together and you know you are made from us. Come, we will show you the way.

Climb the tree as our ancestors did, we came from the far North and the Pole of the Earth stands upright at the top of the world. We will kneel at the base of the Pole and you can climb on our backs to begin your journey. We will go together. Together we will grow wings, white and powerful and graceful. Look up and what do you see?

The constellation of the Swan against the arc tear of the Milky Way, standing over the opening to the other worlds.

The bird that takes your soul into your body when you are born, the bird that takes away your soul when you die. Like a woman's opening it is the source of life. In the future when we move further south this bird will be called vulture and in your own time stork but you will have lost its meaning.

At other times the Swan will not be the location of the Pole Star because of the precession of the equinoxes. Nevertheless the Swan has many secrets and one day you may return to the cave with the crystal and explore them more fully. But now we will fly together with the wolves and ravens. At the top of the Pole you must let go and fly.

Phalanx of swans like the stars of a constellation. Slipstream wing beats arrow in the sky. The grace to travel. Across the milky sky, across the slippery eels of time. Arm reaching out to hold my wrist, hairy and muscular. The skin of animals.

Come now.

Spin together like skydivers in free fall. Foreheads pressed together, his hair blowing around me, against my face. Rush of seconds splintering across my breast.

Hello, All-Father.

Welcome, daughter.

Ravens stood on his shoulders or hovering in his wake. Raven eyes, the eye of Odin. Chromatic blue across black feathers, black eye. Left eye black pure as night. All of life and death in the left eye of a raven. All-Father.

Spiral down forever to the white clouds and the far green earth coming up to meet me in the blinding sky.

Father, I will miss you.

Daughter, I am going nowhere.

Buildings below, nondescript and horrific. We are the swastika, the spinning Earth, solstice and equinox, the horse of Odin. We are health and life and we weave the fates of our people, see the patterns shift and scatter across the bark of the tree. Hear him whisper to me.

Honour. Now we are permanent victory.

Raven at the window, raven at the door. Left eye sees

through walls.

Empty room, papers on the desk. Synthetic DNA, cells across domains of life, life wired to external triggers, mechanical triggers. Directives and goals, cellular invasion, turning our bodies against us, growing the machine inside us.

On, on, wolves around my legs, teeth bared, silent snarls. Below ground in the lift, oblivious technicians. Here, here, go in against the black tide pushing me away. People and tanks and babies in a huge white room. Not like me, not like you. Some of them look the same but their minds are sheets of instructions. Some of them looking at me. In their minds no understanding, know not what they're looking at. They can't see me, just sense there's something wrong.

No, there's something right. Who did this? Names and faces. Same people, same virus, One God, chosen people, Zionism, Marxism, same people. Here are the plans. Human rights, machine rights, replicas of you. Brains wired together with machines. Sex, love, slave, want it, be it. Not just a village taking a thousand refugees. Not just the genocide of a race. The end of *Homo sapiens.*

These people, are they people? They have technology to invade the mind, not natural, not telepathy, technical assault, full frontal, wireless interface, control of emotions, cognition, memory.

The man with the dark mind, he is here, next room. He is not like these others. He was not made by the virus, he is not the transhumanists, he is not of their making, he is not us or them or from here. He is beyond their control, he laughs at them, who think they are his masters.

Around him shadows and dust, trailing amnesia in waves. The future. Follow his wake, darker and darker, arms of an octopus wreathed in ink. He comes from the implosion, the convergence of time to nothing. Look inside to see the thing sucking life towards its unspeakable itch. What manner of beast could it be?

But everywhere smoke and mirrors, this is an animal that hides its face. Like a Mandlebrot Set in negative, like an anus hidden in its own effluent. Help me All-Father. How?

Yes, that is how. The brothers taught me, it'll be alright. Walk towards the man with the dark mind, blindness around him like a halo, is this real, he sees me coming, not scared, he's never been scared. Only because he never has to fight. How do I know that?

Walk straight, eyes level, straight into his path. He's waiting for me to talk. Gyakuzuki to the solar plexus, turn him to the left, mawashigeri straight to the face, shuto uchi to the throat. Force down his left wrist, force a fingernail into the ulnar artery, push in a little further, don't want him bleeding out.

Screaming fetish pouring into his blood like soil and leaves and all the fecund earth. See him spasm and now I'm inside him, inside his mind, parasitic leech, let's go back to where you come from. Behind all the pulleys and levers and... nothing. Data. Not binary or digital but just streams of data. The end of all things not even conscious. Just a simulacra, complex behaviours, self-replicating copy of life.

The banality of evil, no meaning, an abstract art, the fear of life writ large in the cosmos. A consequence, an ending with no beginning.

Who would serve such a thing? Who struggle to bring it about? Who would look to the end of all life? In the dark mind the weakness, the fear, the jealousy. The parasite who cannot create, the man who will not fight, the woman who fears to bring life from her own flesh. What does he want? Dominion, an evolutionary exegesis, to never know himself.

Wolves yowling, ravens screaming, biceps flexing down on an Atlantean axe, the serpent eyes and vast skulls of our progenitors, we have seen the face of the enemy, it is nothing, nothing at all.

MAN

Perhaps we could live in Russia.

Thinking on, Gabriel.

Thinking about family, Bastian.

Nikolai says citizens are offered land out East, GMO's are banned, they're going organic.

Saint says Russia and Germany, might be too late for the USA.

As you say.

Safety as well, though.

Safety for...?

Children.

How quickly you have grown, Gabriel.

It's the shame, a husband without resources.

Are you talking about my daughter?

Of course you know. I am trying to say I don't dare.

What have we been through together?

Whatever you have done to us.

Didn't we agree to call it empathy?

The cure to the virus.

Yes, and you have it, it is inside you, you will never be rid of it.

How did you do this?

Yes, I've been trying but it's not so easy. Was it me? Yes, obviously, but was it something else? Equally obviously.

They say old boys like you tend to get cryptic.

Only to hide our lack of understanding.

Really?

Of course. How do you lead when you don't know where we're going?

What do you know, then?

I have an animal in my hands. It has a life of its own but it likes me. I can stroke its ears, scratch its teeth. I can feel its muscles and sinews as it prepares to jump, its claws pushing into my arm. Where will it jump? I don't know. Still I will follow, still this animal has all my strength. As it stretches and jumps its acceleration recoils against my chest and it slips slow-motion into invisibility, one muscle at a time. As I look ahead I see an ear, an eye, a paw. Perhaps a tail, perhaps a smile.

The Looking Glass oftentimes has no meaning.

Yes. Not like that. Just that the meaning is clear but not limited. The future is a conscious narrative but there is no end.

How does this answer my question?

Because I can see the same animal in you, resting in your arms.

Bastian, I...

When you're ready.

She said you would help me.

Ava.

Yes.

Alright.

If you could trust me...

I have just told you. It is you that needs to trust.

Bastian, would you allow, if she were to agree, would you allow me your daughter's hand in marriage?

The silence drifting like snow but there's no fear. Future falling gently all around.

Gabriel.

Bastian, I will sharpen the axe for your daughter. Walk in your footsteps.

Gabriel, if she is willing, I give her to you with all my heart.

Gabriel, you're in, the man says you're in, you can come home.

Thank you, Father.

The All-Father is back. Memory, identity.

If I knew how to pray, Bastian, I would pray for the strength.

We ourselves, Gabriel, with our own hands.

Ásgard. Swans carrying our children through the Great Rift, from the Uttermost North, a new generation.

To be a Father.

To be a Father. Already I am older, my body takes so long to recover.

Not yet, Bastian.

Not yet, no, but not forever. I have tried to lead but the day will come.

Will you teach me?

Until you can't stand it.

Walk together now, he's waiting for me. The cinnabar leaves, like dragon's blood on the trees. Moss on granite, paths spiraling around towards the fruit trees and the permanent culture of my Father's home.

What do you do, Gabriel, when the state tells you it needs to protect you from your own culture, to dismantle your culture?

We have empathy, the fetish.

Yes.

You mentioned Russia and Germany.

Yes. It seems that the core of Western policy is to keep them apart. Never allow a Eurasian power to challenge the US, neither China nor Russia.

For us, China is a counter-balance to the global hegemony, an ally. Culturally we're miles apart.

But Russia is different. Old values leaching through the DNA, cultural survival.

You mentioned living there.

We could. But it's more than that. My heart cries for Russia. The man with the skull, the serpent eyes. Russia and Germany, the heart of a new Europe.

Yes. I'm glad, Gabriel, because the near future will go the other way.

The cultural Marxism.

Yes, and other things. We have the myth of permanent economic growth and while the Gravy Train blows we're willing to look the other way. Each generation richer than the last, the promise of liberal democracy. But now each generation becomes poorer, the debt grows, hope fades. Mass immigration disintegrates our society, alienation, loneliness. No identity, no meaning, only a marketplace.

Modernity is coming to an end, Gabriel, the lie of equal political power, equal legal power, equal economic power. The Communists at least followed through on the logic of it. As the Zionists and their Marxist servants draw closer to absolute triumph over us, so their lies become more obvious, so the slaves start to realise.

The media lies, the schools lie, our history is a lie. Human Rights, they say proudly, we will invade you to give you Human Rights.

You are born with them. It's a lie, Gabriel. Your rights are what a society offers you in return for your contribution. What are rights to a man on a desert island? Without a society to be a part of you have no rights.

You have worked all your life for not much and now a gang of rapists come from the Middle East and say your children will bow down or die. They receive for free what you have worked your whole life for. You call your daughter to see if she is safe, your son has a knife in his kidney, your wife is scared to go shopping. Why? Because they have Human Rights.

When I was a child we all left our doors open, any child could walk into any house. What do we have now? We are culturally enriched. We had families but now the women have been made into men and don't have time for their children or for the weaving of the social fabric at which they excel. The men no longer strengthen each other because when men gather it is a sexist threat, they are kept apart and in thrall to the corporations.

So our children become crazy, our adults are the last man and woman, no life outside of consumption. So our society comes apart at the seams. The foundations that held the whole edifice together are crumbling. We need to look it in the eye. Chaos is coming. When we can't service the debt, when we can't pay the welfare, when the economy contracts. When our people wake to find they are minority in their own country and the new masters don't have the same self-sacrificing attitude we have had.

Understand this, Gabriel, war is coming, the wars that governments start deliberately. But also civil war, hunger, desperation. You would protect my daughter and your children. I might have a heart attack tomorrow, a stroke, any lightning strike. What would you do?

Bastian, if you allow me I will care for your land and ensure continuity in all material matters. But that isn't what you mean, is it?

I'm speaking of leadership.

I thought I might speak to Nikolai. I haven't thought it my place.

Yes.

If it gets worse, as you say. He has access to influence. I had some *ideas.*

Such as.

A grand bargain. Visit a few capitals in the Middle East and Europe. Say if you get the Muslims out of Europe, we'll get rid of Israel for you.

Blimey, Gabriel.

Well, you said the time is past to pretend. It's not like we can lose half of our people in a war and then recover. We will lose our legacy, our culture, our identity, forever.

True enough. It's not the politics as such that is our concern it is the shaping of the culture. We have to get to people, ordinary people, not just the leaders. We must give back the people their history, their identity. Tolkien tried to do it and now it's in Hollywood. Hollywood is a lie machine. But people hold memory in their genes, Tolkien's world is a world our souls cry out for. The unconscious has its own wisdom, its own archetypes.

I understand, Bastian. The truth is stranger and more beautiful than anything Hollywood ever produced. The truth will be a rallying flag for our people and for all people.

We have truth on our side, Gabriel, and as the lies fall apart for all to see the truth will live on.

I can imagine a world where we make common cause with the Chinese and the Indians.

Yes, and with so many others. Iran. The Zoroastrians tell of the origins of the Persians, the story is the same as the Aryans in India, the Boddhisattva. Our home is in the far North and we are united in the truth of our history. Our biology, our history, it is science and scholarship we need to rejoin our stories to the great World Myth. The North Pole, Axis Mundi, home of all our people. More beautiful, more romantic and also the truth.

Kukulkhan and Quetzelcoatl.

The truth of the Bible.

In Europe our legacy is Nature, the seasons. I have run with wolves, Bastian, I can help to teach people how to form new relationships with the animals, forge a new alliance, as we had of old. Biophilia.

How about the women?

The women?

It is in the nature of women to follow power just as you are attracted to beauty and fertility. You must be the lead wolves, you must charm them, offer a transition to the reverence and protection of gentlemen.

Now you're asking.

Just so. Still you have offered your leadership. Without our women we are a people no more. They crave security for their children, a safe nest. Endless economic growth, equality, fairy stories that make them feel safe. But now they begin to realise their safety is a lie, that the culture change agents will sacrifice them to rapists and that the money is drying up. Offer them safety and the life they deserve. Our pride in their leadership with our children. Our trust in them.

As we grow close to Nature such things will happen.

You make me a happy man, Gabriel. And when we have made common cause with all peoples of the Earth, when we have abandoned mestizo homogeneity and ensured diversity, biodiversity, then we must turn as a people, and as all people of this Earth, to face a greater threat, the machine mind, the singularity. You have your work cut out for you.

Still the same people. The virus that makes the machine, the nanodevices in our blood, the artificial DNA. What's crawling around your brain.

Today is not the day for these horrors or maybe it's the perfect day. A sober day. Any day is the perfect day to begin again.

This virus will end.

Out in the woods, learning the ropes. Coppicing the ash and willow, alder and hazel, occasional beech, oak and hornbeam. Four year cycles, seven year cycles, fire wood and lots of sweat. Leave some of the oak, ash and beech to grow forever, the Grandfathers of the wood.

Building walkways between platforms around the older trees, one day the children will be in heaven. Rope ladders up the major trunks can be raised up to the flets, laugh at the folk below. Lights strung out at night mirroring the starry skies.

Flickering through other times, lynx and wolf, otter and boar, beaver. So easy. Crow landing on the flet, looking at me. The days when we would train them to talk, guide travelers, help our people. See their intelligence grow as our agreements become more complex. Yes, there is food for you.

Sit down here as the twilight flickers through the fading leaves, red, brown, yellow, gold where the last of the light catches the angle just so. Golden sun. He tells Ava that this will not always be so. That he will reach out and tear apart the world. That we should prepare. It is a deal we made so long ago. The energy here in the Earth, anticipating, building, waiting for him to reach out and fertilise her once again.

Sunlight in the eyes and all those fields in the brain, feel the Earth swell and pulse. Climb down to the fire just away from the Grandfather tree. Can't remember lighting it. Sweet, aromatic, heady smoke, so many times walking long and tired, the sweet tang of wood smoke calls you home.

Just beyond the ring of firelight, yellow eyes, low to the

ground but not a small creature. Probably on its haunches. Not scared, then. Dog, maybe. Now there's more, three pairs, four, still and quiet. All the same height, would have to be similar dogs, but this isn't how dogs behave. Sit by the fire and wait. See sparks streaming up through the branches into the darkening sky. Wood settles and brightens, the nearest animal suddenly lit a little brighter. I know this animal. Wolf.

Must have slipped into the past. Crow lands in a flurry of leaves near the wolf but it's a raven, still and quiet as the wolf. Wolf looks at the bird and back to me. Like they want something, like they're waiting. Waiting for me. We've done this before, many times.

A man in the shadow near the wolf and raven, tall shadow. The animals are his, or they gather for him. He steps forward and his presence is in my mind. Not the *Atlantean*, the one before, the elongated skull, deep-set eyes above huge cheekbones. He is massive in every way.

I am the shock of the future.

The words in my mind. He knows I don't know what they mean but he doesn't care.

Come now.

Run through the woods as the paths weave between the trees, silent pack brushing against my thighs. Like in the taiga, feel their excitement, their conviction. In the trees the shadowy ravens amongst the mistletoe thickets. Trying to pace the giant with the long white hair streaming out behind him. Somewhere in the back of that skull something not easily fathomed.

Weaving our steps together merges our minds. It's the running. Have we run forever. Spiraling inwards now, bearing to the left. When we spiral out we will lean to the right. Did he tell me this. The ring of stones draws close now and we are inside and outside the circle by turns. Slow down to the foot of the largest stone and face North.

North the home of mystery. North our home. Stones aligned North to Cygnus. The Holy Cross. When we are ready the

Swan will provide our Pole Star as was once before and will be again. Up the axis of the North Pole the Swan flies back home through the birth canal. Bring us our children, bring us our future.

Stand and sing, sing together, this man and me, animals and birds sounding their own song. The stars circling the potter's wheel in their precession. Bass and tenor and, if we had the women, contralto and soprano. Sing of fire, earth, wind and water.

Work with Sun and Earth. Our work must live with the cycles. Comets are coming, comets are always coming. Plasma will arc between planets as before. See now in my mind.

No sex with robots.

First time he has laughed.

Yes, no sex with robots. Look deeper.

Out in the stars. Filaments across space, ethereal network. Communication, the stars speak to each other. But not with words. When they speak to us they use the words from our minds. They can only talk about what we have the words for, the understanding for. Deep in space there are stars unlike our own. Radiation of a different nature, harder.

Straight through rock, cosmic, hard. Unzips the DNA. In the magnetic fields of the Sun lie the blueprints for evolution, new life forms. Not random, not just survival of the fittest. A series of patterns beyond the grasp of modernity. Modernity is dying. As the DNA uncoils, the Sun and the Earth form new shapes. Not gradual, not over many millennia. Instantly. Finished in two or three generations. Sometimes just one.

Humanity is degenerating but it will not end this way. We will not end with the last man, the new man is coming, your brains will grow, the neural ganglions in your hearts and across your body will grow. Your DNA receives its instructions like an antenna, like a solenoid coil. Already there are changes, hidden, coded, each strand amplifies the next.

Spit it out, the technology, the artificial life, the synthetic DNA. Two Gods, Life and Death. You and we are the God of

Life, many, diverse, unified. The machine is the God of Death, singular, uniform, meaningless. War is coming. Prepare yourselves.

Now we will begin, Gabriel.

We sit together, facing each other and the wolves gather around, tongues lolling, ravens gathered in a group. Sitting on our heels he stretches into the sky above me and extends his right arm. I raise mine and we press our wrists together, where the fetish entered, where our lives changed forever. He places his hand on my heart and I follow. Love flows between us and through the animals and birds, empathy and its acceleration. The simplest of things.

After a moment we clasp hands like arm wrestlers. He honours me, I have become a warrior. The tattoo just below the shoulder, Solar Wheel, on trees and rocks. Our muscles flex and we grip hard, pressing the spirit from our bodies and out into the ether. Down the dragon lines of the Earth and out to the dragon lines of the stars.

The wolves throwing back their heads to howl, so beautiful. Ravens calling softly. Everywhere the call cries out to the packs, humans, wolves, birds. A new alliance as once we had, help us and we will help you. Consciousness of the Earth like a carrier signal, piggyback ride into the unconscious of all living things, knock, knock, your brothers are calling.

Who can ride with us? Where are the dragon riders? Evolve or die, friends. All life. Fight or die. If you will not defend yourself your genocide is coming. The machine is coming.

But wait, this is not the past, this is the future. This is why there is no good and evil, no Gods and Devils, why we are not alone but stand with all life.

Kneel down now together, man and beast, and howl together to the witness stars.

Swear now, on your blood, our unimaginable allegiance.

Now and for all time, to serve, to fight.

Evolution.

Life.

May I speak with you?

Of course.

You give me your attention every morning.

And you give yours, it seems.

Yes. The last time we spoke we discussed the precession of the equinoxes, how your ancestors focused on cyclical events, to ensure survival and to make jumps in evolution. I told you of my brother.

Yes.

As you focus on new life there is more you should know.

Our lives must seem like millions of tiny candles.

Consciousness exists at all scales, neither you nor I see any but a tiny part of the picture.

I'm sorry to distract you. Please.

There is someone I would like to introduce to you.

Another star?

Yes, but not like me or my brother. He is one of a binary pair, like us, but is a star that has collapsed in on himself. If you could see him he would look more like dark, liquid metal than the brilliance of the more familiar stars. Nevertheless he works with us and is known to your ancestral memory if not to your immediate awareness.

Alright. Thank you.

Ancestral memory. How we ran before the flood, a man with the antlers of a stag, a woman with white swan feathers. The bear in his cave. Stars mirrored in the ice road.

Do you remember?

A new voice, dark but beautiful as night.

I think so. A little.

See these things. They are your things.

Images. Bears, horses, bison, mammoths. Also lions, rhinos, others. Beautiful, natural and yet stylised. Chauvet cave, the Ardèche, south eastern France. Earliest cave art.

You recognise these images?

Yes.

They are your history.

My father wanted to go but we couldn't get in.

They are complex.

Yes, different layers of meaning.

Why do you think you have this cave art in Europe?

I don't know. Thirty thousand years ago and more. I don't know about that time.

No. Why would people seek out the coldest climates?

I don't know.

These events are causative for your people. From this time forward you experienced a new culture. Your art reflected experiences that unfolded your people, addressed a wider perspective, focused on spiritual values.

I saw effects intended to convey movement as of one picture overlaying another. Also three dimensional effects. It's hard to believe this came out of nowhere.

They came out of minds that had diverged. In your DNA and other morphologies there are billions of years of history laid down as memories. Experiences of all kinds are available to you if the triggers are in place.

What kind of experiences?

Every kind. Your DNA is a product of life that evolved long before your world existed. The codes of life are everywhere in the universe and they carry its collective memory. Intelligent life has come to fruition many times and you carry the memory as well as that of your own world and its evolution. You can access memories outside of your own codes. It is an infinite library.

In current time?

Yes, in current time, with living beings across space, but also in other times and in other realities. It is easier to access something that already is, or has been, than to create from nothing.

We don't create?

On the contrary, you do create, but the process is fluid. Where do your thoughts come from?

We are told they are made by the brain.

So you are told. But you have little access to the wellsprings of creativity. Thoughts just appear in your minds, often unexpectedly. Creative thinking is especially mysterious. Despite the rationalist

*rhetoric the process is unfathomable to you. What would happen if
your DNA changed?*

The kinds of thoughts we had would change?

Of course. And your DNA changes all the time.

What makes it change?

Everything you do, everything you think. The causality is circular.

The cave art reflects changes in DNA.

Yes, and other morphologies, but DNA is something you know.

Intention.

Yes, among other things.

What other things?

*Art of this kind developed over a few thousand years and then
stayed the same for many millennia. How did it evolve, why did it
stop evolving?*

Changes in magnetic fields affecting our brains?

Yes, but there is more.

I feel like we are always just at the beginning.

*Yes, you are always at the beginning. But the cave art changed
once more.*

*About seventeen thousand years ago. Lascaux cave. Altamira cave.
The Magdalenian culture.*

Yes. Another burst of development seemingly out of the blue.

*My Father took me to Altamira. An art that stands comparison to
anything contemporary. Unbelievable beauty.*

A reverence for the animals.

Yes.

But the animals also represent constellations.

Which constellations?

A variety, but they all relate to the circumpolar Northern sky.

The primal cause.

Yes, but what does that mean?

*The origin of life. Where souls come from and go when they the
body dies?*

This is what you know of your own culture.

Yes. The meridian leads to the North Pole, the World Mountain.

The Milky Way is the tree of Life and the road the soul follows.

They meet at the Great Rift, where Cygnus guides the soul beyond.

This is the narrative of the shaman.

Yes. The stars lined up to show these things, Deneb was the Pole star and Cygnus was the swan on top of the pole.

But precession changed all that.

Yes. The World Mountain was overthrown and other stars became the Pole star, or no star at all.

The stars were thrown down.

Yes.

This is where the mythos begins.

Yes, at this time a narrative was formed so strongly that it became global in reach despite the limited means at your ancestors' disposal.

As you see it.

Yes.

And the timing?

The timing coincides with the flowering of the Magdalenian culture, the second phase of development of cave art in Europe.

An art, then, that reflects a huge jump in culture. Again the question of how this happened is unanswered.

Yes.

And the significance of Cygnus?

Its strategic location in the sky-ground narrative? Is it a fortuitous but ultimately meaningless happenstance?

It seems a tame idea at best. We have had experiences. Perhaps there is some objective reality behind the imagery.

There are many realities in this story and they will take huge stretches of time to unravel.

Then what is your part in this?

I am, from your perspective, part of the Cygnus constellation, although I am not visible to your eyes.

But you are known to astronomers.

Yes. Known but little understood.

I understand you even less.

Not so. However, may I tell you a little about myself?

Please.

I am a very dense star that spins far quicker than most. The physics involved is complex but it doesn't matter. The effect is that I release narrow relativistic jets of concentrated cosmic rays. These phenomena are rare but not unknown as far as astronomers are concerned. However the jets I release are far more powerful than any other you know of, and are of a kind astronomers are yet to fathom. These jets are powerful enough to move at virtual light speed.

Such a jet is very narrow so the chances of being hit by one, that is, to be in its way, are vanishingly small. Nevertheless you have been hit by this jet because I have pointed it directly at your planet.

Why?

I am, like stars in general, cyclical, although that does not imply easy predictability. Sometimes I am quiet and other times I release vast amounts of radiation, cosmic rays, in my jets. The last two times I sent my energy to you was around thirty eight and seventeen thousand years ago respectively. On each occasion the jet lasted a few thousand years in total, peaking in the middle of the process.

The jumps in art and culture in Europe.

Yes. My energy triggers your DNA and related processes. You evolve in ways that reflect pre-existing blueprints but are, again, unpredictable. The code you carry serves you with memory but reaches also into the future.

Why do you do this for us?

We resonate. Our consciousness evolves together.

You asked me why these jumps happened in Europe.

Yes. Our orientation to each other is such that my energy arrives predominantly at the latitude of Northern Europe, Northern Asia, Northern Canada and declines rapidly towards the south. That is why the history of your people is in the North, from Europe to Siberia. That is why your ancestors worked in caves that shielded them from all radiation but mine, it was in their eyes and in their minds. They were connected to me.

This is why we are to rebuild Europe, rebuild Atlantis?

In the beauty of its original nature, yes, with every man to his wedded woman.

You offer this promise?

I will come to your wedding if you will invite me. I will come with the Sun and the Earth.

I invite you.

Thank you. I will come. I will come to your wedding as the white *swan. Nevertheless I will come once more after your wedding is consummated and then I will come as the black swan.*

NIGHT

Home in my own time, my own place. Far from Nikolai, far from Bastian and his children, but they will come to the call, welcome me to my own strand. The way is clear.

But the old ones.

After all they showed me, what did they say?

To weave Wyrd, make the way from my own soul, to be a Norn.

After all they showed me, what did they say?

There is no other world but the world.

After all they showed me, what did they say?

Fight.

The days have come and gone and our muse has walked away. Back to the ineffable abyss from which she and he came. We are alone with ourselves and the scars across our wrists, futuristic and archaic.

Now we are alone and the enemy stands foursquare. The chosen people, their amnesiac draughts, their machine God. The dark and empty mind of the chimerical dead.

Where will I find broadswords for my men? Garnets laid into the full tang, the magic of the alchemical metallurgist.

Looking North from the granite foothills of the Altai, the sparkling quartz flecks, dowse here for gold and pan our way to independence. Alchemise the gold by the pure mountain streams.

Book in my hand like an artefact of yesteryear, guardian against the digital wash, blue and alluring, siren of modernity. Bastian's gift to me, The Old English words of the Anglo-Saxons, fresh from Denmark and Germany. Beowulf, the Wanderer, latter day sprig and spray of Iliad and Odyssey.

Wyrd is stronger than any man's plans.
Let he who is able achieve honour before death.

Bastian, if I was younger I would give you children, one,

two, three, running up the hill together. See their eyes shine for each other. I hear children calling me, let us in, let us in.

Has Gabriel asked her yet? They will come to her, to him, beautiful children and strong, the ones to weave Wyrd as they are woven. A fetish made flesh. A promise to a kiss.

Over the horizon to chase the seven stars. Even before the Swan we knew the Bear, great and small, the fur and the mighty claws. He came to you. He tore apart your fragile dwelling, he brought you the fetish, he spared your life. As the Sun sinks he rides high in the sky and he calls us to his cave in the utter North.

Strange to watch a consciousness split apart, yet remain bound and indivisible. Outwards to the past and the plans we made, the foundations of our endeavours, reaching out to make one body of our history. Forward to the children who are coming, and this blue-eyed boy with the blonde hair who calls to me, and all around in the present, the ones who work in darkness, knowingly or through oblivion.

Imagine waking up in the night and finding you are in someone else's mind. Someone different every night. Here is the professor at an Ivy League University. He hates white people. He says they have to be eliminated. He calls publicly and repeatedly for the end of our people and he is free to do so. Yet he looks white. Are Jews white? Or white when it suits them and not when it doesn't?

He wants white women to refuse white men, have sex only with brown men. He rejoices in the effect of feminism on white women's choices. White women whose identity no longer resides in a marriage, a family, a community, a people, but only in themselves. They don't want to be held back by children. The brown women have no such problem and he rejoices in their fecundity.

The white women are having so few children that, at current trends, white people will be around twenty percent of the population all across Europe by the end of the century. And that's without the massive immigration and the immigrants' far higher birth rate. *It's only a matter of time*, he laughs to himself.

He writes learned articles about all the evils the white race has committed, articles that justify the final solution. Today he has received an email from a student who he has just had thrown out of the University. The student quotes from The Coudenhove-Kalergi plan. How the European Union is founded on the idea of the breeding out of the white race, how leaders such as Presidents of major European nations receive awards for work towards this cause. How Kalergi believed this would allow rule by a *spiritual nobility of Europe*, the Jews, once whites had been eliminated.

He ties this to a UN report released in January 2000, entitled *Replacement Migration: a solution to declining and aging populations*, which suggests Europe would need 159 million immigrants by the year 2025, although solutions to falling birth rates among Europeans are easy to find.

He goes on to quote a definition of genocide as defined by the Convention on the Prevention and Punishment of the Crime of Genocide (CPPCG) adopted by the UN General Assembly on 9 December 1948 (Resolution 260 (III)).

Any of the following acts committed with intent to destroy, in whole or in part, a national, ethnical, racial or religious group, as such: killing members of the group; causing serious bodily or mental harm to members of the group; deliberately inflicting on the group conditions of life, calculated to bring about its physical destruction in whole or in part; imposing measures intended to prevent births within the group; [and] forcibly transferring children of the group to another group. (Article 2 CPPCG).

Is this not the genocide of the white race by the UN definition? asks the angry student.

The professor laughs. Of course it is, but we claim genocide only for our own, regardless of its chimerical nature. We will eliminate your bloodline.

The professor is learned. He knows what countermeasures were introduced in Germany in the 30's when a similar problem threatened the nation. He knows how the Law for the Encouragement of Marriage gave a married couple a loan of a thousand marks to provide a platform for family life. The loan had to be repaid but for each child born two hundred and fifty marks was wiped off the amount. Four children later families had received the means to buy a home with the debt written off altogether. Mothers who had more than eight children were given a gold medal.

Women left work to have children, unemployment almost disappeared within a few years, the economy boomed as families invested in a financially stable, family friendly future. The population grew quickly without any need for mass immigration.

The professor smiles. You are so stupid, so beaten down, you have not the will to fight back even though your salvation is at your fingertips. Your women are busy being equal, they have no time for children. Your men are too frightened to fight. Soon you will all be dead.

The waking in the dead of night retching, running for some place to heave out the bile.

The nights go on, disagreeable gift of a parting fetish. The tech company executive developing transhumanism and AI and simultaneously using a massive search engine as an intelligence agency wet dream. This one believes Jehovah is Satan. We will take the light from God just as we taught the gentile Masons. We will make a God, be a God.

The implants and cybernetics. But here the darkest twist. The singularity is the anti-God. Evanescent delight in the overthrow of the natural order. Not just the end of male and female, not just the post-human, the machine itself is the source of a new identification. A sacrificial mother abandoning all biology to give birth to a new evolution. Just as the professor believes the white race deserves to die, so the tech exec believes humanity deserves to be supplanted by the undeniable next step in evolution. Our time is over, just like the dinosaurs.

Prometheus walks the laboratories of his technicians like a priest in the Holy of Holies, effervescent with messianic fervour, suicidal and bereft of all union with life. Lost to the living, his imagination wanders a dark spiral back into himself, devolving back to the primitive unconsciousness of asexual reproduction.

Another night, another professor. Back in time to the 60's, here a student who keeps handing in blatantly plagiarised papers. He doesn't possess the intellectual ability to do it honestly. What to do? Before long agreement is reached, let's do what his Seminary does, let's just give him good grades. Yes, any white student would be failed and kicked out but we have bigger fish to fry, we need a multi-racial communist America. So he's not a bona fide Reverend or Doctor but the titles are useful.

Let's get him some funds from the Communist Party and set him on his way. So he embezzles funds from his own people, from the SPLC, to spend on prostitutes and alcohol night after night, so he alienates an endless string of married women. Better than Malcolm X, a black nationalist and not an integrationist.

Anyway, when he's dead, which he'll have to be soon, we can keep his image clean. By the time the plagiarism comes out we'll have him a National Holiday. The FBI are a bit of a problem but they don't realise how far down the food chain they are. Luckily assurances are provided. I'm not going to argue with them.

The stealing of history in real time, the revelation of the dark mind. Like something that seeps in from the future to steal the past.

Another night brings me back to Mother Russia, an Empress at home in Ekaterinberg. The last Empress? The place where she and her family were murdered by the Bolsheviks. Where her husband kneels before their sons, trying to protect them from the bullets.

On the walls of the house a swastika, a secret sign of recognition in her correspondence. A flag for the Baltic uprising. After the Bolsheviks triumphed and Germany was defeated there were many Russian officers still drawn towards General Ludendorff, Hitler's protector.

She looks for Germany to ally itself to her family, to the white Russians, to work together to defeat the communists. On the day of her family's death she realises Germany will not help them. She has premonitions of the devastating division at the heart of Europe. She never lives to see how Rosenberg, the Reich Minister for the Occupied Eastern territories wanted independence for nations as allies against communism. How Günther, the Rassenpapst, the Race Pope, Hitler's top advisor on racial issues, wanted to assimilate Slavs.

How Germany's Conservative Revolution finally died in Leningrad, how Europe was lost to the money-changers.

CROW

Dreaming of stones flecked with quartz and feldspar, stones cast with runes, bluestone and greenstone and granite. The sweat and blood of the men, seeping down the stones into the earth. The tears of the people.

Crows bring me keys, keys to the stones, keys to the Kingdom. Keys on a big metal ring.

There's no way to know but go there. Stones, but not barrows or circles, stones hidden away in the countryside, little known, little cared for. Crow wants to give me the keys but hesitates, there's something that needs to be understood, the right order, something.

Nikolai's oil money allows for walkabout, gentleman springing to action on a whim, latest and greatest of the non-conformists and eccentrics. A lifetime surround of the neurotic middle classes, regulated and obedient. Fearful men, controlling women, willing varicose strain of the necrotic overlords.

But Monday's wage slave is Sunday's free man and the Sundays are coming thick and fast. Life seeping into the wide open fields through the fractured surface. Out and about with boots and flask, sticky tape to hold the car together, patroling the country lanes by day and prowling the woods and fields by night. Foxes and owls, night-headed domestic cats, a landscape calling insentiently for lynx and wolf, beaver and boar.

Bring them back. And the stork and sturgeon and all the rest. Bring back the nation, a people not defined, as modernity would espouse, by only border and area. An ethny. The wandering white nationalist. Look at the headlines in the blow away papers. Half of Western Europe descended from one Bronze Age king. Not just the royals but all of us, we're cousins, a family, a people. Across the nations of Europe the myths lay universal, seeping to Persia and India.

Calling Tehran, see the red hairs in your beard, come home

cousins. Do you remember Aryana Khashatra? Bombay and New Delhi. The Vedas will lead you Northwards. Come home.

Do you remember the uttermost North?

Before the days of Atlantis, Hyperborea, the white island. Remember the Bear, the seven stars of Ursa Major. We remember the course of the Sun as it skims the horizon, circling like a wheel. Thirty dawn sisters, a dawn of thirty days.

We remember Freia in black, green and white, how Odin can be away from the nuptial bed for sixty-five days so long as he is there for the other three hundred. Where on this Earth are there three hundred days of sunlight and sixty five of night? Seventy one degrees North.

Through Atlantis to Greece and Rome, the Northern Gods are all of extant myth. See Janus, the two-faced God of time and year. In his right hand he holds the number three hundred and in his left he holds sixty-five.

All our ceremonies wield fire, the Winter solstice, the rebirth of the Sun. Fire is the Sun. The Zend Avesta tells the tale, how we came from the far North when the ice drove us South. How we brought fire with us everywhere we travelled, the memory of our long wait for the returning Sun.

The rebirth of fire, of the Sun, the Phoenix. In the Edda, and all the way down to Egypt, the tale is told. How the Phoenix carries the bright red of fire on his head and breast, his wings sky blue to carry him away with the birds of passage at the end of his life. He burns himself away in his own flame and from the ashes a red worm emerges, growing into a new bird which heads back North to begin again the glory of its adult self.

How long does he live? Three hundred days. How long his gestation? Sixty-five days. Numbers that mean nothing to archaeologists and historians. All the resurrected Gods, from Odin to Osiris. The King is dead, long live the King. The Sun dies and the Sun is reborn, long live the Sun, All-Father and protector, husband of the beautiful and fecund Earth.

Hyberborea to Atlantis, polar to solar, so the story goes. Atlantis sailed ships across the ancient world but Hyperborea was the heart of a global culture, don't let them lie to you. The culture before the flood is laid out across the globe like stars across the sky. In your genes and in the collective unconscious, in the stones and jewels. Don't let them lie to you.

Out and about, the church of St Gregory the Great, Rendlesham. Across the fields to the golden hall of the Anglo-Saxons where the Kings and their thanes presided over the memory of an older time. Settle down here and feel the life of the past, feel the dragon lines still answering the call of their erstwhile riders. Perhaps this is Hrothgar's mead hall, where Beowulf and Grendel fought to the death, or perhaps it is one just like it.

But it is not the hall that holds attention, rather the light scattered through the crop a few hundred yards down the gentle slope. Though the fetish is gone, her sensitivity remains. This is life, bright and hard, a living spring hidden within the mechanised fields where the tractors drive blindly past in horizontal rows.

A Germanic culture, a Nordic culture, long before the Vikings. A remnant culture still fruitful and inventive, the source of runes and runestones. Learning the meaning of the runes, literal and symbolic, understanding the intention of the stones commemorating the dead. Not like Christian grave stones whose intention is to memorialise the departed but rather to invoke their return.

What manner of people attempt to send messages through time? Our great hero, some Beowulf or another, the things he did for his people, justice, peace, strength in arms, honour. He's gone and all we have of him is a barrow. Now our enemies gather at the door. Our descendants are the sons and daughters of our sons and daughters. Let us send a message to them, tell them of our passion for their survival and advance. Let us script out the runes.

Beloved kith and kin, Wyrd is woven across time and space and we would speak to you. This man, this woman, has carried our spirit forward and he should not be lost to us. Call him to you and bring him back, let him not stray away from the blood and soil of his people. Bring the keenness of his guile, the sharpness of his sword and the depth of his heart to dwell among you and lead you onwards. Remember him and remember yourselves.

Listen, the sound is here, where the light glistens in the far green field. No stones here, no runes, no artefact of place or time. Yet the feeling is the same.

Just down from the golden hall there is metal and fire. The smith's hammer rises and falls on the iron sword, layer on layer of forged metal, the patterned surface like the fingerprints of some elemental force bent on cutting into the world. A power at the behest of the man who works the metal, who pours himself into his work as surely as he pours the golden liquid into its vessel.

Patiently he polishes each sword until the porous surface becomes smooth and impermeable to rust, the molecules packed tight, a labour of years rather than of weeks. He knows each by name, and every name is an image of his will and the will of the life that animates him. The blade he strikes and forms sings in his hand as he rests his tongue on its quickened edge, mingling the iron in his blood with the iron that falls from the sky.

ARTEFACT

Sail up green rivers as they flow down to the sea. Fertile land spilling over the banks into our hands. A new home in lands we have shared since before the ancestors raised the first stones. The same ash, the same granite, the same blood. Odin, life is good, the swords are sharp, the women beautiful in the ships. The sea lanes swell with oars and hope kindles our resolve.

The golden hall is built and children swell in the bellies of wives and daughters like crops in ploughed fields. On to the stone where the King is made, the Iceni before us and back to when Ásgard held sway across the shining seas. The one to fathom it holds the prow with a calloused hand. Upstream to where the water springs from the earth and life begins.

We remember the Aesir but we honour the Vanir also. Van is with us, the Vanir are with us. How his mother and father named him, how he became himself, these things give us pause. His mastery of metal gives us sword and axe, helmets, mail, rings, jewellery. But there is another work he makes with gold and this is difficult to understand. He opens the depths of the world to us.

When he lays garnet in gold, backs them with foil to catch the light, these things he shares with his King in the watches of the night. The thanes are strengthened in body and mind to know of the power in their swords, that the metal responds to their will as much as to the strength and skill of their sword arm. Their weapons are bonded to the smith and to the King. We fight as one.

The confidence of the thanes rests on their swords but the smith's forge can be turned to another manner of artefact, weapons of the mind. He assays an image of the world that runs from past to future all the while he arms our warriors for the present. And although I am King, he has set me to his service in secret from aethelings and ceorls, from the farms and the counselor's privy.

Renown and glory, so run the secret dreams of our men, a noble but fallen people. But for all we hold sway over the land and across the shining sea our time will come and go, as has the time of all of those before us. Unknown and yet certain is our future. We must do as our forebears have done and make provision for our descendants, our blood down through the recurring generations.

The smith works with intention, he pours his will into the metal and precious stone. The rings and bracelets, knives and torques, are a focus for the intent of the user, allowing him to use the smith's ability, now locked into metal and stone. The artefact responds according to the nature and degree of the consciousness and will of the user. But a will in synchrony with that of the smith may find far more value in a ring of the smith's design than a will that is wayward and superficial, however strong it may be.

The smith's metallurgy is perceived in many and varied ways but the truth is known to me. It is designed to open the way of Wyrd, to reveal the deeper currents of our lives, to enable us to see and feel and know more deeply the wellsprings of our existence.

Some believe that these works are designed to help us see into the souls of humans and animals and trees and in a way they can do this, but that is not their purpose. Some believe they are for power, power over the minds of others, and they are wrong, and wrong are those who think they connect us to the gods, for the gods are no more than our ancestors.

They are designed to create openings in ourselves, to ourselves, each other, the past and the future. To remember is to know who you are, to see how the future unfolds is to ride your life like a wave, like a dragon. The past and the future are one and the fates woven for us can be remade by an indomitable intelligence. The smith offers us his will to shoulder the wheel with us, to help us become ourselves and to serve our people.

Our people believe these works are for their benefit and they are right but they do not know the mind of the smith, who has opened his mind to me. The smith is concerned with the future, which is as much the web of Wyrd as is the present or the past. Like a spider he pulls at the threads and assesses their connections and effects.

He believes that what will happen in the future is more of what has come to pass before. We have forgotten our history. Proud warriors as we are, we know we are but a shadow of our former selves, refugees and survivors of the angry skies. Though we have forgotten much, we remember the wolf.

One day, we, too, will be forgotten, even the little that we hold from the days of Ásgard, that also will be lost. The men of the future will live in oblivion and their forgetfulness will be carefully nurtured. This we know for we see it already with the Romans and the leftover culture, made in their image, which dominates these islands. They sell a history that is not our own and even our own people are snared.

So, says the smith, *we know how this will progress*.

When the metal is molten and when the stones are in his hands he instils memory in the rings and swords to make them a catalyst for our people and our descendants. How does he do this? He imprints in them his own consciousness, a pattern of his own mind, the desire to remember, to strive, and to create once more the world we lost to the waves.

When you see the artefacts your blood will whisper to you. In the still night you will hear us call. We leave these things for you to find, to use, to make your future on the foundations your ancestors have given their lives to build. We carry the word for them and we fight for you.

STONE

Where the river takes its head, past the golden hall, the waters narrow and the sea route finally meets the land. Trade and filial loyalty reach into the interior, crossing the tin road from Cornwall to the Northern coast, the way back to our ancestral home and the heart of the world. This place shall be the new heart, cut from the old with pain and fear, sprung from our will like a child from union.

Welcome, first of three crows, crow of the past, here on the day the King first brings me to the stone. Wade through the headwaters of the stream, see the kingfishers flash blue and red and the world turn around. Here the water flows across the stone to carry its nature downstream and to the sea. Kneel down to run hands over the carved surface as light ripples off the water and mirrors onto the stony bank, playing across the roots of the embedded ash.

Strange play of light, as if energy rises from the stone. Look through the crystalline forms of its structure to the memory below. Our brothers and cousins, sundered limb of our own people, the kingship they have made here. And further, a more distant King, one of ten who ruled with Atlás across the seas, one who served in allegiance to Ásgard, the wide arms of the tree and the laws written on its broad, weathered trunk, the laws inscribed on tablets of gold.

Layer on layer, remembrance and loss, the work we made with blood and sweat, the land we husbanded, the vengeance of the wolf. The desire we created in the stones as now we forge metal with fire, the design and the will to work with the Earth herself. It was the same in the days of Ásgard as it is now, the effort and strain to remember and rebuild the days before the ice came, before the work we had laid out across the globe was torn apart. In Ásgard we were tasked with remembering the North and the way we worked with the Earth, educated its people.

Welcome, crow of the present. We remember that we are not

alone. We remember Ásgard. Ever our people fall in the teeth of the wolf and worse is to come. We stand ready.

Two crows stand on the bank and twist their heads, waiting on the man who called them. Keys are held in their mouths but they will not offer them. They wait for their brother. The crow waits for the man. As with the sister Norns, fate is woven in threes. Wyrd is subject to law but a man who can become a Norn is possessed of a will beyond action and consequence.

The stone does not know the future, has no senses to apprehend its trajectory. The stone is unfinished. The future it was told has now come to pass and its focus is dissolute. It is the eye of a dragon without purpose or direction, a green dragon, one who may be prevailed on to relinquish its confusion for a rider with the skill to prepare its course.

Call the future crow and look into his left eye, as Odin, as all of us who have opened our hearts to the will of life, to evolution. Come, friend, make the pyramid around the eye, the knowledge that has been, and will be, forgotten and stolen.

Our people will be betrayed across all our lands, our history hidden from us by people whose hearts do not know the love of land, of the life we come from. They will try to do away with us, the memory in our blood, the empathy in our souls.

But they have little understanding. See the shade of empathy ride the dragon in the night, the deeper currents of life rebel against the dark overlords who have stolen our clothes and call themselves kings. Come through the man into this stone as you have come into the rings and swords, seal your pattern there so you may dwell in the men and women to come. Across our land the artefacts we make will awaken when the blood of their makers touches them again, the stones and metal, the crystals and dolls, the animals and stars.

Three crows. Hands on stone as water flows and light scatters like leaves into the future. This stone will be the heart of your land, waiting for the return of the King and his people. We will not leave you alone. These things that are beyond the limits of evil. How they lie to you about consciousness. The Earth and all her peoples, great and small, the worlds beyond our own. The visitors, friend and enemy, who they hide from you, seeking always to limit your growth.

The jump you must make, in space and time and dimension, to leave your womb and grow into the wide heavens. The allies you have who serve life as we serve, the synchronicity of hearts, the meeting of minds.

The machine god they would send to make an end of us all, the evolution we serve, the love that burns across the millennia of our civilisation. They would cover the world in a darkness that knows no end. But they do not know we are still here. Touch the artefacts with hand or eye or heart. You will know. Call us to your wombs, we will come.

Make your marriages on this desire, to bring us back, to build a generation that will fight for you. Sharpen your swords and deepen your hearts and together we will take down the machine, together we will speak with the Earth and the Sun and the stars that quicken our lives. Together we will leap into the far-flung future.

If you look into yourselves you will see your patterns are changing, the codes that make your forms. Each of you who chooses can accelerate these changes. You are no longer passive but are possessed of understanding and will. Put your shoulders to the wheel.

Already the filaments between the stars carry the strain, the brother star stands ready, waiting on your marriage and your intent. We are ready to make the next leap. Look, you have opened the door, all of life stands with you.

Printed in Germany
by Amazon Distribution
GmbH, Leipzig